ALOF·T

ARIBOSLIA BOOK III

J. F. ROGERS

NOBLEBRIGHT
— PUBLISHING —

www.noblebrightpublishing.com

ARIBOSLLA

Cian

Tuath Na Mara

Baladh Sea

Bandia

Cnatan Mor

Kilmara

Nowr

Ardara

Tower of Cuatnw

Readh

Sanaka Cavern

Gnaatabarra

Fárach

Tioram Desrt

Saltmar

Sea of Eirinn

Crai Crat

Diabaloa

City of Nisa

PRONUNCIATION GUIDE

PEOPLE

Aodan Tuama \ **ay**-den Too-**ah**-ma \ Fallon's Uncle

Alastar \ A-lah-star

Badb \ Bav \ Morrigan's Older Sister

Cahal Fidhne \ kah-**hal** Feen \ Fallon's friend

Cataleen \ Cat-ah-lean \ Fallon's mother

Cairbre \ **kar**-bruh \ a legendary hero

Declan Cael \ **deck**-lan Kayl

Fallon \ **fal**-lawn

Faolan \ **fway**-lawn \ Fallon's friend

Fiona \ fee-own-ah \ Fallon's paternal grandmother

Kai \ keye \ an exile

Macha \ Mah-chah \ Morrigan's sister

Maili \ may-lee \ Declan's betrothed

Morrigan \ More-ih-gahn \ the original fasgadair

Pepin \ **pep**-in \ The pech who made Drochaid

General Seung \ say-ung \ A selkie general

Sully \ **sull**-ee \ a seer

CLANS

Ain-Dìleas \ ahn **dill**-ay-ahs \ from Bandia
Arlen \ are-luhn \ from Kylemore
Cael \ kayl \ from Notirr
Dosne \ Dohs-nee \ from Fàsach
Olwen \ Ohl-ven \ from Red
Treasach \ treh-zack \ from Gnuatthara

RACES

Fasgadair \ faz-geh-deer \ vampires
Gachen \ gah-chen \ shape-shifters
Pech \ peck - small, strong people with abilities with stone
Selkie \ sell-key \ gachen who shape-shift into seals

PLACES

Ariboslia \ air-eh-**bows**-lia \ the realm
Ardara \ ahr-dahr-ah \ a gachen village
Bandia \ ban-**dee**-ah \ occupied by the Ain-Dìleas
Bàthadh Sea \ **bah**-thach \ sea to the land to the east
Ceas Croi* \ kase kree \ a mountain city siezed by fasgadair
Cnatan Mountains \ crah-dan \ mountains bordering Bandia
Diabalta \ **dee**-ah-**ball**-tah \ a kingdom seized by fasgadair
Gnuatthara \ new-**tara** \ the Treasach's fortified city
Kylemore \ kyle-more \ the Arlen's tree village
Notirr* \ no-tear \ the Cael's village
Saltinat \ **salt**-in-at \ an underwater selkie city
Tower of Galore \ ga-**lore** \ a large tower city

THINGS

Bian \ bee-ahn \ the gachen's first time shape-shifting
Cianese \ see-ahn-eese \ a foreign language
Drochaid* \ **dro**-hach \ the amulet Pepin created
Neas \ nees \ weasels

Rác \ rack \ Kai's dog
torman-ciùil* \ **tor**-man kyohl \ a lap stringed instrument
Zpĕt \ sp-**yet** \ the amulet that resurrected Morrigan

FALSE GODS
Aine \ awn-yah
Aoibhell \ ee-vell
Camalus \ cam-al-is
Druantia \ drew-ahn-tia

*trill the r

PROLOGUE

Morrigan poured the boiling potion onto the looking glass. It bubbled and spread, filling the frame. Gleeful anticipation burbling up her chest, she clamped her lips tight. The metallic liquid writhed as though sea serpents twisted beneath the silver surface. Then it stilled and hardened.

She gripped the carved handle, holding it up to gaze into the perfect reflection of her lair. Her ancient collection of spell books in various states of disrepair lined the stone shelves behind her. Vials, canisters, herbs, and various ingredients surrounded a cauldron. The mirror reflected everything in its path, but her.

Not that it mattered. She fluffed her hair, envisioning the black lustrousness Dagda had so admired. The lack of reflection allowed her to imagine her eyes as they once were, like a lone star on the blackest night. She'd never seen her eyes as they probably were now, with the same enlarged pupils her demonic descendants possessed. But when she imagined herself with those eyes, her anger flared.

She curved her free hand into a claw, envisioning killing those women who'd resurrected her like this. Fools. Any half-wit could have restored her as she was. Their deaths had been too quick. How

1

she longed to resurrect them to kill them again. Perhaps she would. Once more pressing matters were complete.

But the fool's shoddy efforts had resulted in abilities Morrigan hadn't previously possessed—power and immortality. And, thanks to their ignorance, she had loftier goals than merely wiping humanity from this world. Filling and subduing it with more fasgadair with her as their queen was far better. Her heart burst from her chest, and she laughed. Eagerness coursed through her undead being. Her perfect dominion would soon become a reality. The years studying Aodan and Alastar hadn't been a waste. Her diligence *would* be rewarded. The Enemy wouldn't stop her this time.

Her laughter cut short. The Enemy. This was His fault. He'd stolen both Aodan and Alastar. Her blood boiled as her temper flared, threatening to bubble over. A dim pain emanated from her palms. She released her grip and inspected crescent moon-shaped cuts. A few dripped blood and the coppery scent distracted her, awakening her thirst. She licked the crimson fluid, and the broken skin sealed, erasing all traces of injury.

Blood. That was all she'd needed from Aodan and Alastar, and she'd accomplished that task. Now she had her defense against Fallon and anyone who might attempt to use the zpět against her. Almost.

She needed one more thing.

Morrigan placed her finger on the mirror's smooth surface and chanted the words to cast the spell. She swirled her finger, rippling the image as if she'd tossed a pebble in its center.

She stopped chanting and stepped back. The swirling image smoothed, revealing people crowded around a table littered with maps. But the image flipped too quickly back to the maps to see who stood there, conspiring against her.

"We should use these three"—a man the likes of which she'd never seen waved toward Fallon and whoever stood on either side of her—"to lead the charge from Turas into Bandia." Everything about the man was dark. Black hair, mahogany eyes, and tan skin. Other than the sprinkling of gray in his trim beard.

"That won't work." The top backside of Drochaid came into view. Another trophy Morrigan wished to secure. But she couldn't take it from Fallon. Not yet. Not if she wanted her to communicate. And, for now, she needed her to. "Drochaid needs to stay inside Turas, or we'll end up trapped in Bandia."

"What happens if Drochaid remains behind? Or someone else uses it?" The dark man's slanted eyebrows squished together. Was he one of those people her army had invaded under Alastar's charge?

Alastar. How had the selkie overtaken them? Her connection to Declan severed, then Alastar. Then hundreds in rapid succession. She needed to know what happened. If only her connection with her underlings allowed her to access their eyes, like this connection to Fallon did. She needed a better method to keep track of her minions. Perhaps, since she'd learned with Fallon, she'd find a way with them too.

The mirror's limited view didn't permit Morrigan to see around the table, only where Fallon focused with no periphery. Right now, Fallon looked at the dark man.

Morrigan moved closer, as if that might enhance her view. She stared with an intense desire to control the mirror's focus, as if the power of her gaze alone might turn Fallon's head.

The image blackened.

"No!" She pushed the mirror away. Her dead heart pulsed for three beats, then the image returned.

"Without Drochaid, I can't understand the language." Fallon's voice sounded weak.

"Ah. That's why your words are off." The dark man stood taller and smoothed his coat, heavy with gold adornments. "Are there other amulets that can allow Fallon to communicate?"

The view drifted to Pepin as he cleared his throat. Morrigan wrinkled her nose, disgusted by that little creature. "There are, but not here. The dark pech don't create them. I'd have to secure one from my clan across the Bàthadh Sea."

So, they did intend to return. Good. She scoffed. Fools. Even if

3

their numbers were as vast as the sea, they'd never overpower her fasgadair army. Still, she'd need to consider doubling-up on the shores. Or... Perhaps there was a better way.

"You created Drochaid. Could you make another?" The view shifted to Declan leaning across the table toward Pepin.

Declan wasn't dead? His eyes. Human? What trickery was this? The black monster within her, the thing that returned her life and sustained her immortality, raged, demanding blood. Its anger mingled with her own, tripling in intensity. Morrigan screamed to release the tension. In one sweep, she sent the herbs and canister at the end of the counter flying across the room. Chest heaving. Fists clenched so her nails pierced her palms again.

So *that's* why she'd lost connection with Declan. He was no longer a fasgadair. But how?

Is that what happened with the others? With Aodan?

"Ah." Pepin blushed. Her clenched fists tightened with her desire to squeeze the life from his pudgy face. "I'm not really—I'm not sure I—"

"An angel helped him make Drochaid," Fallon said.

Angels. Those blasted creatures kept interfering.

"Do you think you could do it again if we gave you the supplies?" Dark Man asked.

The blush fading from his already ruddy cheeks, Pepin frowned. "I don't think so."

"We need to get you to the pech." The mirror showed Abracham pulling his grotesque beard. "Surely, they're wondering why no one has met them. Someone needs to intercede before they grow restless and take up arms against the fasgadair on their own."

Morrigan laughed. Those pitiful little cave dwellers dared drag themselves above ground and fight her? Pathetic.

"Using Turas?" Pepin asked.

Turas? She quirked an ear. What weapon was she unaware of?

"Aye," Aleksander said.

Ah. Another king to add to her collection. She raised her hand, poised midair, ready to tear the life from everyone around that table who conspired against her. Black, talon-like nails neared the glass.

"Ow!" Fallon cried, and the image went black.

"Curses!" Morrigan lowered her hand.

"What's wrong, lass?" Was that...Faolan? His connection severed last year, after Fallon's escape. Right around the same time as her guards. Not long after Aodan.

Fallon. This was all her doing. What kind of witchcraft severed her connections without killing the fasgadair? Worse...restored them to their original form? A fire burned within, broiling to eliminate the threat. But she had to keep it under control. Her prior attempts to destroy Fallon had disastrous results. Time for a different tack, one with a more favorable outcome. One which ensured everything would ultimately come under her control.

The image returned. Morrigan's attention moved from those around the table to the maps. Diabalta? What were they scheming?

"My head." Fallon's voice again. And the image blackened once more.

"I'll take her to lie down. Please continue. I'll return shortly." Morrigan couldn't see who spoke, but it sounded like Faolan.

She placed the mirror in a stand and stepped back. She didn't care what pain she caused Fallon by penetrating her mind. But this was not conducive to her plans. She needed Fallon's eyes to see. To remain in these meetings. She'd have to be less intrusive. For now.

The image cleared, revealing everyone surrounding the table from a distance. Alastar was human too. A threatening rumble vibrated from Morrigan's throat. The beast's growl merging with her own as she gripped the mirror once more at a safer distance.

"Sorry." Fallon spoke again.

"There's nothing to apologize for." Sully approached Fallon, reaching toward her.

Morrigan's lifeless heart seizing, she lurched her body as far from the mirror as her arm allowed. How she despised that man. He touched Fallon's forehead, and his lips began to move. Recoiling,

Morrigan dropped the mirror on the counter. She cringed and turned away. "Dùin!"

Once again, the mirror displayed the room minus Morrigan.

Hand to her chest, she caught her breath, then chastised herself. "He's just a feeble old man. He's no match for you. Or your sisters."

But he was praying. Every bit of her recoiled, curling into the blackness within her as if it could shield her from the Light.

The onslaught ending, she smiled.

Soon. She would reclaim the zpět and resurrect her sisters. Then nothing would stop them. She tucked the mirror under her arm. But first, she needed to visit Bandia. This time, she wouldn't fail. This time, Fallon would bend to her will.

CHAPTER ONE

The leaders pored over maps and strategies in the war room while I fought a massive headache. Their maps included not only their own territories but also those of Bandia and the mainlands west of the Bàthadh Sea. All pillaged from gachen ships the selkie had confiscated over the years.

"Ow!" I bent forward and grabbed my temples. The stabbing pain intensified.

Wolf wrapped an arm around my shoulders. "What's wrong, lass?"

"My head." I squeezed my eyes shut as if that might help.

He pulled me away from the table. "I'll take her to lie down. Please continue. I'll return shortly."

The pain subsided somewhat, but it would probably be better to leave. Allowing him to guide me toward the door, I glanced back to the wide eyes all staring at me. "Sorry."

"There's nothing to apologize for." Sully caught up to us at the door and laid a hand on my forehead. Eyes closed, his face aimed toward the heavens, his lips moved in silent prayer. I could almost feel the blessing surging from his hand. He opened his grayed-over eyes and aimed them at me. "You are loved, dear one."

"Thank you, Sully." That man was all the medicine I needed.

As Sully returned to the gathering around the table, Wolf half-carried me out of the war room. He stopped a servant with an apron covering the front of her wide dress. "Have ye anything for head pain?"

She dipped in a small curtsey. "We do. Shall I bring the remedy to the princess's room?"

He nodded. "I'd appreciate that. Thank ye."

"I think I'm okay now."

"Ye need rest." He delivered me to the room I shared with Rowan in the castle and walked me to the bed.

I didn't lay down. "This isn't necessary. My headache is already gone."

Wolf pushed me down. "Ye never recovered from all the blood loss, lass. It's been what, two days since the battle? Rest."

The maid appeared with what looked like the same seaweed substance the selkie in Saltinat had given me, but it stunk like expired seafood. "I don't need this."

"Take it anyway, Fallon. 'Tis good for you." He swiveled to the servant. "Isn't that right, miss?"

The maid bobbed and left the room.

"Take this medicine and rest. I mean it, lass." He threw me a look reminiscent of Stacy's mom when she gave a final warning.

"Okay. Okay." I wrinkled my nose at the foul, low-tide stench strengthening as I neared. I pinched my nostrils, shoved the slimy leaves into my mouth, cringing at the overly salted, decaying-fish, cod-liver-oil taste, and gagged.

If salt enhanced flavor, this was one "food" item that shouldn't be salted.

Wolf gave a satisfied nod. "Now rest." He exited, closing the door behind him.

With my headache gone, my body itched to do something...

anything. How could they suggest I just lie here? There was too much to do. We needed to reclaim the gachen's lands and take Morrigan out. First, I needed to find the zpĕt. Which meant, I had to go to Turas and travel back in time to when the two morons resurrected Morrigan. That was the only solid clue in history as to its whereabouts. I stood up too fast, the room spun, and I dropped back onto the bed, still chewing the impenetrable seaweed substance.

This was so unfair. How many fasgadair had fed on my blood? Over how many days? I wasn't even sure. I had been in and out of consciousness. But Declan drank on the day of the battle when I was already weak. How long would it take to be strong enough to leave the castle? I needed to get to Turas before they began using it as a weapon. There'd never be another chance afterward.

I swallowed part of the seaweed glob, fighting the urge to spit the rest out, and glanced at the table. The piece of parchment I'd asked for lay open with the ink and pen ready. I couldn't believe I lost my journal. Everything I'd experienced since arriving in Ariboslia last year was in that thing. Gone. Along with everything else. I'd left some of my belongings back in my room in Bandia. The small amount I'd managed to smuggle with Rowan in raccoon form were abandoned when we fled from the stronghold. What little my friends grabbed before fleeing Bandia was now at the bottom of the sea. Gone forever. Would I ever get any of the other stuff back?

I choked down the final remnant of nastiness and hung my head. I needed to do something. Anything. Even if I was weak. Perhaps writing would help clear my thoughts.

I sat at the table and dipped the fountain pen in the ink. Blackness dripped onto the parchment. I scraped some off and put the pen to the paper.

Why do I feel so down? Although I've yet to kill Morrigan, we accomplished so much! We eliminated the fasgadair threat on the selkie's shores. And I've grown stronger in my faith. God keeps proving Himself over and over. I have brothers, new friends…Kai.

9

Kai. I get so confused when I think about him. I've never felt anything like this. Do I like him? Yes. Is it love? I don't know. I've never loved anyone…other than Bumpah. But that wasn't the same. And it wasn't permanent. People either hurt you. Leave you. Or both.

It doesn't matter, anyway. I have a quest I need to fulfill. And I'd already nearly abandoned all God called me to do to stay with Kai in his piece of paradise. I can't let that happen.

But he decided to join me in my quest. That he'd give up his amazing home to put himself in danger boggles my mind. Was he following me? God? Both? In any case, I'm grateful to have him with me. His presence is like God's gift for returning to my duty.

And He's given me brothers too. Declan and Alastar. I'm a triplet. Though there's lots of family dysfunction to tackle, I'm glad to have them. And together, we have the power to defeat the fasgadair!

I'm still ashamed to admit I'd had romantic feelings for Declan. But, having never had a boyfriend, I believe I mistook the electric sensation of the triplet bond when we touched as an attraction. The truth is much more amazing. When we're connected with Alastar, we have powers over fire! Now, knowing the cause of our connection, I can see him as a brother. And I much prefer him that way.

And Alastar. Who saw that coming? He was raised by Morrigan, the original fasgadair, and our uncle, their feared leader before Alastar took over. Aside from Morrigan, Alastar became the most feared of all the fasgadair, Na'Rycha.

I moved the full parchment to the bottom, dipped my pen back in the well, and continued writing on a fresh piece.

I still can't get over how God tricked Alastar. He thought he was eliminating the threat to his rule by getting me to turn Declan back into a gachen, thereby severing the connection to Morrigan so she wouldn't know when Alastar killed him. But Declan's blood turned Alastar back into a gachen. Just like mine does! We have yet to unlock that mystery. But it probably has something to do with the fact that we're siblings...triplets.

I hate how we were separated at birth. But with my ability to start fires, Declan's ability to control it, and Alastar's ability to decide what it burns, we probably would've caused damage. According to Sully, God's prophet, we would have died if we'd been together when we were little. I guess that makes sense. When we connected, we had no idea what we were doing. It just...happened. And we were much stronger together. I shudder to think what damage we might have caused as toddlers with limited understanding. I didn't understand it as a so-called adult!

I dipped the fountain pen and tapped it on the inkwell rim. Purging these thoughts from my mind was definitely helping...giving me clarity. Was there anything else to add? I glanced back at my original question: Why do I feel so down?

I still have to face Morrigan.

With my brothers, we have controllable fire. And Turas, known as Stonehenge in my realm, will allow us to visit history or travel wherever we need. We could use Turas to go to Bandia, send troops in to fight, then retreat. But Turas taps into the spiritual realm where both angels and demons linger. The more we use Turas, the more notice we'll get from demons. I've already seen one once. But they can't enter the circle, so how much of a threat are they?

These things will help us push the fasgadair back to reclaim the gachen lands. But how will I get to Morrigan? She'll never come close enough for my brothers and me to set her on fire. She'd never drink my blood. How can I get rid of her?

Someone rapped on the door.

I rolled up the parchment and hid it behind my back. "Come in."

Kai poked his head in the room. Just seeing his face, beholding his beauty, sent a thrill through me. "I heard you weren't feeling well." He entered, leaving the door wide open. "What's that?" Sidestepping, he tipped his mahogany eyes around my shoulder.

"Ah, nothing." The words I'd written rushed to my mind, and my face grew warm. I angled, keeping the parchment hidden.

"Oh, really." Showing off his dimples with a deep grin, he took a few steps toward me and reached for the parchment.

I turned to protect it, both hands behind my back.

His hand didn't make it to the parchment but hovered beyond my shoulder. He looked down at me, his face so close.

I stared into his soulful eyes.

He broke the stare, pulled back his hand to massage the back of his head as if that's what he'd meant to do all along, and coughed. Throwing me a small smile, he watched me out of the corner of his eye. "What's on the parchment?"

"Noth—" I laughed at myself.

"What's so funny?" He ran his fingers through his wavy, black hair, giving me a rare glimpse of his tan forehead.

"Nothing." I handed him the parchment. "Here you go."

His eyes sparkled as he unrolled the parchment and dulled as he studied the paper. He raised an eyebrow. "What's this?"

"English." I hid my laughter behind a fist.

He threw me an unimpressed look as he rolled it back up and dropped it on the table. "Why aren't you resting?"

"I can't rest. Too much needs to be done. My mind won't stop."

"If you're up for it, I want you to meet someone."

"Who?"

"You'll see."

CHAPTER TWO

K ai led me downstairs to the banquet hall. The selkie
transitioned the space into an infirmary for those wounded in
the battle. He pulled open one of the heavy doors.

Moaning and cries for help blasted us through the doorway along
with the metallic stench of blood intermingled with some kind of
alcohol.

My chest tightened as I stood in the entryway, looking at Kai
rather than whatever took place in that room. With one hand still
holding the door open, he gave my shoulder a reassuring squeeze. His
eyes and small smile bolstered my courage. I could do this.

Diminutive women flitted about among the patients. Wide
dresses under beige wraps resembling sleeveless scrubs cinched above
their waist obscured their slim features. Dark braids swung at their
backs. These must be selkie women.

We passed a man propped up on pillows as a selkie woman
spoon-fed him. A bandage covered his neck and shoulder. I touched
the bandage on my neck. It was much smaller than his. Perhaps my
attackers had been kinder. Knowing Na'Rycha had wanted to keep
me alive for his experiments, they must've gone easy on me.

A man in the next bed, with a smaller, yet similar dressing on his neck, sat up eating an apple. He appeared far better off.

We passed several more beds. All men with neck wounds. Fasgadair must not be too imaginative. But at least they were predictable. Good thing they hadn't forced any of these men to drink their blood and become demons like them. Or had they? How long did the transition take?

Keeping a wary eye on the last man, I hurried past his bed and nearly crashed into a woman with a bowl of red water and stained cloths. Coppery alcohol vapors assaulted my nose. My neck burned at the memory the stink invoked. They must've used the same stuff when cleaning my wounds. I pressed my hand against my neck.

"Pardon." She nodded as she rushed by, careful not to slosh the liquid. Worry creased her face creased.

A twang of guilt lurched my stomach. I'd been so out of it the last two days. The first day I did nothing but sleep. Yesterday, when I wasn't sleeping, I was eating or participating in battle plans. I hadn't even thought of coming here to visit the fallen. Or helping.

Kai wove his way through the throng to a man sitting on the edge of his cot, chatting with the bandaged-necked patient on the next bed. He sported a man bun, but, with his chiseled features and stubble, he still looked masculine. The man glanced up as Kai approached. Recognition kicked in, and his eyes crinkled into slits. "That was quick."

"Torian, this is Fallon." Kai motioned between us.

"Nice to meet you," I said.

"And you." Torian twisted to sit facing us without wincing. He didn't wear any visible bandages. Why was he here?

"Tell Fallon what you told me." Kai sat beside Torian and tugged me down next to him.

"What should I say?" Torian held his arms out, palms up as if to illustrate he had nothing to share, then leaned forward, resting his elbows on his legs. "As I told Kai and the nurses, I was a fasgadair. A member of Na'Rycha's army."

"What?" Pain shot behind my eyes, zapping my brain. I squeezed them shut and rubbed my temples.

Kai touched my back. "Are you all right?"

"Just another headache." I forced my eyes open and continued massaging as the ache dulled. "How's that possible? Declan was with me the whole time, neither one of us was bitten."

"I didn't bite anyone." Torian's eyes widened as if willing us to search the depths of his soul and see his innocence.

"But that's not possible. How'd you change back to a gachen?" I squinted up at him, avoiding the sunlight streaming through the window.

"I don't know." He shook his head.

"What's the last thing you remember?" Either this guy was off his rocker, or he was lying.

"I was stabbed in the stomach, just above my navel, by some guy with a dagger. But..." He stood and lifted his shirt to reveal perfect flesh. Not even a scar. "There's no wound."

This guy was messing with us. What was he, bored? "I don't have time for this." I stood too quickly and sent the pain surging throughout my head. Everything swam.

Kai stood and steadied me. "You should lie down."

"I'm fine." I sat back down.

Loosing an exasperated sigh, he kept an arm around my shoulder. "I don't think he's lying."

"He has to be." I aimed a thumb at him. "Or he's nuts."

"Nuts?" His face scrunching in confusion, the liar cocked his head.

Kai closed his eyes and waved me off. "She's not from around here. Not everything she says makes sense. Do you remember who stabbed you?"

"I don't know his name, and I haven't seen him since. He looked like a cross between a gachen and a selkie with the gachen's bright-blue eyes but the selkie's black hair and tan skin."

I stood, careful not to jar my head, and tugged on Kai's sleeve. "Let's go."

"Where are we going?"

"To check his story. Only one person I know matches that description."

KAI and I searched the castle's obvious places. As much as I hated to interrupt the leader's meeting, I had to ask. We poked our heads into the war room.

"Anyone seen Evan?"

They met my request with nays and shaking heads.

"Aren't you supposed to be resting?" Wolf asked.

I closed the door. "Where else might he be?"

Kai shrugged. "We can do this later. You should rest."

"I'm fine, really." The pain was a more tolerable, dull ache at this point. And I needed to know.

We pushed through the main doors into the courtyard where people were still cleaning up the fasgadair ash, spilled blood, and broken carts from the skirmish. But Evan wasn't among them. We walked out the main gate to the rocky cliff where I'd sat with Sully. Evan sat on an outcropping overhanging the water, hugging his legs, staring out at the sea.

Kai helped me across the rocks. My eyes watered from the blaring sun reflecting off the water, compounding its strength. Did anyone have sunglasses in this realm?

We made it through the rocky obstacle course and lowered ourselves next to Evan with me in the middle. A soft breeze caressed my arms, and I inhaled the briny scent it carried. Both comforted me, lulling me back to times with Bumpah on the beach when I was young. Waves crashed beneath us, sending up a spray. But only a mist reached us. I could bask here, soaking up the comforts surrounding me and watch the sparkling waves all day.

But what brought Evan out here? I peeked at him from the corner of my eye. Something in his slumped shoulders and pensive expression concerned me. I put a hand on his shoulder. "We have been looking all over for you."

He glanced over his shoulder, then turned back to the sea and hugged his legs tighter to his chest. "Ya? Why's that?"

"Did you stab someone during the battle?" Kai got right to the point.

"By someone do you mean fasgadair?" He shrugged. "Ya. A few. Why?"

"Did you use a dagger?" I asked.

"No, a sword."

"Oh." I deflated. So, the guy was a liar. Or someone else matched Evan's description. Whoever it was, I'd never seen him.

I pulled my legs up to sit like Evan as a flock of birds dove into the water then shot out like rockets a few feet later. They continued to plunge and reemerge as if sewing the sea.

"Actually, there was one."

"One what?" I asked, mesmerized by the birds.

"A dagger."

Jolting, I sucked in a breath and held it, fully focused on whatever Evan remembered.

He stretched out his legs and crossed them at the ankles and leaned back on his hands. "I lost my sword in the skirmish. So, I picked up a dagger. I stabbed a fasgadair with it." He tilted his face over his shoulder again, his gaze bouncing between me and Kai.

I scoffed. That wasn't helpful. I searched for the birds, but they'd disappeared.

"Where'd you get the dagger?" Kai asked.

"A fasgadair flung it at me. Good thing I saw it and dodged in time. He nicked me in the arm, though." Evan rubbed his upper arm. A bandage bulged under his sleeve.

Wait. I stared at Evan as if his body might give me clues.

Both Evan and Declan used to be a fasgadair. But I never was.

Kai and I gawked at each other. We each seemed to reach the same conclusion.

"No way." I scarcely breathed.

"No way, what?" Evan watched us. "What's going on?"

"Is it possible?" Kai asked.

"Is what possible?" Evan's eyes narrowed at us. "Would one of you please tell me what's happening?"

"Declan changed Alastar back to a gachen." I worked it out in my brain as I spoke. "Because I'd turned Declan back into a gachen."

"Huh?" Evan scrunched his eyebrows together.

A cloud passed overhead, casting a shadow over us, chilling the air. As I spoke the words aloud, the idea grew clearer, and I became more certain. "Don't you see? Because I changed Declan back, he has my blood. *That's* how he redeemed Alastar. You have my blood too. The dagger had your blood on it. When you stabbed the fasgadair with your blood—my blood—you changed him back."

"I did *what*?" Evan's mouth slung open. He gulped, licked his lips, and let out a low whistle. "Does this mean all gachen who were once fasgadair have the power to redeem fasgadair?"

The back of my eyes zapped my brain with a high voltage. I squeezed my head in both hands and fell into Kai.

"Fallon!" He grasped my shoulders.

The pain lessening, I pulled away. "I'm okay." But my weak voice betrayed me.

"No, you need to lie down."

"Seriously, I'm okay." The dull remaining ache was nothing compared with the searing pain.

Kai raised an eyebrow as if to say, "Yeah, right."

"Come on." I grabbed his arm. "We need to get to the war room."

CHAPTER THREE

"This changes everything." King Aleksander practically bounced, his ice-blue eyes sparkling. I'd never seen him so giddy. "If this is true, we can dip arrows in the blood, shoot the fasgadair from Turas, and retreat. The blood will either kill the fasgadair or return them to gachen. This option allows us to end the fasgadair problem with minimal losses and save some in the process."

The king's excitement was infectious. Those surrounding the table nodded and grinned and practically bounced with him.

"We need to test this theory. Collect blood from the redeemed. We've been planning to use Turas to spy out Bandia anyway. Let's fill two holes with one plug. We'll spy out the land. When we come across a lone fasgadair, we'll shoot it to see what happens. Are we in agreement?"

More nods and ayes.

The king shifted to Wolf. "Collect Evan's and Torian's blood. They'll receive the request best from you, who I assume, is also willing to donate for the cause."

"Aye." Wolf nodded. "Of course."

"We're already certain Fallon and Declan's blood changes

fasgadair. And Fallon still needs to recover from excessive loss. We'll test the blood first, then plan to reclaim Bandia according to the results." The king rubbed his trim, blond beard. "Alastar, you'll be willing to donate some blood to test this theory as well?"

"Aye." Alastar scratched his eyebrow. "I'm eager for the results of these tests."

"Splendid." His voice booming, face beaming, Aleksander clasped his fingers together. "Maili, you are by far the best archer in our ranks. Would you be willing to take part?"

"I'd be honored." She placed her right hand over her heart.

"Thank you, Maili. Faolan, collect the blood in the morn. We'll wait for nightfall to test in real time whilst the fasgadair are in human form to ensure we don't unwittingly harm an animal. Be prepared to depart for Turas after the evening meal."

This was it. Once they used Turas to fight the bloodsuckers, it would be all over. I'd lose my chance to search for the zpět. That was the goal, right? Sully said I would need it to defeat Morrigan. I *had* to get it. The trip would only take about four hours both ways. Once I was in Turas, searching for the zpět, no time would elapse here. They could live without me for four hours.

Tomorrow morning. After breakfast. I'd leave whether or not my body was rested enough.

AFTER DINNER, Rowan and I headed to our room. I'd need plenty of sleep if I might spend days tracking down the zpět. We turned the corner. Evan was leaning against our bedroom doorframe.

He met us halfway. "Princess Arabella, I apologize for approaching you like this." He bowed to Rowan. "Might I have a word?"

What was going on with him? Sweat wetted the sideburns framing his flushed face. He looked like he'd just taken a few laps around the castle.

"Evan, we're friends. You needn't be so formal." She glanced around the hall. "But our bedchamber might not be the most suitable place to meet."

"I know." Wetness darkened his tunic in patches. Was he ill? He was producing an unnatural amount of sweat. "I wasn't sure how to meet privately, and I couldn't wait any longer."

"Come." She ushered him back down the hall. "The former king's study should be empty this time of day. Do you mind if Fallon joins us?"

"N—no. Not at all." He smiled at me as if grateful to have rein-forcement.

In the study, stale air smelled of musky books and smoked fish. Seascapes flanked some kind of mounted winged fish above the fire-place, and slits of sunlight parted the closed drapes. Evan stomped forward, dropped into a chair—the wide back scalloped like a shell—and gripped the arms. His knuckles whitened.

"Are you sick?" I asked, placing a hand on his shoulder. It was damp.

"I—I have news of the royal family."

Princess Arabella pulled a matching chair next to him. "They weren't all killed in the fasgadair attack?"

"The immediate family was."

"You know of the extended family?" She settled into the padded pink clammy seat and tucked her feet beneath her. All glowing and pale and golden in its center, the princess could have been the pearl in the oyster.

Oysters—I suppressed a smirk as her coaxing tones reminded me of the silver-tongued walrus in Disney's *Alice in Wonderland* leading those animated little oysters to his pot.

"I do." Evan leaned into her entrancement. He scrubbed his hands together. His fingers had left indentations in the soft leather.

"I came to you," he continued, "not only because you're a friend, but also because you might understand."

"You?" She gasped, hiding her mouth behind a spread hand. Wide blue eyes staring.

He dropped his gaze to his fidgeting hands.

"You're a selkie?" Not just any selkie—part of the royal family. My gut squeezed. Like those foolish Wonderland oysters, he was about to leave the safety of his oyster bed for unknown. And, if it was in my power, I wouldn't let whatever he faced swallow him up.

"Not exactly."

"Tell us your story." Rowan grasped his hand in hers. Blonde curls fell forward.

I dragged a heavy driftwood chair closer to them and plunked onto its bleached seat, my nose crinkling. The thing still smelled like salt and kelp. I smacked my lips. At least, they weren't making me gnaw on it like that nasty medicine. I could still taste it. *Ugh. Focus, Fallon.* I knew some of Evan's story. How he became a fasgadair. Royalty had never been mentioned. And his being even part selkie? I'd say no way, but before I arrived in selkie territory, he was the only person I'd met, besides his brother, who spoke Cianese.

He pulled away from Rowan's grip and took a deep breath, leaning back into the clamshell. "My father was Ryung, King Jum's second son. His older brother, Da Bin, took the throne—his family was the one killed."

"Are you the only living heir?" Princess Arabella's voice came as a whisper.

"If the fasgadair killed Da Bin and his family and there are none left in his line, then yes, I believe so." He slouched in his chair and rubbed his temple, his miserable expression suggesting he'd be quite happy if the clam-shaped atrocity came alive and clamped shut on him. "But my father's totem wasn't a seal, so his father banished him. He married my mother, a gachen woman."

That explained why he looked part selkie and part gachen with his dark skin and hair and light eyes. A stunning combination.

"How did you come to live in the west?" Rowan adjusted herself in her seat and smoothed her dress.

22

"My father wasn't content to remain on selkie lands. He lived in his totem form as a whale. When he arrived on the mainland to the west, he returned to his human form and explored the land. He traveled north to Reòdh. The Olwen found him on the verge of death. He wasn't suitably dressed for the unseasonably harsh weather. They took him in. Then he met my mother and never left."

"Did you come to me because you're afraid to come forward and claim your birthright?"

"If anyone could understand, you could." He scoffed. "Before banishing my father, King Jum gave him the royal seal to mark his children, should a threat ever arise against the crown. My father branded both my brother and me." He loosened the string on his tunic, shoved it over his shoulder, and showed us the mark—a circle with strange etchings in its center.

He pulled his sleeve back up and tightened the cord. "My brother is dead. I'm the last of my father's line. But I'm the half-breed son of a banished heir. A former fasgadair no less. I know little of my heritage and nothing of the selkie lands. Nor of ruling a country."

I blew out a breath. "How is it I happened upon and redeemed two displaced royals?"

Rowan and Evan both gave me looks as if to say, *Seriously? You're making this all about you right now?*

I wriggled. Ouch. Something splintery on the seat stuck me.

"It's no coincidence but part of God's divine plan." Waving my comment away, she leaned closer to Evan. "I'm glad you came to me. If anyone understands feeling unworthy of the crown, I do. However, God saved you for a reason. There's no other heir for a reason. And there is discord among your people as to which family to raise up for a reason. You are the answer. Will there be those who oppose it? Yes. But you are the only remaining rightful heir, returning at a time when your political system is changing, realizing their error, and God is with you. So, if you came seeking my advice, you have it. Claim your right. Fulfill your duty. I will do what I can to help you."

Evan stood and threw Rowan a grateful smile. His face was almost back to his normal color. "Thank you, Princess."

"I'll ask my father to call a meeting with the leaders after breakfast."

Perfect. Everyone will be distracted. No one to stop me from going to Turas.

CHAPTER FOUR

With a full stomach from a hearty breakfast, I headed to the kitchen, trying to ignore the dull ache behind my eyes. I wasn't hungry now, but what if I spent many days searching for the zpět inside Turas? Hunger made sense when I traveled in current time, but it wasn't fair that I'd get hungry when visiting the past for too long, even though time wasn't progressing for me. I could return to the present time, and my hunger would vanish. But I needed to heed the angel's warning. The last thing I wanted was to come across any more demons. I never wanted to endure such complete and utter despair again. Ever. I mean, what if they managed to cripple me, and I got stuck in Turas forever? Or worse, left the protective circle and handed myself over to the demons?

I shuddered.

Wonderful aromas met me as I descended the stairs to the kitchen. My sneakers slapping against stone steps, I sniffed and slowed. The yeasty scent of fresh bread reminded me of the holidays at Stacy's house when her mom baked bread from scratch. My mouth watered for a warm slice straight from the oven.

I hesitated at the kitchen entryway. Unidentifiable spices and broth intermingled with the bread and wafted my way. My stomach growled despite its fullness.

Servants wearing black aprons rushed about carrying dirty dishes. Cooks and food prep staff wore white aprons. They already seemed to be gearing up for the next meal.

One cook inspected a giant pot on a stove. He dipped in a spoon, gave it a taste, wrinkled his nose, and motioned to a boy who hustled over with spice jars.

Flour littered a wooden table where a man and two women pounded dough. Feeding so many people multiple meals a day must be an endless chore.

One woman kneading dough flipped her lump over and was about to give it another whack when she spotted me. She wiped her hands on her apron and rounded the table toward me. "Can I help you, young lady?"

"I need to go out for a while. Is there some food I can take with me?"

The cook curtsied. "I'm sure I have something." She snaked through the oncoming traffic like a pro to a counter along the back wall, hauled a clay lid from a platter, revealing a wheel of cheese, and set it aside. She cut off a generous portion, then wrapped it in a cloth and thrust it into my hand. "Take this."

"Thank you." I put it in my satchel while she fished out a couple pieces of dried meat from a canister. She wrapped those and handed them over. "The king always enjoyed this on his hunting trips." She pinched her fingers and touched her forehead. "May he be at peace."

"I'm—" I almost told her I was sorry for her loss. But I much preferred the Ariboslian saying. "You are loved."

She smiled. "Thank you, young lady." She shot through the bustle once more, reached into a basket full of rolls, and returned with two larger than my fist.

They were still warm. I fought the urge to tear into one now as I stuffed my bulging pack with the food. "Thank you." She'd given me far more than I would've asked for. This should be enough for me and Kai. Assuming he came with me. And assuming it didn't take too long to find the zpĕt.

She waved me off with a smile and returned to her blob of dough.

I made my way to the upper levels and knocked on Kai's door. No answer. He hadn't been in the kitchen, so no point checking there. I trudged down the stairs toward the dining hall. Empty.

Might he be in the infirmary? Guilt wrenched my gut as I picked at a hangnail. I should be helping. Why did I keep thinking like that? Finding the zpĕt *was* helping. And necessary.

Still, I'd leave the infirmary as a last resort. Better to check outside first. I stepped through the grand doors into the courtyard. A breeze swept my hair back. I inhaled the sweet gardenia scent and shielded my eyes from the bright sun as I crossed the cobblestones. They'd done a good job cleaning up. The courtyard glistened. Though last night's rain helped.

Kai stood in a small garden with two guys.

"Wait until Ji Ah finds out you're here. She'll be so excited," one said.

Ji Ah? Who was this Ji Ah?

"Fallon!" Kai beckoned me with a wave. He closed the gap and pulled me to his friends. "Fallon, I'd like you to meet Minho and Tae." He pointed to both guys in succession. Each bowed as Kai spoke their name.

They looked like they escaped from an anime comic. Their chocolate eyes, sparkling with excitement, peeked through wisps of ebony hair. Their perfect cinnamon complexion begged me to ask what they used for skin care products. Both were cute, but neither compared to Kai. They were a little shorter, with less defined muscles, and missing whatever it was Kai had that made my stomach flip whenever I looked at him. More evidence the gachen-selkie attraction was a ruse.

"These are my classmates from primary school."

"Ya. Before the elders banished him." Minho grabbed Kai's shoulder and gave it a shake, his dark eyes twinkling. Then his face turned serious, and he bowed to me again. "I can't express how appreciative I am for what you've done." Tousled hair nearly poked his eyes. "My brother returned home, thanks to you."

"Ya." Tae nodded, his eyebrows disappeared behind thick bangs. "My little sister reached her totem three moons back. She's an otter. We've been hiding it from the authorities. I couldn't imagine her surviving on her own." He grasped my hand in both his and shook, a wide grin overtaking his face. "Many thanks."

"It wasn't me. It was all God. But I'm glad the segregation has ended." Knowing I'd helped accomplish something so major warmed my heart. The elitists' plots wouldn't split up any more families.

Like Kai, his friends had two faces—a smiley, puppy-dog face begging to be cuddled and a tough face making you think twice before getting too close. In mere minutes, I'd seen both in Minho and Tae. Their faces were so expressive.

Kai threw me his tough face. Stunning. "If only everyone were as pleased."

"Who isn't?" I asked. "Didn't most people lose friends and family members? You'd think they'd be happy to have them back."

"You'd think." Kai frowned. "It's mostly the authorities and some older folk."

"Well, then. Why don't you banish *them*?" My old snarky attitude reared its vengeful head.

Kai's friends perked up, glancing at one another. Their eyes, resembling the seals they turned into, widened as if I'd said something brilliant.

"Great idea." Tae tipped his head. His fingers to his temple, thumb to the hollow in his cheek, he squinted as if deep in thought.

"I wasn't being ser—"

"My father is a high-ranking official. I'll ask him to speak with the chancellor." Minho waved Tae forward. "Let's go." He bowed. "Thank you, Fallon."

Tae gave a hasty bow, then tromped after his friend.

"But I—" I held my hand up as if I could stop them.

28

Kai nudged my hand back down. "Let them go. They'll realize soon enough that will never happen." He laughed. "They're very excitable. But you should be careful what you say, particularly around youths. Your words carry a lot of weight."

I grimaced. Being careful with my words? So not my strong suit. "I'll do my best. What do you mean youths? Aren't you all the same age?" Then again, Kai never told me his age.

"Ya. We are twenty."

"Twenty?" Two years older than me. "That's considered a youth?"

"Ya."

"Hmph." Why did I come out here? I touched my overstuffed satchel. Oh yeah. "Want to help me find the zpět?"

"You want me to go to Turas with you?"

I smiled a wide, Cheshire-cat smile.

He waved me forward, flashing his dimple. "After you."

CHAPTER FIVE

"What's your plan?" Kai swooshed a branch out of the way and held it for me to pass through. Trudging through the woods was much more pleasant with him than Pepin. My little not-so-considerate friend would've let the thing smack me. "Are you going to take over where Cairbre left his quest in the Cnatan Mountains? Or go back to the women who used it to resurrect Morrigan?"

Either he had a remarkable ability to recall everything people say to him or he was a good listener. Or both. Impressive. "Well, if I look for Cairbre and follow whatever lead he had, there's two potential problems. One"—I held up my pointer finger—"I don't know that Cairbre actually knew where the zpět was. And two"—I lifted the next finger—"I'm not sure how to get what he knows from him since I can't talk to him." I let out a deep sigh. "But, if I find the women, I don't know that the zpět is still wherever they put it. But at least I'll have a starting point to track it down."

"So, you're saying this could take a long time."

"Yeah. But if we have anything on our side"—I pushed through the brush and beheld Stonehenge across the green plain—"it's time."

Kai shrugged. "Just promise me you'll let me help if you get tired.

It's only been a few days, and you've barely rested. You lost so much blood."

"I'm fine now." Other than a teensy headache. "And I'll be restored the minute we return."

"But we can't keep going back and forth and risk the demons in the spiritual realm."

"I know. I have plenty of food."

Kai grabbed my hand, spinning me toward him. His beautiful eyes stared into my soul with such intensity. "Promise me you'll take breaks when you can. If there's not much talk, I'll translate."

"Okay. Okay." I shook my arm free, and we closed in on Turas. I half expected the ancient stones to morph into a living being. They gave off an aura of something alive—something majestic—with stories to tell, beckoning me near. The more time I spent in their midst, the more I longed to stay.

A crow cawed in the distance. Several others responded. An ominous chill swept through me. Would I witness Morrigan's resurrection and those women's deaths? I shuddered. I didn't care to see either. But what choice did I have?

I thought about those women, their fear, the war, the zpět. There was nothing personal to attach a memory to. No details. Only tidbits of information from stories I'd heard. I didn't even know in which year the resurrection occurred. Probably hundreds of years ago. All I could do was try. *God, help us find these women. And at the right time.*

I placed Drochaid in the depression in Turas's center stone. Pain behind my eyes flared, shooting my brain. "Ah!" I clutched my head. Strange emotions flooded my mind. Frustration, curiosity, and something else...something inhuman.

Kai grasped my shoulders. "Another headache?"

I hunched over and squeezed my head in my palms, my eyes squished tight.

Kai held me. "Let's go back."

The pain subsided into a dull ache and pressure at the back of my eyes. "I'm okay. Let's keep going."

Kai narrowed his eyes. "I don't thi—"

"Please, Kai?" I peered at him, begging. "This might be our only chance."

His chest expanding with a deep breath, he shook his head. "If something happens to you—"

"It won't." I attempted to shut out the ache and the inexplicable feelings of disgust as I swirled my finger over its face and repeated the time to when Turas was whole. "April 24, 1521 BC." The stones groaned, then circled us without disturbing us or the earth. The rocks sped until they seemed to form a gray wall.

Not wanting to chance an encounter with a demon, the moment we appeared in the complete Turas in the past, I did what I could to get us out. The monument had barely come to a stop when I switched gears, focusing on Morrigan. I couldn't imagine anything else since I'd never seen them. So, I conjured the image of Morrigan and repeated the words—*resurrection, women, zpĕt*—in my mind, hoping it would bring us to the right time and place.

Stonehenge swirling around us once more, I breathed easier. Had a demon been there, it was too late to affect us now. The pain, now a constant companion in my head, vanished.

The wall disappeared, and we stood in a modest hut with a dirt floor and a thatched roof. Two women huddled by a stove. Their backs to us. Only their unfurling skirts, ratty shawls, and unkempt hair visible. One red-haired, the other blonde.

Kai reached out for Drochaid.

"Give me a minute." I held up a finger for him to wait.

He gave me a look that said, *I thought you agreed to let me help.*

"I'm okay for now. I promise I'll take a break. Just not yet." I had to see what they were doing. If they had the zpĕt, whatever they did might give us a clue how to use it. I imagined us next to the women. They bent over an amulet on the stove. I sucked in a breath. It must be the zpĕt. Finally! Now I had something tangible to aid me in my quest to find it in the current time. I clapped my hands, hid my smile, and peeked at Kai over my steepled fingers.

He caught my stare out of the corner of his eye. His lips twitched as if trying not to smile. But he didn't need to. His eyes smiled for him.

The zpět didn't resemble Drochaid. It was much darker, as if made from charcoal, and a pentagram covered its face. No other symbols. Just the pentagram.

Nervous jolts set me on edge as the impact of what they were about to do hit me. Every fiber within me itched to destroy the thing before these women resurrected Morrigan.

"What were the words he said to use?" the redhead asked.

"Thoir dhomh Morrigan bhon mharbh," the blonde said.

Words Drochaid couldn't translate?

"Do you think it's hot enough?" Red touched the amulet. "Ow!" She pulled back and brought her sore finger to her lips.

Blonde rubbed her arms and shivered. "Maybe this isn't such a good idea."

"We must." Red grasped the other woman's shoulders. "This is the only way to protect our husbands. There's no way they'll survive this war."

Still shaking, Blonde nodded.

What I wouldn't give to smack some sense into these morons.

Red grimaced. "I'll go first." Her hand hovered over the hot stone. She set her jaw and thrust her palm to its face. Pain twisting her face, she clenched her other hand, probably fighting her instincts and every reasonable thought to keep her hand connected. "Thoir dhomh Morrigan—"

Something about her chanting while connected to the evil amulet and the burnt flesh assaulting my nose made me feel like worms coursed through my bloodstream. I plugged my ears and breathed through my mouth.

When her lips stopped moving, I dropped my hands. She lifted her palm, her flesh a scorched mess bubbling into a pentagram.

33

The blonde, eyes wide, stood frozen.

"Do it. Now." Red's voice came in broken breaths, her face blotchy.

"No!" I yelled and swiped at the amulet to fling it off the stove. But it remained just as it was. If only these fools could hear me. This was torture. Absolute torture. Watching these idiots mutilate themselves, using dark witchcraft they didn't seem to understand, knowing their efforts would result in death and destruction for hundreds of years.

Yet here I stood. A witness. A *powerless* witness. I fought back tears, clenching my hands.

Kai put an arm on my shoulder.

The blonde stuck her palm to the stone. Again, I covered my ears as she hurried through the words. Her mouth wide in silent agony, she shook her palm as if that might ease the pain.

The fools placed their palms together, fingers entwined. As soon as they began chanting again, I pressed my hands over my ears.

An eerie sensation swept over me, like I was bathing in pure evil, soaking it into my pores. Similar to the sensation I'd experienced when the demon appeared outside Stonehenge. Though it didn't penetrate me, making me want to drop to the ground and crawl into a pit of self-pity and despair as before, it gave me chills just the same.

The air surrounding us stirred. Wind tossed my hair, carrying the electric fasgadair scent. Was I smelling Morrigan? The first fasgadair? I twisted my body to Kai. His hair swept up, away from his forehead, then settled back into place. Could he smell it too?

"Uh. Is that supposed to happen?"

I shook my head. Never had I experienced any disturbance inside the circle.

The amulet flew from the stove over the women's heads onto the dirt floor. Their hands broke apart, and they turned as the zpět sank into the ground. Dirt bubbled up in spots until it formed the horizontal shape of a woman with the zpět around her neck. The dirt shape took on nondescript flesh, smooth, like plastic. It opened its eyes. Dead eyes.

Kai averted his gaze, avoiding her nakedness, though her body currently resembled a mannequin. Nothing to feel guilty for watching. Yet somehow guilt washed over me as I witnessed these two buffoons rouse an ungodly creature from its unholy place, knowing it was about to begin its reign of terror. I hadn't caused this. But my body twitched to stop the madness. Anything. But it was like watching a movie, knowing the end, but hoping for a different outcome. Useless.

The demon sat up and turned its head—*Morrigan's* hairless head —back and forth in slow motion without blinking. She could've stepped out of a black-and-white horror film. Black eyes, white skin.

The two women gawked at one another, shut their gaping mouths, then returned to the monstrosity they'd brought forth.

Blonde, otherwise frozen, flapped her hand, hitting Red. "G–Get her a blanket."

Red rushed from the room, but Morrigan had risen. I'd had her in my sights the entire time and never saw her move. One second she was sitting, the next she stood behind Red clutching Red's arm.

Letting out a small yelp, Red fought to remove her wrist from Morrigan's clutches, her face turning purple, mouth twitching with the effort.

Morrigan remained still, expressionless. Red clawed at Morrigan, who never flinched. Then Morrigan drove her teeth into Red's neck.

Again, I hadn't seen her move. I cringed as Red cried out and Morrigan sucked her blood.

Blonde screamed. Hands to her face, eyes bulging. She bolted.

Red's eyes rolled back in her head, and she slumped. Morrigan let her drop, not bothering to wipe the blood from her lips.

Blonde had almost reached the threshold. Morrigan materialized before her and sank her teeth into her neck, cutting Blonde's cry short. Within seconds, she joined her coconspirator on the floor.

Dripping blood, like a living thing, licked down sides of Morrigan's mouth and chin. She pivoted toward Kai and me. Her eerie eyes seemed to rest on me. I held my breath. Could she see us? Those dead eyes remained fixed as she zombie-walked toward us. His grasp on my arm tightened. I grabbed him, just in case, as I visualized us out of her way. She glanced our way but continued toward the door, then leapt and transfigured into a crow in the air. The zpět dangling from her talons.

CHAPTER SIX

I envisioned us in the sky after Morrigan. She vanished into the clouds. I followed but, surrounded by white, lost sense of direction. My gut squeezed. I couldn't lose her. But where should I go?

Uncertainty twisted Kai's face. "Any idea where she went?"

"According to the legend, as soon as the women resurrected her—or partially resurrected her—she flew to the battlefield...." I imagined us above the clouds, scanned the skies for any movement. Nothing. I'd have to check each direction, starting north. I darted ahead.

"What battlefield?" He widened his stance, arms splayed, glancing at the clouds speeding past beneath him.

"To the final battle of the clan wars. Those women thought they were helping their families by resurrecting Morrigan, hoping she would wipe out their enemies. Instead, they gave their husbands a death sentence. Legend has it that Morrigan flew to the battlefield and killed everyone other than a few who escaped and shared the news."

"Can't you imagine us there?" His cinnamon complexion had sallowed to a green hue as he groped for the ground and lowered himself.

"I don't know where it is." Finding nothing north, I returned to the original spot and darted northeast. "Besides, I can't get there without going back to 1521." But what about when I followed Declan's father? I moved time forward by imagining the sun higher in the sky. Could I move us forward and to another place?

"What are you going to do, check every direction?" He crisscrossed his legs and stared at me as if trying to find something to ground him.

"That's the plan." I noted the sun's position to keep my bearings.

"But you didn't know the women's location, yet you found them." He swayed. "Can't you try? We can always go back to where we lost Morrigan and try again."

He was right. I didn't want to waste time checking every direction and fail to find her. And I was already tiring. As much as I hated to admit it, the blood loss had weakened me.

I stopped, and he lunged forward, catching himself on his palms. I'd never seen him so unstable. Was his mind was playing tricks on him as we traveled through the air? We had solid ground beneath us. Even if it was invisible.

With no idea what the battlefield looked like, I closed my eyes and conjured the image of Morrigan in human and crow form as the word *battlefield* swirled around my mind, hoping Turas delivered us to the right place.

Pounding thunder and a roar like a herd of crazed animals jolted my eyes open. A swarm of men in kilts, chain mail, and helmets bellowed in a barbaric war cry as they stormed around and through us. My breath caught, and I brought us back into the sky, over the rushing army. We were mere shadows. But it still unnerved me when people walked through me. Especially these guys.

This looked right. But where was Morrigan?

I searched the skies. This would be much easier in falcon form with my eagle eyes.

"Here, let me take over while we wait." Kai held his hand out. He looked much better. "Go sit."

"Fine." I pulled the cord over my head and gave it to him. "But if anyone says something important, tell me. And if there's a lot of talk, let me take it back."

He nodded.

I rooted around for the invisible rocks, sat in front of one, and leaned back. These lands didn't look familiar.

Something came barreling from the clouds to the north. He moved us closer. A crow. My breath caught. It had to be her. The crow swooped low, cawing as if thrilled by the ensuing battle. If the legends of her bloodlust were true—and from what I'd just seen, they were—they didn't call her the battle crow or the battle queen for nothing.

In the air, with Kai in control, I understood his motion sickness. It was like we were flying a jerky, invisible plane. My stomach rolled as he dipped lower, hovering over the clans as they converged, their weapons clashing together. Arrows crossed paths. One flew through my shoulder. I tensed and grasped the spot, surprised by the lack of pain. Then laughed at myself. Their weapons couldn't hurt me.

The screams dissipated as metal clanged. Grunts and gasps flowed along with crimson rain as weapons met flesh and bodies fell.

What brought Morrigan here? How far had we traveled from the women's hut? Had she sensed blood like a shark? Or had something in the women's spell drawn her to this place? She resumed cawing as if reveling in the destruction, circling over the mayhem. Jutting her wings to slow her approach, she transfigured midair like a pro, landing smoothly on her bare feet.

Kai averted his gaze again, though her body looked just as it had before, like a life-size hairless Barbie with freakish demon eyes. But, rather than point that out, I stood and reclaimed the reins.

Before anyone registered her appearance, she came up behind a thick man with bare, bulging arms and bit his neck as she had the two women. His opponent, an intimidating warrior, stood like a statue, staring as a monster did his dirty work for him. She dropped the life-less body, and the warrior remained frozen. Either he was a horrible fighter, or he was a nonbeliever falling under Morrigan's control. I blinked, and he was in Morrigan's clutches, losing precious blood.

Even if I weren't merely a shadow visiting the past, as a believer in God, I wouldn't be able to experience being caught in a fasgadair's web, stilled, as I once had. But why hadn't the women fallen under her spell? As feeble as their attempts were, they at least tried to flee. But believers wouldn't have summoned Morrigan. Or, like her features, maybe her ability to control nonbelievers took time to develop.

More fighters saw Morrigan drinking another man's blood. They poised their weapons against her. She killed them too. More and more men noticed the monster in their midst. They stopped fighting each other. Some tried to attack. Others stilled. It didn't matter. She was far too quick and seemed to have eyes everywhere. No matter where they came at her, she disappeared and reappeared elsewhere, in a perfect spot to land another bite to a neck.

Between each kill, her features took on more definition. Bloody mud caked her skin, covering her nakedness. Her black hair grew, and her face became more feminine and less crypt-like. But those eyes would never change. Nor would the sick sensation washing over me when in her presence.

Within minutes, dead bodies blanketed the battlefield. An atrocious smell—coppery, sweaty, rotting flesh—defiled earth. I didn't see anyone escape, but at least one must have to tell the tale. The fight was over. Both sides lost. She returned to the air and flew back and forth over the dead bodies cawing, reveling in her victory, just as the legends claimed.

My body shook as my stomach threatened to show me what it had done to my breakfast.

Kai attempted to follow her. He must've gotten annoyed chasing her back and forth and stopped bothering. Instead, we hovered, midair, over the battlegrounds while she continued her victory flight.

I had to fight through this desire to give up. We'd made progress. We now knew what the zpět looked like. We had a starting point from which to locate it. We hadn't witnessed these atrocities for nothing.

But if Morrigan had the zpět, how did it end up in the Cnatan Mountains? Or was Cairbre misinformed? How long would I have to follow her to figure out where it is now?

Something caught her attention on the ground. A body moved. She dove, and we followed. She stood by the writhing man's head, cawing in his ear as he flinched. A gash in the man's side and the lack of teeth marks showed him a victim of a sword, not Morrigan. She transfigured, bit her wrist, and then fed him her blood. He sputtered, then drank. He grasped her wrist and drank like a starving animal.

Morrigan yanked her wrist away. Her head swiveled, slow and to an unnatural angle, like a demon-possessed doll in a horror film. She materialized beside a body a few feet away. She removed a tunic from one of the cleaner bodies and covered herself. It fell like a tent on her small frame.

She returned to the man who drank her blood. His chest was still. No sound came from him. Perhaps her first attempt to create another fasgadair had failed.

The corpse's back lurched with a sharp inhale, and I jumped.

Kai laughed. "That startled me too." He placed a hand on his chest and took a deep breath.

Her new fasgadair blinked, revealing freakish pupils and engorged irises. He touched his stomach where the wound had been, then sat up and lifted his tunic to find pale but otherwise healthy skin. It was like watching someone redeemed in reverse. Rather than fill me with excitement and hope, I wanted to be sick to rid my body of these toxic emotions. I'd seen a creature from the pits of hell create another.

But I couldn't give in to despair. There was hope. I couldn't change the past. But with God, I could help undo some damage and offer hope for the future.

Jaw agape, the fasgadair turned to her. "Na tha air tachairt dhòmhsa?"

"What did he say?"

"He asked what happened to him."

She did her demon-possessed doll-head swivel thing and reached to touch the man's face.

"Dè th 'annad?" The man's face shifted between fear, curiosity, and gratitude.

"He asked her what she is," Kai translated.

Morrigan didn't respond. She rose and walked away. Barefoot, she stepped through the carnage, the soles of her feet dripping with reddish-brown mud.

The man rose and followed.

We tailed her across the field, into the woods, and along a path. She walked without wavering, like someone on a mission, yet slow, as if time was of no consequence. She didn't act desperate or in need of anything. Then again, she'd just gorged on a huge buffet. That should tide her over for a while.

And how did such a little thing consume so much blood anyway? Did her undead body dissolve it somehow? And why was she walking? Why not do her teleporty thing?

The man called to her. "An urrainn dhuinn fois a ghabhail airson mionaid?"

"He asked to rest," Kai said.

She continued forward as if he hadn't spoken a word.

I threw Kai a skeptical look. "He used a lot more words than that."

"That was essentially what he was asking."

"Mmmhmm," I said in a disbelieving tone. "I'm going to have to take over soon if there's going to be much more conversation."

"You needn't worry. Clearly, she's not one for conversation."

She walked in a straight line into a village. A man approached her. As he neared, he slowed. His concerned look morphed to fear. He stepped back, but it was too late. She grabbed him, bit his neck, and then tossed him like a salad.

The other fasgadair lunged after the people, desperate, chasing men, women, and children to get his fill. Fortunately, the kids were quick, and the adults protected them. Still, my body shook in anger. The battlefield was repulsive enough. But this... If only I could jab my arm into his mouth and force him to gag on my blood.

She cut a path to a hut and entered as if she owned the place. We passed through the doorway behind her. A man lay on a pallet in the corner. Somehow, he'd slept through the commotion outside. She drew near what looked like an apothecary chest and rummaged through the drawers.

"Okay. I'm done resting. Hand over Drochaid." We switched places. I couldn't rest if I'd wanted to.

The man stirred, rubbed his eyes, and then bolted upright. "Whoa. Who are ye to be going through me things?" He stood and reached for Morrigan.

She seized the man's wrist and flung him across the room. Then she continued to search his items, unfazed.

Wincing, the man pulled himself up to sit but otherwise remained where he landed. He leaned against the wall and put a hand to the back of his head. It came away with blood. "Bleedin' banshees. Are ye mad? Who are ye?" his voice shrilled. "What do ye seek?"

"I sense it..." She pinched something and held it up to inspect—a smooth, alabaster stone.

"That old rock? What do ye want with that blasted thing?"

With the stone in her palm, she made a fist. Beams of light peeked out through the gaps. She disappeared.

CHAPTER SEVEN

K ai and I both gasped. Frozen, we both seemed to be asking the same wordless question: Where'd she go?

"What was that thing?" I raised my hands and flopped them back to my side. "I have no idea where to go from here." What a waste of time.

He shook his head. "At least now we know what the zpět looks like."

"Can I imagine it and end up wherever it is? In whatever time?"

He opened his mouth.

"Or should I follow Cairbre?"

Again, he opened his mouth.

"What if Cairbre was on a hopeless mission to begin with? Should I try to find Morrigan later in time and see if she still has the zpět?"

One brow rising, he squinted at me. "Do you want answers to these questions? Or are you ranting?"

I slumped against invisible stone. "What should I do?"

"Let's go back." His hands warm, he cupped my shoulders. "We can figure this out later."

"There's no telling how much more time I have, though. The leaders plan use Turas tonight. Once that happens, I may never get it alone again."

"What do you suggest?" He cocked his head and slid his hands from me.

I shrugged. "Morrigan's centuries old. I've never seen her wearing the zpĕt. There had to be a reason Cairbre was searching in the Cnatan Mountains. Should I try to follow him?"

"Sounds like a waste of time. As you said, he never had it and never found it."

My surroundings wavered. I swayed on my feet.

Kai steadied me. "This is too much on you. Let's go back. God didn't put you on this mission for no reason. But maybe you weren't meant to find the zpĕt this way. Perhaps we should regroup. Besides, they'll need you to help test the blood on the fasgadair tonight. You should rest up before then. It will be in the current time, which will exhaust you."

My shoulders sloped. He made sense. Wasn't that where I went wrong last time? This was God's plan, not mine. I was supposed to follow Him in His plans, not try to force Him to follow mine. It seems I either run ahead of Him or forge my own path. But I never sit with Him and wait for Him to show me what to do. "I'm not good at waiting."

"Then that's probably what you should be doing."

When did he become so wise? Defeated, I returned us to our normal time. When the wall stopped, excruciating pain pulsed through my temples, and I fell into Kai. Frustration permeated my mind, then relief. Neither emotion felt like mine.

Kai carried me to a stone and sat me down. He pulled me into his shoulder and wiped the hair from my face, then touched my forehead. "You're sweating."

The pain dulled. Frustration still rumbled somewhere below the surface, but relief washed most of it away. But... I wasn't frustrated or relieved. I was discouraged at returning, expecting to be refreshed, and met with a blaring headache and suspicious emotions. So, where were these feelings coming from?

He picked me up. "We need to get you back."

"I can walk." I strained against him.

"Nonsense." He trudged forward without missing a beat. "I'm concerned about these recurring headaches. You need to stop being so stubborn and rest."

I sighed and leaned into him. My headache had lessened to about a two on the pain scale, but he was right. I didn't have the energy.

Perhaps that was part of God's plan too.

AFTER ANOTHER BIG LUNCH, a long afternoon nap, and dinner, I felt much better. My headache was closer to a one now. And, ready or not, it was time. I recognized most of the faces gathered in the war room—King Aleksander, King Abracham, Maili, Pepin, Wolf, Declan, Alastar, Cahal, Torian, and Kai. Evan should have been there since his blood was being tested. But he'd already given us a sample, and General Seung and a bunch of other selkie officials kept him preoccupied. I wanted to see how he was doing. But at least Rowan was with him. True to her word, the princess was doing what she could to help.

We trekked the two hours back through the woods to Turas. Everyone bore bows and quivers on their back, except me. But I had a dagger at my hip...just in case. Wolf, Alastar, Declan, and Torian held flasks of their blood. Maili carried Evan's and Rowan's.

As we neared, and I should have been tiring, a new energy swept through me. I was eager for this experiment's results. So far, I'd turned six fasgadair back to gachen in total. Declan and Evan each turned one. Only six still lived. Morrigan killed Aodan, and Alastar killed the nameless vampire he forced to feed on me. But, if what Rowan shared with me about her transformation applied to all redeemed fasgadair, those two were in heaven right now.

How many more would be redeemed? This question spurred me on, quickening my step as we went.

Once we arrived in Turas, everyone else pulled out an arrow and dipped the tip inside a flask.

King Aleksander stood beside me and gave me a wink. "Ready?"

"Yes. Everyone needs to link hands with me now. When we get to April 24, 1521 BC, I'll imagine us out of there right away. I don't want to risk us getting caught by a demon. And when we arrive in current time in Bandia, anyone not linked will materialize there. We all need to be linked to return."

"As we discussed"—King Aleksander raised his voice for all to hear—"if you're not commanded to shoot, remain connected to Fallon."

I placed Drochaid in its spot and almost swirled it myself. Oops! Pepin didn't know I'd been taking Turas for drives without him. I dropped my hand.

Pepin eyed me askance as if he suspected I might've done this without him. But he swirled his finger along Drochaid's face as I repeated the date. The rocks whooshed around us. The minute the stones ground to a halt in the spiritual realm, my traveling companions oohed at the complete Stonehenge. But they only got a brief glimpse before I imagined us in the fields beside the castle in Bandia. A fasgadair spun around and looked right at us.

"Maili, shoot!" King Aleksander shouted.

CHAPTER EIGHT

The fasgadair lunged toward Maili. In one swift movement, she nocked her bow and shot the monster square in the chest.

Declan caught her wrist. "Go!"

Heart pounding, I watched the maimed fasgadair falter, then step forward, determined to destroy at least one of us.

"Fallon!" A collective yell came from the group.

I collected myself and imagined us back to our time in selkie lands, just as the fasgadair grabbed Maili. Fangs bared, he neared her neck. The rocks groaned to life and, with Maili still in his clutches, the fasgadair spun as they picked up speed. The ground didn't move, but the fasgadair seemed off balance. He released Maili, splayed his arms, and stepped back to catch himself, eyes bulging with unanswered questions. The demon clutched the arrow in his chest and fell to the ground, writhing. He gasped for his final breaths just before his skin sifted to dust.

Everyone stood still.

I broke the silence. "How did it see us?"

"Perhaps because it's an abomination, somewhere between life and death, a demon. You said demons travel the spiritual realm, correct?" Wolf asked.

"It makes sense." Kai ran his fingers through his hair. "Morrigan could see you when we traveled in the current time.... She even seemed to sense you in the pa—"

I glared at him, sending him a silent message to shut up. But it was too late.

"You used Turas without me?" Pepin's scowling face mottled many shades of red before settling on a deep purple as his eyes skewered me. His fists shook at his sides.

Kai threw me an apologetic look and lifted his shoulders.

"Sorry, Pepin. I had to find out about my brothers. And try to find the zpět."

"How many times have you used it?" He quaked like a boiling pot.

I pinched my fingers together and backed away. "Just a couple."

He rubbed his face, pulling his lower eyelids down, giving me an extremely unattractive view. "This is your fault." He jabbed a chubby pointer finger my way. "That's how the demon found us. I warned you not to overuse Turas, Fallon. The angel warned you. Yet you chose to ignore us to follow your own silly notions."

I gulped a spoonful of guilt.

King Aleksander stepped between us. "We have bigger concerns." He motioned toward the pile of dust still in human shape, except where the arrow fell to the side, caving in the surrounding area. "Evan's blood worked to kill the fasgadair. We have yet to witness its redemptive power. But since we know they're able to see us in the present time, even when we're connected"—he smoothed his embellished coat—"we need to come up with a new plan."

Alastar cleared his throat. "Not that I want to remind everyone I was the lead fasgadair in charge of the seize of Bandia... but I believe my knowledge, and the fact that the fasgadair possessing the castle still believe themselves to be under my command, puts me in a unique position to assist."

"By all means." King Aleksander swept the air, prompting Alastar to speak.

Alastar's gaze ping-ponged between me and Pepin. "This thing will allow us to go anywhere, right? Even the sky?"

Pepin snarled and gestured for me to answer.

I picked at my hangnail, attempting to ignore Pepin's blaming stare. We couldn't deal with this now. I had to help reclaim Bandia. "It should."

"We should secure the fortress first. My men, er...the fasgadair will expect to see anything coming from any direction, even in the air. They may not see us coming if we materialize on the roof. We can drop in through the windows and cut the fasgadair with knives laced with redeemed blood."

"How do we take over the castle from there?" King Aleksander sheathed his dagger.

"We should attack during the day. They don't know I'm no longer a fasgadair. They'll think I'm still in control. Therefore, they will be in the formation I commanded when I left. The men outside will be sparse, weakened, and in animal form. Most will be asleep in the dungeons. Once we've tested the blood-dipped knives on the fasgadair in the fortress, we'll infiltrate the caverns and cut them with dipped weapons in their sleep."

King Aleksander grasped Alastar's shoulder, giving it a squeeze with a fatherly smile. "Alastar's plan is sound. We'll return on the morrow with the first battalion and the second on standby."

"Agreed." King Abracham stroked his Merlin beard. "Return to the war room to solidify our plans and prepare for battle."

I YAWNED, wavering on my feet, bracing myself on the map table to keep from falling. It was late, and I was tired. Two trips to Turas in one day were a bit much. Eight hours just walking. And even though time hadn't actually passed during my first trip to Turas following

Morrigan, and my body revived when I returned to the present, my mind felt like it had been days and needed a break. But King Aleksander seemed eager to reclaim his lands. So here we sat, gathered around the strategy table when I'd rather be sleeping.

King Aleksander rearranged the maps so Bandia was on top and slid stone paperweights onto the corners. He placed three silver figures on the fortress, then pointed to Wolf, Declan, and Alastar. "You three. Fallon will deliver you to commandeer the fortress. We'll need a skilled archer." His eyes lifted toward Maili. "Are you up to the task?"

"Most certainly, Your Highness." She straightened and raised her chin. "My people are adept at hand-to-hand combat fighting within trees as well as archery. I'm quite agile. This is a quest I'm well suited for."

"Very well." He placed another figure on the fortress. "You will join them."

"Yer Highness." Wolf motioned toward Declan and Alastar. "Do ye think it wise to split the triplets? We may need their fire."

"Right." King Aleksander rubbed his eyebrow. "Wolf, I'll trust you to choose another soldier to accompany you and Maili."

Wolf tipped his head, acknowledging the command.

Aleksander pushed more figures onto the fortress. "Once the fortress is secure, we'll drop more soldiers. But hold your position until you receive my command." He continued to rub his eyebrow. "What happens if they're killed in animal form?"

Having been asleep for the past seven years and so far removed from the fasgadair threat, he still knew little about them.

"A fasgadair in weasel form bit me on the way to Bandia." I rubbed my fingers together as if I might still feel the bite. "It died."

"Interesting." King Aleksander scratched his blond beard. "We've yet to see any fasgadair redeemed through these methods. But no matter, as much as I'd prefer saving lives and having more reinforcements with which to secure the castle, as long as we devastate their numbers, we will succeed. That is the end goal."

"Our plans to secure the fortress are solid," Alastar said. "Once we've eliminated the fasgadair in the dungeons, storming the castle will be easy."

"We should use the triplet fire," Wolf said.

Burn them up while they sleep? "But we haven't tested it. We don't know what will happen if the fire ignites while I'm connected to Turas. And if I'm disconnected from Drochaid, I won't be able to communicate." No way did I want to risk attempting to survive in Ariboslia among fasgadair without communication. "Also, they'd all die. We wouldn't redeem any."

Wolf quirked his lips. "I was referring to the point in which we storm the castle. But be on the ready, lass. If we get into a situation where we're overrun, we may need ye three to act."

Declan motioned his head toward Alastar. "We should stay close to Fallon, just in case."

King Aleksander took a deep breath. "Do you know where they're taking up residence in the dungeons? The cells, the wine cellar, the underground tunnels?"

"The majority are in the cells and the guard's quarters. Though some are likely in the wine cellar, despite my orders." He rolled his eyes. "Miscreants."

"Have you seen these underground lairs?" King Aleksander asked.

"Aye." Alastar nodded.

"Then we have another problem. You're best suited to lead us." He squinted at me. "Do you need to have been there once before to transport us?"

I tipped my head back and forth. "Uh. Not necessarily. I mean, I can get you there. But it's not an exact science. It would be better if I'd been there before."

"Is it possible you might deliver us to the wrong location?"

I didn't like the direction this was taking. "Yeah."

"Then it's settled." King Aleksander gave a firm nod. "Alastar will lead us."

Drochaid...taken away? I sucked in a breath. "But how will I communicate?"

"You simply need to be connected to Drochaid to understand us, correct? Even if that connection is through another person?"

Something within me didn't like being pushed aside. But it made sense. Why had I never thought of that? All those times I could've just held Kai's hand, and I might've understood? "I don't know. It might." Then I remembered my manners. "Your Highness."

"Good enough." King Aleksander clapped so loud, I jumped. "Everyone rest up. I'll ask the kitchen staff to prepare an early breakfast at sunup. We'll leave for Turas promptly thereafter. King Abracham and I will remain to work out minor details. Alastar, we could use your assistance for but a few moments, if you don't mind."

"Not at all." He clasped his hands behind his back as the rest of us vacated. I held the door for Pepin, but he remained at the table.

"Is there something I can help you with, Pepin?" King Aleksander's kind eyes peered down at him.

Pepin tugged on an ear. "We're delayed in meeting the pech in the Somalta Caverns. I'm concerned they may attempt to attack without us." He glanced at me from the corner of his eye. "And it seems Fallon can use Turas without me."

Ouch. Why did that sting?

"Are you suggesting we deliver you to the pech?"

Pepin drew his lips into a thin line and nodded.

"Very well. If there are any pech you'd like to bring with you, alert them. We leave in the morn."

"Thank you, Your Highness." Pepin's eyes shone, his solid shoulders loosening. He bowed, smiling as he left the room.

I closed the door after him and sighed, hoping he wasn't upset with me. I didn't want him to leave on a bad note. But, for the moment, we had bigger issues.

The battle would begin tomorrow.

CHAPTER NINE

I woke feeling as if I hadn't slept at all. My legs and shoulders ached, and my head still didn't feel right. Perhaps it was something in this place.

By the time we arrived at Turas, I felt great. It made no sense. I'd just walked more, but somehow recharged and ready to go...other than the annoying sensation behind my eyes. That remained. But my biggest concern was the bloodsuckers overtaking us, breaking the line, disconnecting me from Drochaid. What would happen if I got separated and had no way to communicate? Or worse, what if I was left behind?

I shook it off. No point worrying about all the possibilities. I couldn't do anything about them, anyway. God had a plan. He'd see us through this...somehow.

Kai grasped my hand and squeezed. "Be careful."

"I'll be fine. God's got us." I smiled to reassure him. And myself.

He opened his mouth as if to say something more, but he closed it and stepped back, releasing my hand. His gaze made me uncomfortable. I gave a little wave and entered Turas.

Our army filled most of the circle. Weapons hung at hips or

behind backs as everyone linked hands. Pepin's comrades took up the ends of the row, ready to disengage. Reinforcements awaited our return outside. Even when we traveled back to the current time, when we returned it would be as if no time had passed from the perspective of those waiting. But we'll have felt the passing time. Hopefully, this wouldn't take days.

Since our first mission was to transport Pepin to a place no one had ever been and I had the most experience, King Aleksander permitted me to lead with Drochaid. I placed Drochaid in its recess and repeated the date to return us to the time Turas was whole and fully functional. Pepin held onto my arm as he manipulated Drochaid. The second we arrived, I sensed demons. Their presence pressed upon me, and I wanted nothing more than to drop to the ground and wallow in self-pity.

Moans and cries rang out down the line in both directions.

Everything terrible that ever happened in my life flashed before me. It was all God's fault. He took my brothers from me when I was just a baby. Then He took my mother away and had my father murdered when I was three.

"Fallon!" King Aleksander doubled over.

"No one let go." Wolf dropped to his knees.

If it weren't for God, I wouldn't have been left with my grandmother, and she wouldn't have hated me so.

Pepin's grip was like a tourniquet around my arm, cutting off the blood to my hand holding Alastar. "Get us out of here!"

I fought to capture the rogue thoughts. Part of me knew it wasn't God's fault things were so bad. But my heart wasn't getting the message. A prick of light pierced the looming darkness. *You are loved.*

Was that God? Only He could love me even as I blamed Him for everything horrible in my life. I held on to those words. "Pepin, help."

Pain twisted Pepin's face. He looked up, tears welling in his eyes.

"You are loved, Pepin."

His face twitched. Understanding crept into his eyes, overtaking the fear. He set his jaw, nodded, and swirled the stone face, and I imagined the redheaded pech huddled together, awaiting their retaliation in the Somalta Caverns.

The vice of misery lost its grip.

Everyone took a moment to get their bearings after the spiritual onslaught.

We appeared in an underground cavern full of redheaded pech.

Pepin released my arm. A few pech spotted him and gasped. One fell out of his chair garnering more attention. Awareness spread until all eyes riveted on Pepin.

"Pepin?" An elderly pech with long white hair and a sparse beard approached with a wide smile and open arms.

"Annar." Pepin closed the gap and gave the man a hug.

So, not all the pech from Pepin's past were bad. Then again, he didn't talk about them much. I only knew they'd sentenced him to the death penalty for believing in God. But he survived somehow, so they had to release him. And, though he traveled a lot, he was in the Tower of Galore when we found him last year. So it couldn't be all bad.

"When I caught word we were joining forces with the gachen to fight the fasgadair, I wanted to help. Then, when I learned my former student and charge was leading the pech, I joined the council." The old man's toothy smile grew wider still as he clasped Pepin's upper arms. "We've been waiting for you...somewhat impatiently, I might add." Annar leaned in as if whispering in Pepin's ear, but loud enough for me to hear. "I can't wait to see Magnar take orders from you." He winked.

Pepin snickered, giving a feeble attempt to hide his laughter behind a fist. What was that all about? An inside joke? I'd never seen Pepin like this. He collected himself. "I've brought others." He motioned for the dark pech to join him.

The dark pech released their hold, severing the connection. Whether it was their sudden or physical appearance, or both, the red-haired pech gasped again.

"Torsten's beard!" someone cried.

King Aleksander broke away from us and bumped his head on

the low ceiling. He stooped and addressed the gawkers. "I'm King Aleksander of the Ain Dìleas in Bandia." He pounded his chest twice as Pepin had taught him. "We thank you for your patience and apologize for the delay. Fasgadair overtook Bandia. Pepin can explain further. We are returning to reclaim the kingdom. Once Bandia is secure, we will join you to purge the fasgadair from these lands as well. We have new weapons, which Pepin can also share. Until then, forgive our departure. I trust you will continue to await our arrival."

The pech responded with gaping mouths, unblinking eyes, and slow nods.

"Very good, Pepin." He thumped his chest twice, then grasped the hand at the end of the line, disappearing from their view. "Fallon?"

"Right." Time for the battle.

CHAPTER TEN

Alastar gripped my wrist while I manipulated Drochaid and imagined the fortress rooftop in Bandia. A bird swooped down at us. Maili broke formation and shot the bird from the sky. She then slung her bow over her head to free her hands. She, Wolf, and another male gachen with a shock of red hair eyed one another and nodded. Silent and stealthy, they darted across the roof and paused. Once each was in position on three sides, they flipped from the roof into the windows below ninja style. Thuds rang from below us, then a whistle. My cue. I imagined us down inside the fortress.

Maili stood over a jaguar. Blood dripped from her knife and seeped from the cat's wound. "There was only one."

"That we saw," Wolf added.

Cahal poised his battle-axe over his head, ready to strike. The feline jerked, and Cahal's triceps twitched.

"Hold your position." King Aleksander held up a fist.

A breeze swept through the wide, open windows, rustling the leaves, carrying a faint whiff of electricity.

The animal writhed on the ground, its tongue lolled out. Then it stilled.

I held my breath. With each second ticking by, I doubted it would revive. I stared as if watching a pot, waiting for it to boil, not breathing. It jerked, and I jumped, then loosed a nervous laugh. The jaguar shuffled to its feet, blinked, then cowered from those not linked, standing over him. He skulked backward into a corner and bared his teeth.

One man pulled a cloak from a sack and threw it at the animal.

The jaguar jumped back from the covering, eyeing it as if it might attack. Crouched low, he crept nearer, keeping an eye on those he could see. They backed up, giving him space. The jaguar snatched the clothing in its teeth and tromped down the stairs. Within seconds, a boy of around fifteen reemerged wrapped in the cloak, inching his way up the stairs. "Who are you? What's happened? I'm not a fasgadair anymore?"

Maili smiled. "God has redeemed you." She turned to us, her eyes shining. "That was Wolf's blood. It worked."

Thank You, God! That must mean the blood of all the redeemed could convert fasgadair. Even in animal form.

"How? Why?"

"We can explain later." Wolf fingered his sword hilt. "This is their land." He motioned toward King Aleksander. "And we're taking it back. Care to help?"

"How'd you get in here?" The boy glanced around as if he expected to find a portal.

"The bird is gone," the red-haired ninja said.

A crowd shuffled to look out the window.

"There's the arrow, but no bird," the same gachen said.

"The dust might've blown away." Wolf backed away from the window.

"Or there's a redeemed out there among the fasgadair." Why'd I always have to imagine the worst possible scenario?

"Let's continue with our plan." King Aleksander tipped his head toward Maili and the red-haired ninja. "The fortress is in your hands. Stay alert."

Maili bowed. "God be with you."

"And you." King Aleksander fixed his gaze on me. "As we planned?"

I placed Drochaid around Alastar's neck. A surge of electricity shot through me as we touched, just like with Declan. I looked around, making sure Declan wasn't too close. I didn't want to start the triplet fire accidentally. But he stood a few people away. I held my shaking hand out to Alastar. "Don't let go."

Please, please, please, don't let me get disconnected without a language translator.

"Not to worry." Alastar grasped my arm and gave it a reassuring squeeze. Once everyone attached, I swirled my finger along Drochaid's face for the next jump.

He closed his eyes, and we reappeared in a dim cave. It reeked of mold and electricity—fasgadair. They slept like dead bodies on the stone floor. On their backs, hands folded over their chests. They didn't even appear to breathe. They all wore the same dark cloaks that blended in to the stone floor. The stark contrast of their white faces made the ground look like a sea of disembodied heads.

Our men broke off in formation. Four stood in front of the king, Alastar, Declan, and me. The rest crept toward the sleeping demons. Alastar kept his grip on me and Declan hovered close by, should we need to ignite our fire.

The crew between us blocked my view. Slashing knives and gurgles broke the silence. Screams of rage and cries of surprise. Then thumping shook the cave. I imagined human-sized fish flopping against the floor. The second battalion pushed back, squeezing us in, probably to give the fasgadair room to flounder.

Our men gasped at whatever they were witnessing. I craned my neck. But they blocked my view. Perhaps it was better that way.

"Well done, men." King Aleksander spoke in a hushed voice.

I understood him. Was it because I was linked to Drochaid through Alastar? So, King Aleksander's assumption was right.

"What happened?" a bewildered voice asked.

"God has healed you," said someone else.

Similar conversations muffled into the background as Wolf approached, parting the crowd. "I'm uncertain of the death toll. The dust was disturbed in the skirmish. But there were only about fifty fasgadair here to start."

"How many were saved?" King Aleksander asked.

"Twelve."

"Out of fifty?" My heart compressed and my lungs refused to draw in air as though an elephant sat on my chest. "That's all?"

Cahal grimaced. "'Fraid so, lass."

So not a good ratio.

King Aleksander cleared his throat. "Remember the plan. With each attack, we'll leave behind two men with the redeemed. Give us time to clean out the other lairs before moving up into the main floors."

A bloody person I didn't recognize, probably one of the trans-formed fasgadair, stepped into my view. "You plan to leave us here? With no weapons?"

"I assure you, you have the ultimate weapon. Should a fasgadair attack, your redeemed blood will protect you. I'll leave Faolan to explain." King Aleksander eyed Wolf, who nodded. "We have God and surprise on our side."

Wolf signaled a man to stay behind with him and the redeemed.

King Aleksander swiveled to Alastar with his hand out. "Ready for the next attack?"

"Aye." Alastar gave a firm nod.

Ready or not, here we come.

CHAPTER ELEVEN

How many underground lairs did this castle have? By the time Aleksander was satisfied that we'd cleared every possible hiding spot, only Alastar, Declan, King Abracham, King Aleksander, and I remained. Every attack played out much like the first. But I was tiring. My stomach growled.

"Time to return to the selkie lands for our reinforcements. Then we will finish this battle and reclaim the castle." King Aleksander looked tired and giddy at the same time. Eyes wide, he vibrated as if he'd just emptied his third bag of an intravenous coffee drip.

Alastar held Drochaid's cord out to me as the amulet remained in its depression in Turas. "You know where you're going now, right?"

"Right." I threw the cord around my neck. "Thank you." Tension eased in my shoulders as Drochaid returned to its rightful place. No more worries about getting disconnected without being able to communicate. I snuck as big a bite as I could manage from the jerky in my pocket, grabbed Alastar and King Aleksander's hands, and waited for the word that everyone was connected.

When we arrived at Turas's home in the selkie lands, the sun hung high in the sky. The wall came to a grinding halt.

The awaiting battalion stood with bulging eyes and gaping mouths, weapons ready. From their perspective, we'd left Turas with a full enforcement of soldiers. Now, six haggard and blood-splattered people stood before them.

"What happened?" A selkie man pushed forward.

"All played out according to our plans." King Aleksander approached the troops. "We've decimated the fasgadair army. We have one hundred and two warriors lying in wait, ready to storm the castle from below. Our men have the fortress secured. If Alastar's calculations are correct, we now outnumber the fasgadair in the castle. Once the castle is recovered, we'll fan out to where his former troops are stationed throughout the kingdom."

The man waved his troop forward. Once again, we filled Turas's inner circle.

But what if demons awaited us? My heart wrenched, and I shuddered at the complete despair that had met us on the last trip. I never wanted to experience that again.

"All joined!" someone shouted.

My hand hovering over Drochaid shook. Part of me wanted to remove the amulet and refuse to use Turas ever again. But we'd left so many men in Bandia, waiting for us.

Kai. I glanced behind me to where he stood, near the end of the line. His smile and nod reassuring me, I took a deep breath. *God, help us.* I squeezed my eyes shut. "April 24, 1521 BC. April 24, 1521 BC. April 24, 1521 BC."

We returned to the past, and despair pressed in on my soul. I couldn't let it take root. I remembered God's words—*you are loved*—and let those words tumble around in my mind as I pictured the underground lair where we'd left Wolf. He snapped to attention at our arrival.

King Aleksander broke the connection. "Greetings, Faolan." He eyed the redeemed fasgadair standing to attention. "Ready to fight?"

"Bandia will submit to your rule before the day ends." Wolf bowed.

"Ha! I like your enthusiasm, Faolan." King Aleksander smacked Wolf on the back. "I believe you're right. And I leave you with more soldiers. Keep them at the rear. They don't have redeemed blood to protect them. We'll reconvene at the bottom of the main stairwell to the kitchens. Hold your positions until then." He swiveled on his heels back to me. "Do you remember the next one?"

"I think so." I imagined us in the next lair.

He left the remaining groups with similar instructions. Once we'd deposited the last of our fighters in the final hideaway, he brushed his hands. "That's the lot. Now to the kitchen stairwell. Do you know where that is?"

I shook my head.

When Alastar switched places with me, we appeared at the top of the stairs above a seemingly endless crowd of warriors. King Aleksander stood in the front, holding a fist to keep us back, then thrust his hand forward and charged through the kitchen door.

A fasgadair stood in the entryway. He spun, freaky eyes bulging, then charged. One of the selkie warriors ran him through with a curved blood-dipped sword. The men from the lower levels continued to swarm around us, stampeding toward the throne room.

Alastar, Declan, and Kai remained with me. As the fallen fasgadair turned to dust, the weight of his death settled on my shoulders. Why couldn't I be happy for those who were saved? Why did the lives lost burden me so?

"Fallon." Alastar gripped my shoulders. "We should follow the others. Will you be all right to control Turas?"

"Yeah." I sniffed and switched places again. With King Aleksander leading the other soldiers in their charge, Kai acted as a buffer between me and Declan. Though I doubted we'd start the triplet fire in a line, we all needed to be connected.

I brought us to the throne room. Our soldiers streamed in from multiple secret passageways. Night hadn't yet fallen. But the windows were boarded up, and the fasgadair were in human form. Mayhem filled the grand room. Fasgadair flooded in from other parts of the castle. Enemies collided. Our troop slashed at the fasgadair while the beasts, using their instincts, bit our allies. Some of our men nursed wounds on their necks, but none appeared to have fallen. In their midst, fasgadair writhed on the ground. Most turned to dust, but a remnant returned to their gachen selves.

"Spread out!" King Aleksander shouted. "Secure the castle, the grounds, and the temple." He pointed to us. "Check the temple."

I sneered. How I hated that place. But I delivered us inside the door and froze. Among the statues of gods at the back stood Morrigan. What was *she* doing here?

Pure horror intermingled with my rage at her existence. She was to blame. Not God. She destroyed my family. I wanted to charge her, sink my dagger into her flesh, or watch her melt in our triplet fire. Anything to remove her from my life forever.

She swiveled her head in its eerie demon-possessed way, and a sick smile snaked across her face. "I wasn't expecting company. Not so soon anyway." She snuffed. "But your timing is impeccable. I wanted you to see this."

This was our chance. My brothers and I edged toward each other. My hand clasped with Declan. Alastar's hand was inches from mine when a breeze swept through and he was gone.

A crash sounded against the far wall, and Alastar slumped in the corner near the statues. He pulled himself up, then was on the ground again, eyes shut, head lolled to the side.

Morrigan turned her attention back to the idols as if we didn't concern her in the least.

Had she done that? She didn't appear to have moved.

She sauntered among the gods, her fingers lifted, caressing their faces as she passed. "Badb, Macha, we'll be reunited soon." She continued along the line, stopping at a male in the center. Her hand neared his face but didn't touch. "Dagda, we could have ruled together. Did you think I didn't know about your affair?"

"Burn her," Declan whispered.

Another unnatural wind passed, and Declan landed beside our brother.

She laughed. "Do you honestly believe a weak thing like you can kill me?"

He winced as he attempted to stand.

We had to do something. I stared at her, imagining her in flames. A spark fizzled midair where she'd been standing.

I aimed my fire at her again. And again. And again. Each time she simply transported to another spot.

"Are you finished?" she asked.

All fear melted away, replaced by frustration and determination. I would get her. It was prophesied. "Not even close." I made several more attempts.

"Quit interrupting my family reunion." Morrigan returned to where she'd left off at the statues, then continued past a gap to the next idol. Another female. "Boann." Her threatening tone would've skewered this Boann, had she been alive. Morrigan wrung her fingers around the statue's throat. "I know every detail of your betrayal." She squeezed her fingers. The statue's head and neck cracked and fell to the floor in chunks. She stooped to pick up something.

Was that? No.

"Well, well." She raised her hand. The zpět dangled from a cord. "Just as I left it. Safe among a rebellious nation...fools." She smiled, her eyes tracking the swinging amulet. She lowered it into her other hand and gazed upon it, touching its face as one might a precious heirloom.

My heart compressed as if crushed by a boa constrictor. God had commanded us to smash the idols. If only we'd obeyed. We would have found the zpět.

Holding his back, Declan hobbled across the room toward Morrigan, then went flying toward the wall again.

She appeared in front of me and placed the amulet around her neck. "You can have all this." She spun her finger at the mess surrounding us.

I tried to burn her again, but she evaded my attack. *How* did she do that?

"Now that you are no longer a threat, I can resurrect my sisters." She materialized back by the male statue and glided a finger over his face. "Such a shame, Dagda. You could have been king. I have the power to resurrect you. If only you'd been faithful." She stood before me again, feet away. With every movement, I never even saw her twitch.

"You fools." Her face remained calm. But her voice deepened, reverberating like something from the pits of hell. "God put us in this realm because humans worshiped us as gods. So, I'm told. I died in the human realm prior to such events. And you, gachen, among those worshiped, look to these as gods?" She let loose a laugh that bristled every nerve.

I tried to set her on fire.

She emerged inches from my face. "You needn't fear. You haven't angered me. Your foolishness worked in my favor. And when my sisters join me, we *will* be as gods." She transported to the gap in the statues. "You should replace the statue of me. Perhaps if you worship us as gods, we'll allow you to live." She extracted something out of her cloak. A mirror?

What should I do? How am I supposed to fulfill a prophecy to kill her when she keeps dodging my attempts? She's much too fast.

Morrigan peered into the mirror.

Searing pain pierced the back of my eyes, and my vision went white. "Ah!" I grasped my head and bent over, desperate to end the torment.

A wind tossed my hair, and pain shot from the back of my head.

Morrigan now stood before the statues as if she'd never left. Not a hair was out of place.

The pain in my temples stopped, but I touched the new ache expecting to find a bald spot. I stared at Morrigan. "Did you pull out my hair?"

Evil glee formed as a twisted smile, and she laughed again. A nails-on-the-chalkboard sound. My body shivered in protest. She held up her hand, and strands of my hair fell from either side of her clenched fist. "Now I have all I need."

I swallowed. Why did she need *my* hair? And what was that mirror? Was it connected to my headaches? My stomach clenched as tight as her fist. Whatever it was, it wasn't good. Why didn't she just kill me?

She pocketed my hair and recovered something small, which she rubbed in her fingers. A stone. The same stone that had made her disappear? "One more thing."

Another gust of wind stirred around me and pushed me across the room. I spun midair. My shoulder struck the wall, then the back of my head. Pain jolted me from the impact sites as I slid down the wall and slumped between my brothers. I fought to remain conscious. My vision blurred. I blinked until my eyesight cleared and my head steadied.

Oh no! Drochaid. My hands flew to my breastbone where Drochaid rested. My fingers curved around the cold stone. Drochaid was no longer in its place in Turas. The connection was severed. We had no way back to the selkie lands.

The door opened. King Aleksander froze in the entryway. Abracham peered over his shoulder.

Once again, Morrigan stood by the statues, and I'd never seen her move. "Aleksander, as much as I'd love to add you to my king collection today, I believe a better opportunity will present itself soon. And, Abracham, you're no king. But no matter. You'll still make a fine addition as well. In due time. Congratulations on reclaiming Bandia. Bask in the victory. You won't have another." She tightened her fist around the stone and held it up. "See you soon, Fallon." Her evil smile spread as light burst from the gaps between her fingers and she disappeared.

She was gone. A roiling sludge of dread pooled in my stomach. My death would've been better than whatever she was planning.

CHAPTER TWELVE

Bandia was a mess with dust, blood, and wreckage strewn throughout the kingdom. The throne room in the castle and the courtyard got the worst. But it was secure, and guards returned to their posts surrounding the perimeter. Though we were exhausted, we needed to attend to the injured and clean. People dressed wounds and set up an infirmary in the ballroom. Others swept and scrubbed floors, beat rugs, and carried debris out to the courtyard to be burned.

Since I'm too squeamish for nursing, I joined in the cleaning efforts. Alastar, Declan, Kai, and I pushed wheelbarrows full of trash to the burn pile.

"I can't believe I lost Turas." A giant serving of guilt churned in my stomach. "How are we going to reclaim the stronghold now?" My wheelbarrow caught as it transitioned from cobblestones to grass. I gave it a good push and rejoined the boys. "What would happen if we left the fasgadair there?"

"They need to eat." Alastar stopped to wipe his brow. "If they're in fasgadair form, they need blood. If they're in animal form, they need whatever food that animal needs to survive. But, since they're somewhere in between living and dead, if they don't get either, they will become emaciated and weak, but they won't die."

"How long does that take?" I paused to give my arms a quick shake and rub my sore fingers.

"Mmm." He tipped his head as if that helped him think. "It doesn't take long to weaken. A few months maybe? It takes decades to appear mummified." He grasped the handle, and we all set off again.

He hadn't been a fasgadair for long. "How do you know?"

Alastar clenched his jaw and focused on his wheelbarrow contents. "I've seen Morrigan's king collection."

"Oh." An image of mummies locked in a dungeon somewhere sprang into my mind. Were they aware of the passing time, unable to move, trapped in their immortal, yet useless bodies? No one deserved such torture.

"We must find a way, even if it's a bold approach on a ship full of men," Kai said.

"Or..." Why was I even suggesting this? "We could fly in, transform, and use our fire."

Kai gave me a stern look. "They'll shoot you out of the sky."

"Are there any aquatic creatures among us?" Declan asked. "Enough to create a distraction?"

I glared at Declan's back. What was he doing, trying to get Kai to volunteer? He knew Kai's totem was a dolphin. But it was too dangerous. His blood wouldn't save him.

"Good question. We should suggest King Aleksander take a census," Alastar said.

"I'm a dolphin. Most of the selkie who came through Turas with us are seals." Kai's muscles tightened as his overloaded pushcart jostled across the field. "But it would be better to wait until my people join us to ensure success. With their numbers, the appropriate attire, and weaponry, we can't lose." Kai threw me a sideways, dimply smile.

I scowled.

His eyebrows drew together, and he cocked his head. How could he wonder what ticked me off? How would the fact that he's a dolphin help him once he got to land? With no redeemed blood or triplet fire? And how would he carry a weapon?

"Perfect." Declan glanced back at me, faltering as he studied me, then nodded as if understanding. "We should wait for the selkie to arrive. 'Tis a far better strategy for the reasons you mention. And the more time passes, the weaker the fasgadair will become."

Thank you, Declan.

I squinted, wishing I could shield my eyes from the sun as we pushed our loads across the field. But a nip in the air begged me to put on a sweater. Something screeched from my right, and I nearly toppled the cart. A masked face peeked out over the grass and squeaked. It turned, and a bunch of furry backs undulated through the grass like a dolphin pod hopping in and out of the water, cheeping as they went. "What was *that*?"

"Neas." Declan stared after the disappearing pack. "A type of weasel. You don't have them in your realm?"

"I don't think so." I picked up the cart's handle and used my hip to help get it started through the grass. "Not that travel in packs like that."

We continued toward the clearing to the burn pile looming in the distance.

"I hope the selkie realize we no longer have Turas and leave soon," I said. "It will take them forever to sail here."

"They'll know." Kai stopped to pick up a broken chair that had tumbled off his cart. The others paused to wait, but I kept going, not wanting to lose momentum, taking the opportunity to get ahead.

Kai caught up with ease. "We always reappeared as if we'd never left. Within minutes, they knew something went wrong."

The boys overtook me once more.

"Aye. There aren't many fasgadair left in the stronghold, anyway." Alastar stopped at the pile and dumped his load. "Since we

71

weren't concerned that the gachen might reclaim it, we left few to occupy it. In Morrigan's years, none have recovered land she's claimed. Until now."

"Good." Declan threw his wood on top of Alastar's pile. "That will make it easier."

"But still dangerous for the selkie." I pulled up next to Kai, leaving the cart for them to decide where to unload it. "When they arrive on the beach, they'll be vulnerable without weapons or redeemed blood." My heart ached at the thought of Kai storming the beach with no protection. He'd be a sacrifice for those who came in with the proper gear.

This was why getting attached to people was a bad idea. They died. It was an inevitable fact of life. Everyone dies.

Kai emptied his cart, showing off his muscles. "The selkie won't be as vulnerable as you think." His smile deepened, as did his heart-melting dimple. He sidled up beside me. Not fair. Why did I feel like I'd give in to anything he asked when he looked at me that way? "But I like that you're worried about me."

I smacked his shoulder. "I'm not worried." Maybe if I said it often enough, it would become true.

We headed to the castle in silence.

"That's everything." Wolf met us in the courtyard, wiping his gloved hands. "The injured are receiving care in the great hall. Cooks are preparing meals. We can help serve when it's ready. We'll have a bonfire tonight. But first, time to tear down the idols. Who's with me?"

My hand shot up. "Me!" Oh, how I wish I'd snuck out and destroyed them when God commanded us through Sully. I'd have the zpět in my hand now. I swallowed another serving of guilt, adding to the weighty helping still overloading my stomach from losing Turas.

I had to quit beating myself up. I couldn't do anything about the past. At least we were obeying God now.

Wolf held out a sledgehammer. Just as I was about to grasp it, he yanked it back. "Are you sure you can do this with your injuries?"

Injuries smingeries. Nothing would stop me from rampaging on those false deities. "Absolutely." I yanked the thing from him. The weapon of destruction was heavier than expected. It dragged my arms downward before I righted it. I rested the head at my shoulder, then sauntered across the courtyard through the temple doors to the line of statues. A thrill swept through me as I gazed upon the creepy statues, knowing I was about to crush them. I took a batter's stance, attempted to ignore my bruised shoulder, and swung with all my strength. The hit sent a shock up my arm. The so-called goddess's arm dented. Cracks spider-webbed from the spot.

"Ha!" I jumped. Pure joy coursed through my being, and I danced like I scored a touchdown. Who knew smashing the idols would feel so good? Kai, Declan, Alastar, and Wolf laughed at me.

Kai motioned for me to continue.

I swung again, aiming below the dent. The thing shattered with a satisfying crack, sending pieces of plaster raining, jingling against the stone floor. The thing looked like a kid had bitten a chunk from the side of a hollow chocolate Easter bunny.

"That looks like fun." Kai plucked the sledgehammer from my grip, gazed down on me out of the corner of his eyes, and flashed a dimple. He put a hand out, pushing me back, then readied a swing over his head. His face tensed as he swung at the next statue, sending the weapon crashing down on the god's head, which imploded on contact. Pieces raining down echoed in the statue's empty cavity.

I clapped, and his face shone. "That is oddly satisfying."

Wolf, Alastar, and Declan approached.

"Don't hog it for yourselves," Alastar said.

We took turns annihilating every statue, making it last as long as possible as if savoring a dessert we'd never get to enjoy again. White powder and chunks of porcelain covered every surface, including us. The room silenced, and we stood, chests heaving, looking like we'd been caught in a dust storm. Grit coated our hair and our clothes, lengthened our eyelashes, and caked to our skin. I cracked up, and the others joined in.

Our laughs morphed to coughs as we choked on dust. But I didn't care. It felt so good to take out my frustration on these overrated hunks of plaster and finally obey God's command.

The temple door opened. Soon-to-be King Abracham stepped in, coughed, and waved the dust away. Dust settled in his Merlin beard. "When you're through, we could use your help."

I surveyed the disaster before us. "Shouldn't we clean this mess first?"

Abracham shook his head, his face somber. "This can wait. No one needs this temple anymore. The whole thing should come down. I doubt God wants it restored even for His purposes. I'm sure He'd rather we build a temple dedicated only to Him. But that's for King Aleksander to decide another time. Right now, we need help with the kids."

"Kids?" I walked toward him, swiping the dust from my hair and clothes. The others followed. "What kids?"

"The fasgadair didn't want to exhaust their food supply." Abracham's frown deepened. "They left women and children trapped in their homes."

"That's awful." Those poor kids. How long were they trapped? Did the fasgadair feed them? Or only feed *on* them? My heart squeezed, and I forced the welling rage down and questioned Alastar. "Did you know about this?"

He sucked in a breath, then hung his head.

"Don't be too hard on him." Abracham placed a heavy hand on my shoulder. "He's the one who alerted us to check for captives the moment the castle was secure."

Alastar's Adam's apple bobbed as I shook my head at him. I followed Abracham into the courtyard. Good thing I'd released so much pent-up anger on the idols. Forgiving Alastar would require a lot of strength.

But was I innocent? I'd made my own share of mistakes. Didn't I want others to forgive me? And if he was anything like me, he probably beat himself up more than I ever could. Yet even more guilt compacted in my gut. Why did I have to make him feel worse than he already did?

I'd need to deal with that later. For now, I needed to be strong for the kids.

CHAPTER THIRTEEN

W e walked through the villages. Soldiers carried dirty children along the stone path toward the castle. Matted hair clung to grimy faces. Eyes squinted in sunlight they probably hadn't seen in... How long were we away? Two months at least.

The path thinned as the cement homes grew closer together and stacked. We wove through homes, climbed stairs, and traversed atop other homes. Abracham better not leave us. I feared getting lost in this maze. The doors we passed had been ajar. But here, the doors were closed.

"Check that one." He pointed to a closed door. "Check all the closed doors until you have a child to bring to the castle or every home is cleared. Leave the doors open as you go so others will know it's cleared."

As I entered a dark house with Kai so close behind, his breath wafted my hair. It took a moment to adjust my eyes in the dim lighting. There were no windows. And nowhere to hide. A ratty carpet and a low table were the only furnishings. I peeked under the table before moving to another door in the back. Half the room was open, overlooking the land and sea beyond the kingdom's protective border.

A cook stove dominated the small space. Soot caked the surrounding walls. I'd never complain about my bedroom or how little my grandmother provided for me again. I was rich compared with whoever lived here.

I snooped over the edge of the wall—two stories high at least. The scent of sewage wafted up, ruining an otherwise beautiful ocean view. Had the prior residents dumped their chamber pots outside the wall too? Or just the captives? Flies buzzed, and I ducked back inside to a different stench, probably from mold.

To the right, we found another room. This one had a dresser with a chamber pot and a sleeping mat. Something stirred. I inched closer. Children, huddled in the corner, squeezed tighter to each other and whimpered.

I couldn't tell how many. Not wanting to frighten them, I squatted. "You're safe now. The fasgadair are gone. We're here to bring you to the castle to get you some food. Are you hungry?"

They rustled. Someone whispered. Then a child emerged from the shadows. Greasy hair hung in clumps. She splayed her hands as if ready to protect the children who followed. Her eyes narrowed at me as she cocked her head. "Fallon?" she asked, her voice weak.

A lump formed in my throat. The small face was familiar. A bit older and haggard. But could this be? "Colleen?"

"It is you!" She flung herself into my arms.

I fell backward onto my butt. She burst into heart-wrenching sobs as I rocked her, smoothing her hair. As much as I wanted to know what happened, I couldn't traumatize the girl by making her relive whatever horrific events had taken place here. This poor kid. She'd started as an orphan, left to die from the Treasach, rescued by the Cael. She must've escaped Notirr and spent the last year in this place only to live in fear for all these months as fasgadair terrorized the city. I kissed her head, not caring how dirty it was. I tried to blink back my tears, but a few escaped, landing in her hair.

Although I had my parents until I was three and my grandmother raised me, I, too, was an orphan. And my heart broke for this poor kid who had experienced so much more heartache than I had at such a young age.

Three more kids emerged, one crawling.

As if sensing them, Colleen stood, swiped at her eyes, and smiled at the kids. "It's okay. We really are safe now." How old was she now? Five or six?

I moved to my knees. Two of the other kids seemed a little younger than Colleen...three or four. The other couldn't be more than two. Had she been caring for them all this time? My eyes welled up again.

I shimmied toward the littlest and held my arms out. "Can I carry you?"

The toddler searched Colleen, then crawled into my arms when she nodded.

Turning to the other two, I pointed to Kai. "This is my friend, Kai. He's very nice. Would it be okay if he carried you?"

When they approached him, Kai squatted, wrapped his arms around each one, and stood. The kids eyed each other as they rose into the air and giggled. I'd never seen him look more attractive than with a filthy child in each arm.

I grabbed Colleen's bony hand. "Are you okay to walk?"

She wiped away more tears, still smiling.

THAT NIGHT, before heading to the bonfire, I returned to the room I'd shared with Rowan. I held my breath as I nudged open the door. The bed had been made. Everything had been straightened. I vaulted over to the dresser and yanked the top drawer open, then sighed at the welcoming sight of familiar items: jeans, T-shirts, underwear, the selkie dress... I could thank God I'd only had time to shove Rowan as a raccoon in a pack with a few other things before I was kidnaped. And thank Him my friends didn't grab much before they set sail.

I rummaged through my stuff. Where was the rest of it?

I crossed the room to the bathroom. My brush, toothpaste...all my toiletries were in a basket by the tub. *Thank You, God!*

"Whoa!" My mirrored reflection was frightening. Grimy from cleaning the castle and holding Colleen, I looked like an elderly person with mostly gray hair from plaster dust. How had she recognized me? I wouldn't have come to me if I'd been her. Then again, after what she and those poor kids had been through...

I choked down the thought. My overactive imagination wouldn't make things better for her. They were being cared for now. And it would be quite the job after months of uncleanliness, despite Colleen's efforts. And I'd come in close contact.

My skin itched. I desperately needed to scrub myself.

After cleaning up, I headed to the bonfire feeling better than I had in a long time despite my exhaustion. My friends sat on a grassy mound. Peaceful, warm firelight flicked shadows across their faces. They smiled and waved, motioning for me to join them.

I ran my fingers through the soft grass and reflected on all that had transpired. The kids were clean, fed, and tucked away snuggly on their cots, which, at first seemed meager. But now, after seeing their clean faces and smiles nestled in blankets, they had what they needed. And I had extra jeans and T-shirts again. And the selkie dress. I'd need that for our mission.

No. I wouldn't spoil the mood by thinking about that now.

People played flutes while others beat drums. Many danced around the fire. The scene reminded me of the celebration at Notirr when I first arrived in Ariboslia. The warmth from the fire and memories filled my soul.

And, unlike our last stay in Bandia, we no longer felt separated by race or culture. Bandia may not be our home, but we were connected. United by our experiences and faith.

How did I get here? A confused, lost girl with only one friend, raised by a grandmother who hated her. I had been so lonely, miserable to the point of cutting myself. What a difference to be sitting here with friends and family, my heavenly Father among us and within us, uniting us. I was so blessed.

King Aleksander handed Kai a stringed instrument. "It's not a torman-ciùil, but perhaps you can play it."

How did King Aleksander know Kai played a torman-ciùil?

Kai accepted the instrument, placed it in his lap, and plucked the strings.

"You're supposed to hold it—"

The beautiful sounds coming from Kai's plucking stopped the king's correction.

"Or play it like that." King Aleksander smiled and closed his eyes, his head floating to the melody.

Kai's song fit right in with the flutes and drums. Sounds of pure beauty drifted into the night sky and my soul. I half expected the warm fuzzies inside me to burst from every pore as if my body couldn't contain such bliss and wanted to share it with everyone around me.

I leaned back, bracing myself on my palms behind me, and breathed in the fresh air. The fire's flickering light mesmerized me. Shadows danced. Sparks swirled and popped like fireflies. How could something so dangerous be so calming? I sat up, wiped the grass from my pockmarked palms, and placed a hand on Declan's arm, no longer fazed by the electrical charge. "I'm curious..."

"Hmm?"

"When we left Kylemore, a fur—no, a *fire* dragon—spit fire at me. The flame split in two. I could never figure out how that happened. Was that you?"

He gave a sheepish grin.

I nodded. "I thought so."

His emerald irises reflecting the firelight as if to confirm his control over it, his face grew serious. "I wasn't trying to stalk you. Morrigan wanted you followed. I volunteered to keep you safe. Another fasgadair might have given in to temptation and killed you. I don't think Morrigan wanted anything to happen to you either."

That made no sense. She tried having me killed before I was born. Then Aodan attempted to kill me, which I'm sure was part of her plan. Why would she want to keep me alive now? She must have something worse than my death in mind. I shuddered. Best not to dwell on whatever evil schemes she had brewing. For now, something else piqued my curiosity. "What happened? How did you become a fasgadair?"

Declan folded his arms across his knees, then hugged them close. "Your mother, Cahal, and I went to Diabalta. We planned to unite with the pech and Ain-Dìleas to reclaim our lands. To succeed, we needed to know what we were up against. But we never made it near the city. We passed burned villages along the way, searching for anyone who might still be alive. We didn't find anyone." He dug his chin against his right knee, pain contorting his face and glazing his eyes as he gazed into the fire. "Though we kept to the woods, a fasgadair pod found us. We fought them off... for the most part."

My hand slid off his arm. Even as I shied from causing him pain, the question escaped. "What do you mean?"

"One got me. It sucked my blood until I was nearly dead. While Cataleen and Cahal fought off the others, that one dragged me away."

"I tried tracking him." Cahal's deep voice boomed behind me.

I jumped, and my hand rose to shield my pounding heart. "You scared me."

Cahal sat, and we shifted to include him in the conversation. Sitting higher on the hill, he loomed well above us. Alastar moved next to him.

"I protected Cataleen. Once she was safe, Declan was..." He squeezed his eyes shut and swallowed hard. Then his remorseful gaze fell on Declan. "Gone."

Declan patted Cahal's shoulder. "You did the right thing. Everything worked out according to God's plan."

A man of few words, Cahal tipped his massive head and quirked his lips, acknowledging Declan's forgiveness.

"So, how'd you become a fasgadair?" I asked.

"The fasgadair didn't give me a choice. He poured blood into my mouth while I was half-conscious. I thought I'd go berserk like the stories I'd heard." He quirked one side of his face in a mixture of pain and disgust. "But I never killed anyone. God spared me from that. He never left me, even in that demonic state. I was a believer first, converted against my will, and He protected me, helping me not to give in to the temptation."

He lifted his face. His intense sea-green eyes delved mine. "That's why I didn't want you to change me. I believed God allowed me to be changed into a fasgadair so I could rescue you. I never could've predicted God's actual plan."

I snickered. "It'd be nice if He let us in on His plans, wouldn't it?"

"Sometimes He does." Declan shrugged. "Through Sully and others. Sometimes He speaks to us directly."

True. And sometimes we don't listen.

"We need to remember what He's done for us already when we confront seemingly impossible odds." Declan stretched his legs out before him and drummed his hands on his thighs.

Right. And a nagging feeling told me it wouldn't be long.

CHAPTER FOURTEEN

I didn't know what to expect at the stronghold or during the upcoming war. So, I attempted to prepare for everything. In a twisted way, it reminded me of high school. Each day was so regimented. I developed a strict routine in two weeks. The schedule comforted me.

Before heading for breakfast, I stepped outside into the courtyard.

"Fallon!" Colleen raced to me, blonde curls bouncing. Her face had filled out, and her cheeks were rosy from fresh air.

I crouched to receive her hug, inhaling the calming lavender the Ain Dìleas infused into their soaps. Her charges fell in behind her, squeezing themselves in for a giant embrace. Though they had adults to care for them now, they still followed Colleen around as if she were their mother. So cute. Seeing them each morning warmed my heart. They provided the strength and determination I needed to push myself. My little reminders of what I was fighting for.

They backed away, offering breathing room.

"Was breakfast good today?"

Exaggerated nods bobbed their heads.

"Something with apples and cinnamon." Colleen rubbed her stomach and rolled her eyes as if in ecstasy. "So good."

I smiled at the return of her little overly dramatic personality. And she'd always been a mother hen. Almost as if God knew what would happen and created her for that purpose. My eyes teared up. More evidence He was always near, going before us, providing everything we'd need to get through troubles ahead.

"What are the guardians doing with you today?"

Colleen's blue eyes grew big as she closed in, invading my personal space, her breath warming my face. "They're taking us up the mountain."

"Wow. Are you strong enough to hike the mountain?"

"Aye." One of her charges, Corwin, flexed his muscle. "We very strong."

Her other older charge, Nialla, beamed with confidence. "Colleen will help us."

I pointed to her youngest, sitting with his thumb in his mouth. "And what about Beagan? Will someone carry him?"

Colleen confirmed by sending her curls bouncing again. "The nurse has a sling. She attaches him to her back."

"Well, that sounds fun." My stomach rumbled, and the kids laughed. "I guess it's time for me to eat." I hugged them once more and kissed their sweet, lavender-scented heads. "Have fun on the mountain."

A spicy scent met me as I entered the foyer. I dragged the heavy dining room doors, and a blast of cinnamon, fresh-baked bread, coffee, clinking china, and conversation launched through the crack. My stomach rumbled again. It had grown accustomed to a fabulous meal this time of day. I swooped to my usual spot with Wolf, Cahal, my mother, Declan, Alastar, and Maili and found my empty seat, next to Kai. King Aleksander and King Abracham sat at the head of the table.

How was King Aleksander managing without Rowan? I know I missed her. I lost my roommate, traveling companion, and confidant.

But the king had only just found her after believing she was kidnaped. And now he'd lost her again.

The familiar guilt clenched my gut. If only I hadn't lost Turas. Rowan and Evan would be here. The selkie would be here. The stronghold would be ours already. And we'd have access to more resources.

At least I was back with my friends and family.

I scraped my chair out along the tile. Kai turned from his conversation with Declan and flashed me his dimples. Would I ever grow tired of that smile? Doubtful.

"What's on the menu this morning?" I grasped my chair seat and hopped it forward until I was close enough to the table. "I hear there's apple and cinnamon. It smells wonderful." I glanced around at the waitstaff serving plates, making their way toward this end of the room.

Kai shrugged.

Declan leaned forward to see me past Kai. "It's 'breacag'."

Okaaay... I grimaced. "That doesn't sound as wonderful as it smells."

"It is, trust me. It's been so long since I've had any." He licked his lips.

A servant came by with a carafe. "Care for coffee, miss?"

"Yes, please." I grabbed the cup resting upside down on a saucer and held it for her to pour the steaming liquid.

She filled the cup and curtseyed.

"Thank you." I sipped the buttery brew I'd grown to crave each morning. The hot liquid warming my insides, I held the mug in both hands to heat them.

Another servant came by and set a plate before each of us.

King Abracham rose. "King Aleksander has bestowed me with the honor of thanking God for our meal." He bowed his head. "Heavenly Father, thank You for this meal and, again, for returning King Aleksander's kingdom. May peace and prosperity reign throughout these lands as You bless Your servants. I pray the selkie would arrive safely and soon so we may resume our quest You've set before us, amen."

A chorus of amen rang throughout the hall. Abracham returned to his seat and adjusted his Merlin beard in his lap. Shuffling and clinking filled the hall as people donned their napkin and dug into their meal.

"What is this again?" I asked, cutting into the long roll dusted in cinnamon.

"Breacag." My mother leaned in from my left. "It's like a rolled pancake. This one is stuffed with a baked apple mixture."

The slice fell on its side, spilling dark juices. I cut a smaller piece, speared the doughy goodness and a fragment of apple, dragged it through the sauce, and plopped it in my mouth. Oh. My. Deliciousness. A cross between cinnamon rolls and apple pie sent my taste buds into instant ecstasy. Colleen hadn't been exaggerating.

"Delicious, isn't it?" my mother asked.

I nodded, hiding my mouth behind a hand as I chewed. So good.

Yet again, I'd found a refuge. I closed my eyes in silent thanks to God for giving us times of reprieve between the trials. I wanted to help the Ain Dìleas and everyone else get their lands back. But to a lesser degree than when I was in Kai's little paradise. I recalled the serene blue waters lapping against the submerged balconies and sighed. It was the closest I'd ever experienced to a true home. Perhaps I'd return someday.

Although Bandia didn't compare to Kai's sanctuary, it was nice, especially now that our faith was not only tolerated but also shared and welcomed. Though Pepin was probably the only pech in our ranks who believed in God. And many of the selkie probably weren't believers either. But they didn't complain. Hopefully, they'd become believers. I snuck a peek at Kai. He'd never professed any kind of belief either. Should I talk to him about that?

Kai chewed a mouthful. He must've felt my eyes on him. He viewed me askance and smiled.

This probably wasn't the best place for such a conversation. Instead, I stuffed my mouth with more breacag.

How much time did we have left? The selkie could arrive any day. As soon as they did, we'd resume our mission. The minute we set foot on another ship, I'd lose my comforts, and life itself will become a battlefield once more with my constant companions—fear and uncertainty—threatening to devour me. My gut clenched just with me imagining it. Life on board a ship was horrible—rations of indigestible could-survive-the-apocalypse food, including biscuits that broke teeth and salted meats that caused instant dehydration. My mouth suddenly dry, I reached for my water glass and gulped it down, then almost snickered over what so much liquid would lead to. And shipboard, the facilities left much to be desired.

Then, once on land, we'd be in fasgadair territory. We'd have an army, including many redeemed and the triplet fire. But we'd also have limited food. And the journey alone, constant walking—sometimes through muck and rain, steep inclines, thorny bushes. My back ached as I thought of sleeping on the ground again.

Bandia may not be Kai's paradise or home, but I *really* didn't want to leave.

CHAPTER FIFTEEN

"You sure you don't want to come for a swim with me?" Kai wiped his mouth, threw his napkin on his plate, stood, and pushed in his chair.

"I wish I could," I half-whined. Swimming with him in dolphin form was tempting. "But I—"

"I know. I know. You need to build your wings' strength in case you have to fly." He spoke in a mocking tone. "You're so predictable." He quirked his lips. "I assume we're still on for a hike?"

"Of course. Every day." I nudged his arm. "See you in an hour." I trekked outside the castle, uphill to the field just right of the fortress and ducked into a shielding mass of shrubs. My changing spot.

After removing my clothes, I transformed into a falcon and hopped free of the shelter. The sunlight warmed my little body. I stretched and shook my feathers, then preened to rid those that had molted and align them for flight. It was nice to have the opportunity to keep myself in prime shape. Once the battle began, I might not have the chance.

Prepped for flight, my pinions lifted me off the ground with less effort than when I'd begun training. People and all my cares shrunk beneath me as I rose. My enhanced eyesight noted the slightest movement with crystal clarity. I inhaled the sweet air, allowing a westerly wind to carry me toward the fields between the castle and the mountains.

For the next forty-five minutes, I practiced evasive maneuvers—flips, spirals, and dips—anything to help me avoid arrows or fasgadair in bird form. And the most important maneuver with which I had an advantage over every other type of bird—the dive.

I climbed higher and higher until the air thinned. The few clouds in the sky floated below me. I ducked back below the clouds and spotted the kids on the "mountain" and chuckled in my mind. As I suspected, they were bringing the kids on a walk on the hills before the mountains. I swooped low. Colleen spotted me and waved like crazy. Corwin, Nialla, and Beagan saw what caught her attention and waved too. I circled around for another pass. Every kid on the hike jumped and waved. I squawked at them as I soared past.

Then I ascended back through a cloud, banked toward the water, and tucked into a dive, hoping Kai might see me show off my speed. I gained momentum as I plummeted and sensed I was approaching a new personal record. I wished someone could clock my speed. Pepin might be able to with his internal clock. But he wasn't here. It had to be upward of two hundred miles per hour. The air whizzed through my feathers as the sea rushed toward me. Just as I feared I might crash into the water, I spread my wings. My feet skimmed the water, and my tiny heart pulsed like a strobe light.

Kai leapt from the ocean. And, for a moment, it was as if we were flying side-by-side. Then he fell back into the sea. I banked back around, and he reemerged before me, undulating to stay above water, cackling as he went, before flopping sideways with a splash. I returned to the heights and flew into the headwinds to strengthen my wings.

When my time was up, I circled my changing spot to ensure nothing lurked about, then dropped to my clothes hidden in the shrubs. I changed back to my more familiar human form and gravity settled in, weighing me down along with ever-looming heaviness of what was to come.

Trying to shake it off, I dressed and headed to the fortress to meet Kai for our hike.

A guard poked his head from the open window on the upper level as I walked past. "I could set my clock by you."

I laughed. My bird-self had a keen sense of time that required no thought. It was instinct.

But what I still couldn't understand was—how did I have no fear when flying? In human form, I'm still afraid of heights...among many other things.

Kai jogged up the hill, shaking water from his hair. This was my favorite time to watch him. Swimming invigorated him. He looked so alive, like he could conquer the world. "Ready?"

I nodded, and we fell in step with each other, passing the fortress to the trail into the Cnatan Mountains. The first few times we ventured this trail, I wanted to turn back. Between the unseasonable heat and difficult terrain, I wasn't up to the challenge. But two weeks had done wonders. I breezed down the hill and up the rocky path. I still wished I had thought to pack hiking boots. But they would've added too much weight and bulk to my already overstuffed pack.

It was probably just as well. I'd lost much of what I had at the stronghold and in the shipwreck. It would be easier to travel without so much stuff. I managed just fine last year when I was dragged through the megalith with nothing but the clothes I wore and Drochaid. And I never considered how much of a burden it would be on my friends. An image of Pepin sandwiched between my pack and his own sitting on Wolf's laden back sprang to mind. I cringed at the thought. Yup. Better to have less.

Still, I was happy to have recovered some of my things from my first visit to Bandia. Extra jeans, T-shirts, and my selkie dress were most important.

But my journal. Losing that hurt. I could only hope I'd find it in the stronghold.

We reached the ridge and started back the way we'd come.

"Are you going to practice archery with me today?" I followed Kai down a steep slope. Unable to stop my momentum, I ran into him.

He turned just in time to catch me.

My face warmed as my forearms braced against his chest. "Sorry." I stepped back.

"My pleasure." His dimples made another spectacular appearance. "I'm happy to catch you."

I let out an unattractive snort as I pushed past him down the hill. Why did he always say things like that? Why did it make me react in unpredictable, repelling ways? Was I *trying* to push him away? Better get a grip before I succeeded.

We walked the rest of the way in silence. I didn't have much breath, anyway. We'd chosen the most aggressive trail I was willing to take. There were worse trails in the Cnatan Mountains. Much worse. People usually returned battered and bruised from those hikes. No thanks.

We arrived in the archery practice field where Maili assisted others with their aim. Kai had never answered my question. But he stuck around, so he must be planning to practice.

Maili waved as we approached. She never smiled. She'd lost Shimri not too long ago. Zakur's father. Judging from the goodbye she gave Zakur when we left for Bandia, they had feelings for each other. Was she still mourning Shimri's loss? Or missing Zakur? Probably both.

And she had none of her own people here. I mean, we're all gachen and she's among our family of believers, but she had no other tree folk from Kylemore. She must feel like an outsider. As the only half-human from America...or anywhere in the human realm, I could understand. But it was different for me. I wasn't among the last of my clan. If anything happened to Zakur, would she be the last of hers?

Ryann sprang to mind, and I kicked myself for doing the same thing with Maili. She didn't make it easy, but I should at least try to get to know her better.

Kai and I headed to the rack of bows. I picked the same one I always chose with the grip wound in a leather strip adorned in aqua beading. The tension was perfect and offered me more success than the other bows I'd tried.

I nocked my bow, anchored it against my mouth, and channeled my anger as I focused on the bull's-eye. Morrigan. The reason every-thing went wrong in my life. The reason my family split. The reason my father died. The reason my nasty grandmother raised me. Hate and fury rose within me, through my eyes and arms as I focused on my mark. I released the string, and the arrow shot forward, straight into the target's center. And the string didn't smack me in the arm.

"Woohoo!" I raised my arms in the air and jumped.

Kai lowered his weapon. "This is why I don't like shooting with you." But his grin belied his words. He shook his head, waited for me to simmer down, and set up his shot.

"Pfft." The arrow whizzed through the air and shot the target dead-on.

A smug smirk curved his full lips. "I believe that's closer to center than yours."

I scoffed. "It's in the target." I left my mouth hanging open, feigning hurt, as I motioned toward the arrow sticking out of the center circle. "It's a perfect shot."

"It's not as in the center as mine is." He waited for the other trainees to take their shots, then stepped toward the targets.

"And this is why I don't like shooting with you." I chased after him.

Upon closer inspection, he was right. But I couldn't give him the satisfaction. "See? It's in the center." I yanked my arrow from the target.

It was his turn to pretend to be upset. "Uh—You just—" He pointed at me. "You did that on purpose. You know it wasn't as centered as mine."

"I know no such thing." With an air of superiority, I spun and returned to the practice line.

"Are you two finished?" Maili approached us.

Kai and I grinned at each other and laughed.

She crossed her arms, her scowl reminding me of Ryann once more though they looked nothing alike. Maili resembled the selkie with her dark eyes and hair that shone like obsidian. But her skin wasn't as dark. And her deep-set eyes, arched eyebrows, and high cheekbones looked like no other selkie I'd seen. Ryann was the polar-opposite in features with dazzling green eyes that, had she lived in my realm, I would've believed were colored contacts and wavy, reddish blonde hair. But their motherly, no-nonsense personalities were similar.

It had taken a while to warm up to Ryann. And I'd wished I'd done so sooner, particularly after she was killed. One thing Ariboslia taught me—you never knew when your time was over.

CHAPTER SIXTEEN

Maili hung around as Kai and I practiced. What did she want? Perhaps I should take this opportunity to get to know her. As Kai set up his next shot, I edged closer to her. "What's up?"

She squinted into the sky.

"No, not up." I changed tactics. "You look like you want to say something."

"You're doing well with the bow. You should practice your hand-to-hand combat."

I hated nothing more than practicing with Maili. I rested the bottom of the bow by my foot, careful not to put weight on it. The thing was solid, but I didn't want to risk snapping it in half. "If I end up in a face-off with Morrigan, with or without weapons, trust me, nothing you teach me will save my life."

"Trust *me*, Fallon. Repeated practice is necessary to instill the movements into your muscles, making your responses automatic. You may find yourself in an altercation with another fasgadair."

"The only things that will save me against a fasgadair are the triplet fire, a blood-dipped arrow, or letting the thing bite me."

Face scrunching, she threw me an unimpressed look. "There's a good chance Morrigan is aware of the power of redeemed blood. If she hasn't figured it out yet, she will soon. When we arrive on my homeland, the fasgadair will likely be too smart to risk biting anyone. And what if you're separated from your brothers, lose your bow, or run out of arrows? I thought you wanted to be prepared for anything? That's what you keep saying, isn't it?"

"I do. That's why I've been practicing." Why was I arguing with her? It was a waste of time, and I was *supposed* to be bonding. "You're right. Sorry. I'll try to quit being so negative."

Kai waved. "I'm off to help with swords." He sauntered away.

"Fallon, I need you to take this seriously. Ridding Ariboslia of Morrigan depends on you." A flash of doubt broke through her stony expression. She set her jaw and rested her hands on her hips.

Yeah. Get rid of Morrigan. No pressure.

"If you don't..." Her eyebrows twitched, threatening to break her façade. She took the bow from my hand.

Was this the opportunity I was waiting for? I had to reach her before she shut down again. "What's really bothering you?"

She stared at me, and an uncomfortable silence reigned between us. "Shim—" Her voice broke, and her hand flew to her mouth. She clenched her jaw.

I'd never seen her falter. I squeezed her shoulder, wishing I could say something—anything.

She backed away from my grip and steeled herself, forcing the words out. "I pray Zakur is still alive." She blew out air as if attempting to release her emotions as her fingers played with her tunic hem. "I'll be all right. God is with me." She regained control. "But I fear I may be the last of my clan."

I sucked in my breath. "But the kid—the cheetah. We sent him to Notirr and Kylemore." The Cael made it out. Why not the Arlen? "Didn't you get the warning in time?"

"The boy you sent fulfilled his quest. But we received the news a day behind the Cael. They'd borrowed our only ship for trade with Bandia. Our only chance to escape was to meet them."

The trainees lined up their shots, and several arrows flew in succession, filling the air with the sound of rubbing corduroy.

"But the boy never returned, and we were running out of time. We couldn't leave on foot and live as refugees on the land without splitting up into smaller groups. So, the elders opted to stay and fight, trusting our abilities among the trees and our hidden homes to protect us." Maili rubbed the gooseflesh on her arms. "We didn't know there'd be so many fasgadair or that they would burn our village." She worked to keep her voice steady.

"As you saw. A portion of our forest village survived along with three elephants. I pray Zakur and the elephants are still okay, so I can return and we can rebuild our clan." Her shoulders slumped. "And I still have to tell him his father is dead."

"But what about the watchmen, surely you and Zakur aren't the only two Arlen left."

"There are two, both elderly. I can only hope they—" Maili's voice cracked. She blew out a breath and clenched her jaw. "I just hope they're all still alive. Many of the children were taken prisoner." She straightened to her full height and squared her shoulders. "I must find them. And I need your help."

And I thought I had problems. It sounded like she planned to marry Zakur, not Declan. I was curious how she felt going against her parents' wishes but couldn't bring myself to ask. Given the extreme change of circumstances, wouldn't they approve? What little I understood of Ariboslia had flipped upside down since my first visit last year.

I scanned Maili. Her set jaw. Her hardened charcoal eyes that, when scrutinized, betrayed her uncertainty. Her firm grip on the sword by her hip. She was preparing for battle, and I was goofing off. How would I feel if my hopes to rescue my people—kids—came down to a twerp like me? Humbled, I nodded. "Okay. I'm sorry I haven't been taking the combat portion of this mission as seriously as I should. Train me."

Before I knew what was happening, she wrapped me into a head-lock, reminding me why I hated training with her.

I attempted to escape her grip as Sloane had shown me last year. I tucked my chin, pushed her arm up, and ducked through the hole to the side. I'd never succeed against a fasgadair. But if this made her feel better...

"So, why the elephants?" I asked after escaping her grip.

The question seemed to confuse her. "What do you mean?" She tossed me a wooden stick, a mock dagger, and armed herself. "Time for offensive maneuvers."

"I mean, what do you need elephants for?"

"For travel. My clan are tree folk, we prefer to keep to the trees or ride elephants. We will walk on the ground." She waved at the grass beneath her. "Obviously. But we prefer to remain above ground level." She motioned for me to come at her.

I thrust the dagger toward her in a lame attack.

She blocked. "You won't hurt me. I'm a skilled warrior. Come at me like you mean it. Like your life is at stake." She threw me a mischievous smile. "Like Kai's life is at stake."

Oooo... She knew how to get to me. I laughed, then tried to summon the rage I'd feel if Kai's life really was in danger.

"Agh!" I came at her full force.

She knocked me off balance and pushed me aside.

I came at her again.

She sidestepped and disarmed me in one swift motion, then retrieved my weapon and lobbed it to me. "Again."

I faked left, then swung with my right.

Maili must've seen the fake-out coming. She didn't falter. Again, she disarmed me in seconds. How was this helpful? I flopped onto the ground and grabbed a flask.

"Is this...?" I pointed to the flask, not wanting to accidentally drink blood.

"'Tis water." She sat next to me. "Have a drink."

"So, what's your totem?" I took a long swallow.

"Gibbon." She reached out, waiting for me to hand her the water.

"What's that?"

She cocked her head and narrowed her eyes. "Do you not have gibbons in your realm? They're similar to other monkeys, but much more agile. I can perform stunts in the trees." She glanced off into the distance. There weren't too many trees around here. Just a few in the hills before the mountains. "Most of my clan are tree-dwelling animals."

"Like, what? Monkeys?"

"Zakur's a sugar glider. He's very sneaky. And adorable." Her dark eyes sparkled. "When my friends and I reached our totems, we'd play in the trees after our lessons. My best friend was a lynx. I remember how jealous she was of the rest of us: a spider monkey, a flying lemur, a squirrel, and a fire dragon."

"Why was she jealous? Lynxes are cool."

"She didn't think so. We were better suited for trees, able to hop from one to the other. Her determination to keep up with us improved her skills, but there were many places she couldn't follow, and she'd occasionally get stuck." She capped the flask, and we both stood. "Ready?"

Before I could answer, she took me down.

After about an hour, Maili released me. By this time, I was thoroughly exhausted. And bruised from head to toe. My legs were tired, my arms ached, and my stomach rumbled. Hand-to-hand combat didn't suit me. But I'd humor her. It was the least I could do.

It wasn't time for lunch yet. I trekked across the field to where Kai was helping others with swords. The sword he'd found for me from the armory stuck out of the rack on the wagon. As the only one with something resembling a Celtic knot on the pommel, it was easy to spot. I retrieved it and gave it a swing. Despite my sore arms, it felt good, like it was made for me. Unlike most swords, I could lift it over my head and strike with accuracy. I just needed to work on increasing the power behind my swing.

While Kai was busy with a boy I'd never seen before, I practiced the maneuvers he'd shown me on a log jutting up from the ground, wrapped in a thick rope.

Kai left the boy to practice and approached me, sword drawn.

The sword was growing heavy in my overtaxed arms. Still, I held it up, waiting for his attack, trying not to get distracted by his flexed muscles...or the intensity in his eyes. He swung, and I blocked, sending a shock traveling up my arms. "Why do you spend so much time teaching me this? A sword won't save me." Ugh, echoes of my conversation with Maili. Why was I stuck on repeat today?

"Stop being so bleak. You keep saying you want to be prepared for anything, but when fighting is involved, you complain." He struck again.

"I'm just not a fighter." I swung, intercepting his attack, but I was losing strength, our swords came way too close to my face. "Whatever is going to happen, I don't think it will come to me fighting, weapons or no."

"Well, I don't know how to defeat an opponent any other way. And I'd feel better if I knew you could at least handle yourself in a battle." He shimmied forward, clashed my sword with his, then swirled it in such a way that I dropped mine and fell backward. He lowered his weapon to his side and caught my fall.

I scarcely breathed as he held me, his dark eyes staring into mine —intent. His face lowered toward me. This was it.

"They've arrived!" someone shouted. "The selkie and pech have arrived!"

"Fallon, did you..."

That sounded like Alastar.

Kai released me, and I caught myself from falling, then tugged my T-shirt.

"...hear?" Alastar's gaze flipped from me to Kai and back a few times, his mouth forming a small smile. "Am I interrupting something?"

He was becoming like a little brother. Just how Matty would've been with Stacy.

"Not at all." Kai sheathed his sword, rubbed the back of his neck, and avoided eye contact.

"The selkie and pech are in port."

"So, we heard." I stepped toward Alastar and waved to Kai. "Let's go."

If only the selkie had arrived a minute later.

CHAPTER SEVENTEEN

"Evan! Rowan!" I shouted as they disembarked. I expected Rowan, but I wasn't sure if the selkie would make Evan stay back and take his rightful place as their king.

He threw me a toothy grin, his white teeth gleaming against his dark skin. The time on deck, exposed to the sun must've deepened his tan. His blue eyes sparkled. He would make an exotic-looking king.

I fought through the crowd.

Evan dropped his pack, grabbed me, and pulled me in for a hug. Considering he hadn't washed properly since boarding, he didn't smell bad. Just a tad musky.

When Kai raised an eyebrow, I released Evan and gave him an awkward pat on the back.

"It's so good to see you." I didn't realize just how much I missed my friend. We'd grown close over the past months.

"It's good to see you too." Evan kissed my forehead.

Kai draped an arm over my shoulder. "Ya, you too."

Evan shouldered his pack as Rowan neared. Were you supposed to hug a princess?

"'Tis good to see you, friend." She gave me a quick nod.

Guess not. Was I supposed to bow? I nodded back. "You too."

We headed to the castle and fell in step together.

"Sorry we didn't return. Morrigan tore me from Turas." I kicked a pebble on the road. "I can't believe I lost it. There's so much we could've done."

"Morrigan?" Evan stopped short and pushed my shoulder, forcing me to face him. He stared as if wondering how I was still alive. "We assumed you disconnected with Turas, but Morrigan? I didn't expect you to cross paths with her yet."

"She didn't try to kill me." Answering his unspoken question, I waved him forward, and we resumed our walk. "We'll fill you in later. Tell me about you?" I raised a hand to block the sun. "Did the selkie make you king?"

Sunlight crowning him, Evan tipped his head back and forth. "Yes and no. I haven't been sworn in yet. There's a good number, particularly among the older officials, who don't want an exiled half-breed to claim the throne. But that's a battle for another day. I insisted on returning to aid in the war. They're entrusting the day-to-day decision-making to the council until my return. The choice to wait placated most everyone."

"But he will be king." Her posture regal, her chin tilted, Rowan spoke with confidence. "The people are in an uproar from lies and broken families. They're ready for change and consider Evan the perfect candidate to honor their traditions and overturn corrupt laws."

I almost said, "You mean *if* he returns."

But I held my tongue and shuddered at the thought. But it was true. Some of us might not return.

BEFORE DINNER, we gathered in the courtyard before moving into the dining hall to eat. The environment differed with the new arrivals in our midst. How long had it been since gachen and selkie coexisted? Had they ever? It warmed my heart to witness the walls keeping us apart, the ruse of the gachen/selkie attraction started and fueled by selkie elitists, tearing down. The truth was out.

And the pech emerged from hiding. Hadn't they retreated below ground when the gachen first arrived? How many years had they been avoiding the gachen and selkie? Hundreds? Thousands?

This room. At this time. With these people. This was history in the making. Was I the only one who recognized it as such?

I stood with my friends, listening to Evan share what happened after we left.

"Even when you travel within the current time, you return at the exact time you left. So, when you didn't return right away, we knew something went wrong. Still, we gave it two days, readying the ships. When the ships were prepped and you still hadn't returned, we set sail."

"Kai?" A petite girl with hair that shimmered in rippling black waves like the ocean after midnight and dark eyes that took up most of her diminutive face tapped Kai's shoulder.

Who was this? She looked like something from *Toy Story*. An animated doll.

"Ji Ah?" He gawked.

She smiled the most adorable smile and opened her eyes wide, full of adoration. Kai scooped her into his arms.

The green-eyed jealousy monster I never knew existed within me surfaced, and I was overcome with the desire to "accidentally" make this adorable creature disappear. Seriously, who was this girl? She had better be his sister.

Ji Ah disappeared in Kai's strong arms as he lolled her from side-to-side. Just as I readied to peel them apart, he released her. Gripping her arms, he bent to look into her eyes. "How are you?"

The girl, Ji Ah, opened her mouth to respond.

Kai glanced around. Then his eyes darkened. "Why are you here? I thought only soldiers were arriving."

Her smile now crinkled up her bewitching face. "I'm here for my nursing skills." Her mouth transformed into a pout as her dark eyes widened, resembling a baby seal. "Though I hope I'm not needed. I'm sure I will be. And I want to help."

"Of course, you do." Kai caught her head and tugged her into his chest yet again.

I clenched my fists. The monster within me seethed.

Kai turned to me, grinned, and released her. "Ji Ah, there's someone I want you to meet." He motioned toward me.

Ji Ah raised her eyes expectantly. I stood about a foot taller than this little thing.

"This is my—Ah. This is Fallon."

"Hello." I plastered a smile onto my face and attempted to unclench my jaw. This is my *what*? Was he going to say girlfriend? He should have. Perhaps my smile wouldn't be so forced.

Ji Ah flashed me another darling smile and bowed. "Pleased to meet you, Fallon."

Kai introduced Ji Ah to the rest of my friends and family. Stars filled their eyes as they gazed upon the bundle of cuteness.

Maili glanced my way as if wondering what I thought of this, then addressed Ji Ah. "How do you know Kai?"

Thank you, Maili! Good question.

"Oh." She patted his chest in a way-too-familiar way that made me want to bite her hand. "We attended primary school together. We were very close." Her expressive face morphed from adoration and joy to concern and fear. "But when we went swimming one day before our bian, Kai changed into a dolphin. I hid him from our friends. That was so sad, wasn't it?" She peered up at him, the pout returning. "He pretended his totem was delayed. But, once you turn seventeen, if you can't prove you turn into a seal, the elders assume you're hiding your true totem and banish you." She rubbed Kai's chest. "That was the last I've seen of him...until now." She rested her head against his chest, then smiled up at him.

If this girl wanted to help anyone on the battlefield, she'd better get her hands off Kai. She was about to become a casualty.

The guys stared at her—spellbound. The little witch.

Mercifully, the crowd moved into the dining hall. Kai grasped my hand and pulled me along. Ji Ah noticed our linked hands. I couldn't read her face, but she stopped touching Kai. Good call.

Kai sat beside me, as usual, with Ji Ah on his opposite side. She kept him engaged in conversation. I couldn't hear her, and I couldn't see past him. I slumped against my chair and held an impromptu pity party.

What was my issue? Kai and I weren't a thing. He'd never asked me out. Did they even do that around here? How did that work anyway? It's not like we could go to dinner and a movie. And it didn't matter. We were on the brink of war. Starting a relationship made no sense.

Then why was it such a struggle to tame the beast within me?

King Aleksander stood and waited for the chatter to simmer down. "It warms my heart to welcome the selkie and dark pech. We've been awaiting this moment with much eagerness. Bandia owes you a debt of gratitude. Thanks to your efforts, our kingdom has been restored. It's an honor to stand before you today as king of a revived nation that will become better, stronger, with our religious and racial barriers torn down. I'm honored to have the pech, selkie, and gachen dining together in my home. This fills me with great hope for the future." He aimed adoring eyes at Rowan sitting beside him. "And I'm grateful beyond measure to have my daughter here by my side."

Evan sat at the head table next to Rowan. How strange to see him sitting there. This must be Bandia's public acknowledgment of Evan as royalty.

King Aleksander faced heavenward. "God, thank You for going before us and preparing the way to restore our lands. Thank You for returning my daughter and the redeemed fasgadair. Thank You for tearing down walls, rooting out lies, and shedding light upon the truth to unite us. Knit our hearts together and be with us, I pray, as we prepare for the battles ahead."

He lifted his glass. Others followed suit.

"Tomorrow we reclaim the stronghold, then the lands of those who are still displaced. Ariboslia will be restored!"

Cheering and whistles echoed through the hall, chased by silence as everyone drank to his toast.

Tomorrow we would follow King Aleksander's plans to reclaim the stronghold. After that, I'd have to figure out how to handle the Ji Ah situation. If I could take out a fasgadair, I could eliminate this petite threat.

CHAPTER EIGHTEEN

I stood on the ship's deck, watching the line of similarly dressed selkie embark on the plank like ants in formation, climbing along a limb, and waited for the crew to sail it out of the harbor toward the stronghold. A wave of doubt swept through me. What were we doing running to a fortress full of fasgadair? Even if Alastar was right and their numbers were sparse, there was no way to sneak onto the shore. How would the selkie survive this without redeemed blood?

The setting sun cast an orange and red haze flaring up over the mountains. The remaining yellow orb peeked through wispy clouds. Water lapped the dock and boats bobbing in the harbor. Splashing drew my attention. Two men paddled a rowboat past us. Gulls squawked, waddling along a shallow area on the harbor's far side. The air was chilly, and the boat offered no reprieve from the wind. But I'd be in my bird form soon enough, and the cold wouldn't bother me.

I was as jittery as if I'd just pounded twenty double espressos. Where was this doubt, this uncertainty, coming from? I tended to run straight toward trouble.

Time. And waiting. Too much time to overthink wasn't good for me.

Keep your focus on Me.

I sucked my breath and rubbed my arms with shaky hands. *Forgive me, God. Help me keep my eyes on You.*

The captain belted out orders as the crew scurried about preparing the ship for sail. Selkie wearing sleeveless tunics to their knees with no pants cluttered the deck. They donned swords on their backs in sheaths strapped around both shoulders. They looked like men in nightgowns ready for battle. But I was too nervous for them to laugh.

Kai stuck out wearing his usual tunic and leather pants.

He spotted me, and his eyes widened. I glanced at the rippling aqua material hugging my waist and tugged. It was too form fitting. He'd never seen me wearing a dress...other than his oversized tunic. His gaze heightened my discomfort.

He waded through the crowd without taking his eyes off me. "You look amazing."

"Uh, thanks?" I returned the compliment with a crooked, uncertain smile.

"You always wear those—what are they?—American clothes." He touched my upper arm, sliding the material between his fingers. "Did a selkie make this?"

"I assume so. A girl from Saltinat gave it to me."

I didn't realize his eyes could grow wider, but they did. "Once this war is over, let's go there."

He was making plans for the future with me? He wanted to stay with me? Even if he did, now wasn't the time to discuss it, if ever. One thing was for sure—I was growing more and more uncomfortable in this dress. I crossed my arms, missing my jeans and T-shirt.

The main sail puffed with air with a loud whoosh.

He mercifully averted his gaze to the horizon. "Why are you wearing a selkie dress?"

"It's easier to carry when I'm in bird form. And it's waterproof."

He frowned at the reminder of what I was about to do. "Promise me you'll be careful."

My brothers appeared over our shoulders donning the dresslike tunics the selkie wore. I snickered. More practical, yes, but oh so hilarious.

Declan glared at me.

Alastar snarled. "Shut your gob."

I gave them my most innocent look. "I didn't say anything."

Declan smacked Kai's back. "Don't worry. We'll take care of her. I've a good many months perfecting sneaking around. These two just need to follow my lead."

Spoken like a real older brother...even if it had only been by minutes. But it was true. Somehow, as a golden eagle—a giant bird—he'd followed me from the megalith, snuck on board two ships, stole food, flew into my room, and never got caught...well, other than by Valter. But no one believed him.

Valter. So sad. He could've had a better life. At least he believed at his heroic end. He was in paradise now.

"Not to worry." Alastar pushed his way in. "The selkie and the ships will provide ample distraction. They'll never see us coming." He must've misread my mourning of Valter's wasted life.

But I wasn't concerned about us. Not really. I feared for the selkie. But, even if they weren't believers, they joined us in God's mission. He would protect them. Right?

Declan raised his hand. "Ji Ah!"

Great. Just what I needed.

The boys waved her over. A smile overtook her face, and she waved like a little girl as she hopped. The crowd parted for her, and she bounded to us, reminding me of Stacy.

No. I could not allow myself to like her.

Alastar and Declan gushed as Kai advanced with a scowl. "What are you doing here?"

"I'm a nurse, remember? They'll need me if anyone is injured. Don't worry." She punched his shoulder. "I'll stay on the ship until it's safe." She shook her head and held up a hand beside her mouth, as if speaking only to me, but loud enough for everyone to hear. "He so protective." She rolled her eyes at him.

I glared at the nymph.

We left the harbor. The sun set, the sky darkened, and the air grew chilly. What day was it? I'd lost track. It must be September by now. The days were growing cooler. Though the selkie dress felt like nothing, the miraculous material kept my core warm. The wind swirled my hair, chilling my neck. I shivered.

"Are you cold?" Kai stepped behind me and wrapped his arms around me. "This better?"

Something within me wanted to resist, but Ji Ah was watching. "Yes." I pulled his arms tighter. "Much."

He rested his chin on my head.

Why did it take the threat of another girl to make me stop pushing Kai away? What was I doing? How many times had we almost kissed? We spent so much time together—it was as if we were dating already. What was this push-and-pull thing I was doing? Why did I resist?

Because we were headed into war. I might lose him.

I shivered again and fought the urge to push him away.

Pinpricks of lights emerged along the horizon. The stronghold.

"Positions!" General Seung yelled.

The selkie men wearing nothing but tunics and swords lined up along both sides of the two ships.

"Go!" the general ordered.

They jumped from the ship, transformed into seals midair, and dove into the sea. They shot ahead and disappeared. Apparently, seals could swim faster than this ship could sail.

The rest of the fighters, those who didn't transform into seals, flooded the deck from below.

"Are you ready?" Declan looked to Alastar and me.

If only it were so easy for us to transform, then reappear clothed.

We'd have to carry our clothes and hope we didn't get skewered midflight.

"We need to go now if we're to stay out of sight." Declan tucked his arms into his tunic and transformed into a golden eagle. Alastar freed Declan from the material.

This was the closest I'd ever been to Declan in his bird form. He was massive. As if he knew I was checking out his impressive size, he spread his wings. His wingspan was wider than my height.

"Okay, you can stop showing off." Could he understand me with Drochaid?

He tucked his wings and hopped on his massive legs from his clothes. Alastar shoved Declan's tunic inside a bag.

Alastar changed next. I'd never seen him in his owl form. The markings around his eyes made them appear huge though they were tiny. And his face was flat. Declan and I looked like real birds with eyes on both sides of our heads. Alastar's were close together on the front making him look grumpy. I laughed, and he looked grumpier still.

I stuffed Alastar's shirt into his bag. Then I slid my own pack to the deck. "Guess I'm next."

"Wait." Kai snatched my arm, tugged me close, and kissed my forehead. He released me. His intense gaze bore into my soul. "Come back to me."

A moment passed as I regained my senses. I nodded, then turned to my brothers, grateful they couldn't speak and birds didn't have facial expressions. Ji Ah stood frozen, her hands covering half her face. Her shock was clear in the way her eyes formed perfect Os. But I couldn't read her beyond that. Shocked and disappointed? Shocked and happy? Or just shocked?

I couldn't concern myself with any of that now. It was just a kiss on the forehead. Did that mean something more in their culture? Didn't matter. I needed to focus on the mission. Lives were at stake. I transformed into a falcon. He stuffed my clothes into my pack along with Drochaid.

"Chan fhaca mi a shamhail anns na thig is na thàinig." He smiled.

I ruffled my feathers and attempted to throw him an unimpressed look.

"Tha mi duilich."

"Kak!"

Kai laughed and pressed a finger to his lips. Then he patted my head, and I ducked.

Declan squawked. Alastar and I hopped over to him. I'd never stood beside another bird. As a great gray owl, Alastar was bigger than me, but Declan towered over both of us as a golden eagle. More than double my size. How in the world did he sneak anywhere?

He spread his imposing wings and cinched his bag with his talons. Kai backed up to give him room. Declan fanned us with gusts of wind as he lifted, his colossal legs dangling as he climbed. Alastar and I snagged our packs and took to the sky with ease. We overtook Declan in seconds.

Declan flew to the left of the island, circumnavigating it and staying low, close to the water's surface. Alastar and I flanked him. I swooped too low, and my pack dipped into the water. I climbed, hoping I hadn't soaked everything. Not that it mattered. Everything would be drenched soon enough, but not the selkie dress. It was impenetrable. Liquids slid right off, like water off a duck's back.

We kept the island to our right. Declan's wings occasionally skimmed the ocean. He seemed to be giving it all he had but staying behind him was challenging. Even gliding I had more speed. And I couldn't drift too much unless I felt like swimming.

I kept losing sight of Alastar. He struggled to follow Declan too. Times like these it must be nice to be an owl. His night vision must be incredible. But, with his eyes in front, he couldn't have the peripheral Declan and I had.

When we passed the island, we banked a sharp right to approach its backside. I couldn't hear anything. The seals must not have arrived yet. When we weren't far from shore, Declan plummeted into the water with a big splash. Alastar and I dove underwater after him. I transformed, removed Drochaid, placed it around my neck, and threw on the selkie dress. Whatever this wonder material was, it made changing underwater a less painful task. Jeans would've been a nightmare.

I followed Declan and Alastar to shore. My feet slipped on algae-covered rocks, and barnacles pricked my toes. I picked my feet up and swam instead. An image of the fasgadair ships I'd burned came to mind. What if a fasgadair lingered under here, drowning and regenerating over and over again? My heart beat quickening, I paddled faster.

Wait. They'd be on the other side of the island. And if I could stand, so could they. They shouldn't drown at this depth.

I slowed my pace and laughed at myself.

But what if there's a shark? Two notes rang through my mind...Da da.

I chanced touching the nastiness below and used my legs to propel me faster through the water as the *Jaws* theme song chased me. Once the water only came up to my thighs, I relaxed.

They headed toward shore, and I followed. When we were knee-deep, a shadow crossed the beach.

"Get ready." Declan edged closer.

"What—"

A fasgadair materialized before us.

CHAPTER NINETEEN

D eclan and Alastar grasped my hands, but no flames appeared. The fasgadair clutched Declan's neck and sunk his teeth into his flesh. Alastar punched the thing's side. It released Declan and roared, its eyes glowing in the moonlight, then leapt for Alastar. The demon stopped short and clutched its throat. A gurgling rose as he fell into the water and writhed like a sea serpent.

"Grab him!" I yelled. "Pull him out or he'll drown."

Alastar and Declan eyed each other as if thinking it might be a good idea to let him die before grabbing an armpit and dragging the demon to the beach. Once all but the beast's feet were on dry land, they dropped it. The monster stilled and turned to dust.

We must be downwind. I never even smelled the thing. Could they smell us? Nothing else moved on the beach. "I hope we didn't show up on this island with no weapons and no triplet fire." I pulled my sopping hair, wrung it out, and flipped it behind me. Maybe the water would cover our scent.

Declan pressed his bloodstained collar against his wound. We needed his hands free...assuming we could create the fire. He needed to keep applying pressure. I stopped in front of him and snatched his hand away, leaning in in the darkness. "Let me see."

When he released the pressure, blood flowed from the twin piercings.

"Rub dirt in it." Alastar scooped a handful of mud.

"What? You're actual—"

Alastar dipped his fingers in the mud and scrubbed it on Declan's wound.

"Okay...?"

"Good idea. Thanks." Declan winced. He eyed me. "You've never put dirt in a wound? It helps. And it will act like a bandage."

Yeah. That was a new one on me. But whatever. It should help mask the smell too.

"Let's try again." Declan ushered us up the beach where the fire was less likely to be spotted. "I'm hoping it just doesn't work when we're standing in water."

Please let this work. I clutched Alastar's damp hand then Declan's. We connected, and the fire ignited.

Thank You, God.

I hadn't realized I was holding my breath until I let it out.

We broke contact, and the flames disappeared.

"We shouldn't meet another fasgadair on this side of the island," Alastar said. "But stay close, just in case."

Declan led us across the rocky surface to crouch behind the shrubbery. Clashing metal sounded. We ducked behind shrubs, peeking over them, but we were still too far to see.

He motioned us to follow as he dashed over the dunes to the next thicket. We caught up and paused as he spied the situation. He crouched back down. "The selkie are here. Follow my lead. When I say now, we'll link hands." His eyes widened. "Ready?"

Not really. But Alastar and I both nodded.

We ran toward the fight.

"Grab hold!" Declan reached behind as he jogged in front, facing

forward. Alastar reached for me as well. I grasped both their hands.
The moment Alastar connected with Declan, the triplet fire shot up,
and we rushed into the skirmish, sneaking up behind a Fasgadair
swinging his sword at a selkie and melting the beast. The selkie
tipped his head and moved to the next fasgadair. We came up on two
more unawares before the remaining fasgadair kept their distance.

Arrows skewered fasgadair from archers arriving in longboats.
Felled fasgadair cut with swords without redeemed blood began to
regenerate. Our men from the dinghies took advantage of their weakened state and pierced them with blood-tipped swords. We were
winning.

Still, many selkie lay dead or dying on the rocky coast, just as I
feared.

When no fasgadair remained on the shore, we approached the
wooden gate and set it aflame. Kai and others stormed across the
beach with a battering ram they brought on a dinghy. They rammed
the door three times. The weakened wood splintered. The fourth stab
left a gash wide enough to push through. Fortunately, everything
surrounding the flaming gate was stone or sand.

Cahal knocked more of the splintered wood with his battle-axe.
Wolf peered through.

"No!" I called. Was the fool about to enter on his own? And he
lectured *me* for running into danger?

He winked at me, then disappeared through the hole. What a
hypocrite. The flame flared again.

Moments later, the remains of the door lifted. We passed underneath, watching out for falling, flaming debris.

"It's empty." I pointed out the obvious.

"Looks like they were outside, waiting for us. But let's spread out
in groups and check the entire stronghold, including the underground passages." Wolf waved us forward. "Keep the redeemed in
front in case you come across fasgadair."

The redeemed. So, the name for restored fasgadair had stuck. I
liked it.

Declan released us, and the fire vanished. "Stay close."

"I'll go anywhere but the tunnels." I wasn't as likely to have a panic attack without the droves of escapees sucking up my air supply like last time. And they were roomier than the pech tunnels. But why not let someone without claustrophobia make sure they're clear?

Declan nodded. "We'll check the upper rooms."

Alastar and I followed him up the stairs. We checked the room where God restored King Aleksander's health after seven years in a coma. Kagan's potions still littered his room. Was it possible Valter had stolen one and killed Kagan with his own poison?

Next, we inspected the room I'd shared with Rowan. The bag I used to stow her in peeked out under the bed. I examined the contents. A pair of jeans and a T-shirt covered with raccoon fur and my journal. I pulled it out and kissed it. My words weren't lost forever. I shoved it back into the pack and hugged it to my chest and practically bounced back to my brothers.

"Find something good?" Alastar raised an eyebrow, making one purple eye large.

"Yes. I thought I'd lost it forever." I squeezed it closer.

"Put it over your shoulder. We need your hands free." Declan stuck his head behind a tapestry and knocked on the wall. "This room looks clear."

I threw the pack over my shoulder.

We returned to the hallway and continued checking the rooms. The final chamber had a small door. Declan ushered us toward it. He eased it open to keep it from squeaking. We tiptoed up the stairs to a covered landing that opened to a path. A half wall shadowed the outside edge while a full wall towered over the other. We crept along the path to the backside of the stronghold. It was too dark to see much beyond the trees, but the sea rippled in the moonlight.

Keeping low, Declan spied around a corner. He waved us forward to an identical path and still no door in the high wall. We rounded the next corner. The carnage on the beach was visible in the firelight below. And in the path's center, we came to a door.

Declan motioned for us to huddle on the opposite side behind him, so he could pull the door open and keep us close. He inched the door forward. The door flew open, smacking his forehead. We fell like dominoes, Declan into Alastar, then Alastar into me, landing in a pile with a fasgadair looming over us.

CHAPTER TWENTY

The fasgadair wrapped a meaty claw around Declan's neck and lifted him off his feet. Alastar grasped Declan's arm as he stood, then groped for me. I grasped Alastar's outstretched hand, scrambled to stand, then reached around Alastar and latched onto Declan's arm too. Declan and I connected, and fire burst forth. The fasgadair's teeth loomed inches from Declan's neck. Its arm melted, the rest of its body followed within seconds. Declan dropped to the ground, pulling me and Alastar down, breaking our connection.

Crouching, Declan raised his hands behind him, ready for us to grab hold should we need as we entered. The room appeared clear. We relaxed as we inspected the space, searching the walls for any signs of a secret passageway.

"You won't find anything over there." Declan tapped the stones along the wall to the right.

"What makes you think there's a passageway on your side?" I asked.

"You can tell." He returned to the doorway. "The door is in the center of the path surrounding this room. But see how the room is shorter on this side? There's something here. Probably a stairwell."

"If that's true, let me check the rest of the outside wall before we descend to make sure the top level is secure." Alastar made his way toward the exit.

"By yourself?" I asked. "Are you crazy?"

Alastar pressed a finger to his lips and slipped out the door. Declan held the door as I peeked out to watch Alastar shimmy along the wall. He peered around the next corner and disappeared.

"Alastar!" I yelled in a hushed voice.

"Hold this." Declan released the door.

I caught it before it slammed against me. "What are you doing?" These guys would get us killed. Or me. I glanced back at the passage-way. Had it moved? Or was I being paranoid? I sniffed the air. No electric scent.

"Fallon!" My blood stopped in its tracks. Alastar.

I leapt from the room. The door crashed behind me. I dashed down the path, darting around the corner. The electric scent hit me. Still, I ran around the next bend, slamming into Declan. He and Alastar stood over a fasgadair thrashing on the ground.

The demon stilled, gave a final twitch, then turned to dust.

I punched Alastar's upper arm, then Declan's.

"Ow." They complained as they rubbed their arms, eyes wide, staring at me as if I'd just destroyed their favorite toy.

"What was that for?" Alastar asked.

I pointed at each of their faces in turn. "Don't do that again. You hear me? We stick together."

"Okay, okay." Declan held his hands up.

Alastar grinned.

I studied the stone wall before us. "Didn't we go full circle? This pathway must surround the room we were just in." Other than the fact that this path ended here.

"Yes. The covered stairs where we came up must be on the other side of this wall," Declan said.

We returned to what we believed was a false wall and tapped on stones. But I didn't know what I was looking for. I pressed a stone, and it budged. "Is this it?" I asked, sucking in a breath.

Alastar shoved the stone, and a door opened. Now that I saw the seams, I wondered how I hadn't noticed it. Electricity wafted from the gap.

"There's a fasgadair in there." I dragged Alastar away from the entrance by his collar.

Declan nudged ahead of Alastar, yanked a torch from the wall, and thrust it at me.

I lit it on fire, and the pale glow of a fasgadair face appeared over Declan's shoulder, fangs bared. I grabbed him and groped for Alastar as teeth sank into Declan from behind. His eyes widened.

Alastar kicked the fasgadair in the gut. The blood must've been doing its work because the fasgadair fell down the stairs, crunching bones echoing as it descended.

"Why didn't you connect with Declan and light him up?" I asked Alastar.

He hung his mouth open in mock hurt. "Aren't you the one who wants to give them a chance for redemption before just killing them? He'd already bit Declan. Might as well see if it will live."

We followed Declan to a landing where the demon's flattened clothes lay in a pile of dust. That one died in record time.

I'd never understand why some lived and others died. Just one of those things I'd have to leave in God's hands, where it belonged. Salvation didn't belong to me. I just helped it along...if possible.

We squished together on the landing. Alastar released a wall lever, and the opening stones made a grinding noise. I held my breath, expecting another vampire to attack. But we arrived in a room we'd checked earlier. Still clear.

"How can we know the place is secure when there are so many places for a fasgadair to hide?" I asked.

"We can't," Alastar said. "But the top levels are as secure as we can make them. Any fasgadair that slip by us at this point won't last.

They're outnumbered. And, unless they hope for redemption, they won't want to bite anyone once word of the redeemed has spread. They'll die off, eventually. One way or another."

CHAPTER TWENTY-ONE

The harbor bustled. Trunks of supplies, sacks of oats, and casks of wine and salted meats clogged the piers. A wooden crane hauled the awaiting supplies on board while crewmen lugged smaller items up the planks. Boys cleaned awaiting ships by dumping buckets of water while others came up behind with mops, swabbing the deck.

I adjusted my pack over my shoulders, waiting to board. Though it was somewhat lighter than when I'd first arrived through the megalith, it was quite heavy. It was jam-packed once more with everything I owned since I may never return to this place.

God, please don't let me lose my journal again.

If I made it through all this, I'd love to write of my adventures and share it with the world. I'd have to pretend it was fiction, of course. Probably fantasy. As wonderful as it would be to show people just how amazing God is, they'd never believe me anyway. And I might get myself incarcerated in the process.

But that was okay. If any part of my story drew them nearer to God, I'd have done my part in my realm too. But writing such a story would be a much simpler task with my journal. Already I was forgetting so much of what I'd experienced. And I'd hate to lose those memories.

"What's occupying yer mind, lass?" Wolf squeezed between me and Kai.

"Oh... Just thinking about the future." I pressed myself closer to Declan to give Wolf more room.

"Aye." Wolf pursed his lips. "I can't believe 'tis time. The selkie and dark pech are here. King Aleksander has his country back. God has been good to us. Nothing more stands in our way."

"Other than these guys still loading the ship. I thought this was supposed to be done yesterday?"

"There was a problem with the crane. 'Tis no problem. We're not far behind schedule. The ship'll be loaded up, and we'll be off to meet the pech in the Somalta Caverns in no time."

The men attached the last cask to the hoist, and my heart flipped. We'd be boarding soon.

"Yeah. Kagan's plan is finally happening." I sighed. "Too bad he wasn't here to see it."

Wolf nodded, his face somber as he hung his head.

Though Kagan manipulated me to set fasgadair ships on fire, I didn't hate him. He made choices he thought would protect the king and the kingdom. Unfortunately, he was wrong. And his insistence on clinging to his gods to the end and refusing to acknowledge the One True God meant he wasn't with Him. Not from what I could tell.

Chances were, we'd never meet again.

An image of a world without God, with nothing but all the horrors I'd experienced in this world, absent of all of God's goodness —flashed before me. A dark place, cold, surrounded by angry faces and gravestones, brimming with fear, hatred, and self-loathing. I shuddered. Would each person be isolated in their own personal hell? I didn't want to imagine such a place. If heaven was everything good, then hell was everything bad. Since the world comprised both and I was desperate to escape the terrible aspects, I wouldn't be able to handle even a nanosecond in a place like that.

I must prevent as many people from being separated from God, damned to hell for eternity, as possible. No one would go there if I had any choice in the matter.

But it wasn't up to me. God gave everyone a choice, and I needed to do the same. I had no power to do otherwise. I could only use the gifts God gave me and hope people would be saved. I just had to do my small part.

The fasgadair sought to devour and destroy with Morrigan in the lead. God put me here to bring as many people to Him as possible. I had to focus on Him and remember that end goal.

As I stood on the pier waiting to board, a renewed desire to save lives fueled me, but the method of transportation did not. I envied Pepin. If only I'd been dropped off at the Somalta Caverns with him.

But then I'd be trapped underground in a land crawling with fasgadair.

I shuddered. No thanks. I'd face that soon enough.

A crewman shouted something I couldn't make out and waved us forward. We boarded the ship like cattle, jostling each other onto the lower deck. I had no space. No breathing room. The low ceiling made it worse. I gulped for air as I pushed through to the stairs accessing the deck.

Free from the crowd, I took deep breaths and calmed myself, then headed toward the aft to watch Bandia drift out of sight. Pressure built at the back of my eyes, pricking my temples. I rubbed them and groaned.

"Another headache?" Kai, his elbows braced on the aftrail, looked over his shoulder at me. Wind blew stabs of dark hair into his eyes as he twisted in place.

I nodded. "It's not as bad as the others." It had been days since my last headache. I thought I'd gotten over whatever had induced them. They better not overtake me on the battlefield.

The pressure settled into a dull ache as a sinister sense of curiosity and glee overtook my mind. It was almost as if...

No.

I shook off the thought before it rooted in. It wasn't possible. I haven't had another dream since Alastar. No, not Alastar...Na'Rycha. Better to view them as two different people. Alastar was a new person. Na'Rycha was gone forever.

But what was this? The sensation of a malevolent presence in my mind was strikingly similar to the dreams when both Aodan and Na'Rycha had pervaded my mind. But I was awake. And I had no more family members with the ability to take over my mind. Did I? How many evil family members could one person have?

Ever since Wolf yanked me into Ariboslia last year, I've been stumbling upon family members. I've only known that Declan and Alastar were my brothers, triplets, for a couple months. Who knew what else I'd find? But at this point, I think my mother would have told me if I had any other family I should know about.

The pain slipped away, and I lost myself in Kai's concerned gaze. My heart melted. If only I could run away to his tropical paradise with him. But now, I needed to focus on the battle ahead. I couldn't allow anything to distract me.

"There you are." Ji Ah huffed and puffed in an exaggerated fashion. She approached Kai, bent forward, braced one arm on a knee and another on his arm. "Woo." She let out one final breath, then straightened and gathered her dark hair, pulling it over her left shoulder.

What had I just been thinking about distractions?

WE SPENT an uneventful week at sea, bored out of my mind. I'd lost my deck of cards in the shipwreck, so I found scraps from discarded sails, convinced the cooks to give me some beans, and had Kai stitch up crude beanbags. I snagged clay pots, and we played beanbag toss.

The boat's sway made the game more interesting. Everyone got involved when they had downtime. Wolf was the reigning champ.

We couldn't practice archery without losing arrows. Maili forced me to keep practicing fighting. And, since we were so far out to sea and the sailors recognized us, they let Alastar, Declan, and me take off as birds. What a relief to fly and get off the tiny boat. Okay...it was an enormous boat. But every day it seemed to shrink, stifling me.

The only thing that got me through was transforming and flying away from this cocoon. I approached a crewman with a bandana tied around his head. "Is it okay to fly today?"

"Sorry, lass. We're too close to land." He shuffled away.

I found my friends mending masts. Why had I never learned to sew? It seemed like something everyone in Ariboslia could do.

Ji Ah appeared over my shoulder. "Need help? My stitching could use some practice." Declan and Alastar both called out, holding up material, but she sat next to Kai and took some of his bundle. "Remember that time you stepped on coral?" She held a hand over her mouth. Crinkled eyes peeked over the top.

Kai cringed. "That hurt so bad."

She tipped her pointer finger in the air. "That was my first time stitching a person." She patted his arm, then giggled again. "Thank you for giving me a chance to learn."

She stitched his foot? I gagged.

Kai squinted against the sun, then put his needle down to shield eyes with a hand. "Are you going to fly?"

With Ji Ah cozying up to him, I wasn't sure I wanted to if I could. "No, they say we're too close to land."

"That's good news," Alastar said. "Why do you sound so sad?"

I shrugged.

"At least you got to fly." Kai sucked on the end of a string, then threaded a needle.

"Ya." Ji Ah adjusted the material on her lap. "Imagine being a selkie, so close to the water yet unable to touch it." She stabbed the needle into the canvas. "It's torture."

"I still don't understand why they wouldn't let you swim." I lowered myself to sit crisscross on the deck.

Kai poked the needle through the sail and tugged. "Swimming as a dolphin would have been fine. I can swim faster than this ship can sail with a strong wind—"

"As can a seal," Ji Ah interrupted.

"Ya." Kai tipped his head, acknowledging her comment. "But dressing in the water and climbing back on board a moving ship in human form would have been impossible without slowing the ship. I understand their concern."

I sighed. "At least we'll be off this floating coffin soon." Life at sea was beyond tiresome.

So was Ji Ah. Although she was starting to grow on me. Like a fungus. She seemed oblivious to my brothers who were clearly infatuated with her. And her relationship with Kai seemed close and comfortable, but less threatening than a week ago. Still, I wasn't entirely sure I could trust her.

"Land, ho!" The man in the mast spoke those beautiful words.

A handful of crewmen jumped along the rigging like monkeys. Gachen brought up flasks of blood and poured some into cups to dip swords and daggers. Selkie flooded the decks with their battle tunics and swords. Covering their swords in the blood was impractical since it would wash away when they swam to the beach.

The first battalion of redeemed boarded longboats from all nine ships. Archers prepared to shoot any animals that dared approach on the beach.

As the dinghies paddled closer to the shore, the selkie leapt from the ships, transforming into seals midair, as they had when storming the stronghold. But this time, we sent the redeemed ahead first.

Then I remembered the shark. I scanned the ocean for protruding fins. We'd killed the one that attacked us, but what if there were more? My heart stilled as I watched the selkie, flying through the water to shore. But so far, no signs of fasgadair. No scent. Nothing visible in the water or on land.

The dinghies delivered the redeemed and returned for the second battalion. Though a sizeable group now crowded the beach and stormed the forest, not one animal approached.

I boarded a longboat to join the crowd of confused fighters ready for action but finding none. Still nothing. Not one sign of a fasgadair. I sniffed. Nothing but salty air and dirty men. At least the selkie were cleaner after their swim.

Nervous tension filled the air. It was like preparing to confront someone, getting all worked up on the way to their house, and finding them not home. The heavy weight of an unaccomplished task settled on my shoulders. Fasgadair swarmed this shore when we left for Bandia. Where were they now? Had we found the perfect spot at the right time? Or were Morrigan's minions waiting to ambush us when our guard was down?

Keeping watch for anything suspicious, we loaded the necessities onto wagons. Warriors surrounded the supplies, and we walked in silence toward Kylemore. Trudging feet and squeaky wheels. All else quiet. Not even a tweeting bird. Men flanked us. I trekked along somewhere in the middle of the brigade.

Where were the fasgadair?

Not finding a fight was disconcerting. With each step forward, I felt more and more certain—we were walking into a trap.

CHAPTER TWENTY-TWO

Spindly trees surrendered to massive trunks, their thick canopies filtered the lowering sun, allowing dapples of dim light and promising night hadn't fallen yet. Hundreds of birds twittered, flitting about from branch to branch, scattering at our approach. Their song wafted through the sky. The path widened and smoothed with hard-packed dirt. So we had either entered or neared Kylemore. Maili's nervous energy radiated to me. Her face tenser than usual, only her shaking betrayed her. Like a surgeon's, that girl's hands never shook.

She picked up her pace, passing trees broad enough for cars to drive through. The trunks grew in girth. She ran to one capable of housing a Piper or Cessna airplane. She twisted a knot at the base. A smooth plank pushed out, then another and another, forming a spiral staircase along the trunk. Maili didn't wait until the steps ejected fully. She darted up the stubs still in motion and disappeared into the leafy canopy. A few soldiers followed.

I waited on the ground with Kai and my brothers, breathing in the sweet woodsy scent unique to Kylemore. The neighboring trees weren't quite as large, but they must be part of the treehouse village.

Did they have their own staircases? Or was this tree the key to gaining entrance to the village's bridge network concealed in the leaves? Good thing the dwellings were well hidden. They seemed untouched by the fires in the fasgadairs' attempt to burn the village. But then, perhaps that gave the Arlen a false sense of security so they ignored our warning to flee. The fasgadair didn't need to burn the entire village to decimate the Arlen. I shuddered. Hopefully, we'd be able to rescue some in this war so Maili wouldn't be the last of her clan.

God, please let Zakur and her elephants be okay.

"Okay, men." General Seung stood on a crate. "Welcome to Kylemore, our first destination. Ready the camp."

When he stepped from the crate, everyone dropped their things. Leaders barked orders. Men scattered, collecting supplies to raise tents and prepare fire pits while others spread out to hunt.

Maili burst through the cover, descending the staircase like a mountain goat running along a cliff's edge. She nearly knocked General Seung over. She muttered an apology as she passed, worry scrunching her face.

"Maili, did you—"

She dashed past me toward the pond where I'd first met her with the elephants.

Please, please, please let her find Zakur and her elephants...alive.

The men who'd followed her descended the stairs, frowning.

I walked among the sweaty men hammering tent pegs or dividing rations, with an armful of kindling, seeking fire pits ready to ignite.

Maili reappeared with Zakur. Her face more relaxed than I'd seen since we picked her up early this summer—a lifetime ago. Zakur grinned and squeezed her shoulder as they neared. She stumbled into him and flashing a shy smile in return.

Thank You, God.

Declan watched his betrothed. Judging from his goofy grin, he was as relieved as I was. I guess he wasn't in love with her. Or perhaps he cared about her happiness more than his own.

"Thank you for protecting the elephants." Maili seemed to notice the onlookers and adjusted her hair to block her view.

"Eh-hem." Zakur scanned the crowd. "When I heard your army, I knew you'd prefer I hid them in the ravine and hope the fasgadair would pass through without realizing portions of our village were still intact." His eyes lit up, and he danced a couple of steps. "Where's my father?"

Maili's face fell.

Zakur slowed. His face twitched as it morphed through many emotions. "Wh–what?"

She squinted at the people around her and snatched Zakur's hand. "Come with me."

He tripped in his reluctance to follow as Maili yanked him along, lumbering up the stairs behind her.

Blinding white light crossed my vision, accompanied by a scorching pain at the back of my eyes and something evil. I blinked repeatedly, desperate to regain my sight. Declan had just been standing nearby. Was he still there? "Declan?"

"Are you ill?" His voice closed in on my right.

I reached out for him.

He gripped my hand. "What's happening, Fallon? Should I fetch the apothecary?"

"No!" I said a little too forcefully. What if this is Morrigan's doing? I didn't want to call attention to myself and worry people. Whatever this was would go away as the headaches had.

"Why not? What's happening?"

"I can't see," I whispered.

"What?" He must've heard me right because he led me to something. "Here, sit."

I felt the air until my fingers contacted a rough log. Then I lowered myself.

"Let me fetch the apothecary. I think he's around here somewhere. Or Ji Ah. Maybe she can help."

"No."

"Why not? Are you getting better?"

"I don't want anyone to see me this way."

"Fallon, this is silly." The log jostled as he rose. "We need to get you help. The selkie have other healers in their ranks too."

I groped for his arm and pulled him to sit. "I just—I just want to sit here for a minute." *Please, God. Please let my vision clear.* What would I do if I couldn't see?

Another wave of blazing pain shot through my temples. I bent over, compressing my head as if it might split apart otherwise. Declan clutched my shoulder.

Oh, God! Oh, God! Oh, God!

What was happening? It was as if someone shot both sides of my head simultaneously. The steady jolt of pain lessened to twinges. Face down, I clutched my head as tears fell to the ground. Declan spoke in a whisper. I couldn't make out the words, but it sounded like he was praying.

The pain eased, and I sat up. Dancing lights obscured my view of a cloudy forest. "I think my vision is coming back."

As my eyesight came into focus, so did a niggling sensation at the back of my mind. Whatever it was, it bothered me. I shuddered.

"What's happening? Can you see?"

"I can. But something is wrong."

A scream rang out, sending fresh throbs surging through my head. I groaned and tried to pull myself up. The tent was dark, but a campfire outside revealed the outlines of my mother, Maili, Rowan, and Ji Ah sitting up on their bedrolls.

"What was that?" I whispered.

My mother, Cataleen, stood and threw on her cloak. "Stay put."

We sat in complete silence for eons. Finally, shuffling feet and hushed voices broke the void.

"What happened?" I asked, holding my breath when Cataleen returned.

She lit the lantern without a match and sat on her bedding without removing her cloak. She trembled. "Six of our watchmen are dead."

"What?" The rest of us turned to each other. Their masks of disbelief and shock probably matched my own. "How?"

"Fasgadair slit their throats." My mother clutched her cloak tight around herself.

A chill sweeping through me, I shivered. "What? Are they following us? How'd they know not to bite the guards?"

Cataleen stared at me, her eyes vacant. "They knew. Somehow…"

CHAPTER TWENTY-THREE

I lay on my bedding inside the tent, shaking with a cold sweat. Kai wiped my forehead, concern lacquering his mahogany eyes. Part of me wanted to get up and ease his burden. Another part wanted to smack the look from his face. I shuddered at whatever prompted such unwarranted thoughts, wishing to push it out of my system. But it persisted.

Aside from the flulike symptoms, something was wrong. Impressions that weren't my own invaded my thoughts. Like when I dreamed, Alastar's feelings permeated my mind but a little more distant. But yesterday, with the blindness, something changed. It wasn't a faraway feeling while I slept. Something lurked under the surface, something evil. I couldn't shake it, even when I was awake.

Whatever this is, God, please make it go away.

I tried to shift myself, but my limbs weighed a thousand tons. My body ached. "Why is it so cold?"

"It's not." Kai wiped hair away from my forehead. "And you have a blanket. This illness gives you a chill."

I shivered hard enough to make my teeth chatter and clutched the blanket. "Where is everyone?"

"Ji Ah went to fetch a healer. Your mother and Rowan are making plans with the leaders. I'm not sure of Maili's whereabouts."

Ji Ah entered the tent and held the flap. A male selkie, presumably the healer, carried a steaming mug. "Lift her," he commanded Kai.

Kai squeezed himself behind my head to elevate me.

"What is this?" I eyed the man.

"Medicine," the man said. "It will help."

"He's a healer. A good one," Kai promised.

The man gathered his robe and knelt beside me, then brought the mug to my lips. The crinkles around his brown eyes gave him the appearance of smiling, but his lips pressed into a thin line over the finger-length strands of black-and-white hairs protruding from his chin. "Drink." He tipped the cup.

Hot liquid sloshed into my mouth. The excess ran down my chin. It tasted like roasted fungus in swamp water thickened with pureed earthworms. I tried to push the mug away, but the healer persisted.

"Just a little more." He tipped more liquid into my mouth.

The so-called medicine's boggy scent made it taste worse. I tried not to breathe as the thick liquid slurped down my tongue. A sudden urge to spit the broth into his face overwhelmed me. I swallowed hard to keep from giving in to the impulse.

The healer mercifully removed the mug and placed it on the dirt floor. "Make sure she finishes that."

I'll make sure to finish you.

Where did that thought come from?

Kai jostled me as he nodded. "Thank you, uncle."

The healer patted Kai's knee. "It's good to have you back, son." He stood with a groan, then left the tent with Ji Ah trailing.

"That's your uncle?" Chattering teeth played castanets to my question. Part of me was curious as another part groaned with disinterest.

"No. He was a close friend of my family. Selkie address people depending on familiarity. Close adults address the younger as son or daughter, even if they're not a parent. If I were closer, I might call him father. If I wasn't familiar at all, I'd call him sir. Given our familiarity, I call him uncle."

"Oh." That was confusing. "Names are much easier. Will I offend the selkie if I use their name?"

Offend them. Offend them all.

"Not at all. We come from different cultures. They understand as I'm sure you do."

The tent flap opened, sending a breeze. My mother's face appeared. "How do you feel?"

Kai lifted me, eased his way off the mat, and replaced my makeshift pillow of rolled-up T-shirts under my head. My head swam as I adjusted myself.

Cataleen knelt and touched my forehead. "You're burning up."

"I'm freezing."

She motioned to Kai. "There must be a spare blanket among the supplies. Please find one."

I shivered violently.

"Or more."

He disappeared outside the tent.

"'Tis not appropriate to be alone in a tent with him."

Really? That's what worried her right now?

She sat beside me, pulling the covers to one side. If only I had the strength to push her off. "I'm sorry. That's not the main concern at the moment."

You think?

"Tell me what happened."

I didn't want to talk to her, especially after that ignorant intro. But I was desperate to get well. And how would I live with myself if I single-handedly stalled the mission? We needed to get moving.

She can't help you.

Where were these thoughts coming from? Whatever it was, it wasn't God. I couldn't trust it. If it was so sure my mother couldn't help, then she probably could. "I got one of those awful headaches yesterday. The worst yet. It blinded me for a few minutes. My headache isn't as bad now, but I feel like I have a flu." And I think I'm possessed. Was anyone around here qualified to perform an exorcism?

"You went blind?" Cataleen pushed my hair over my ear, her eyebrows squeezed together as she frowned. Other gachen have purple eyes, but we also had the same upturned, almond shape. How old was she? In her forties? Her face was still smooth. If she had any grays, they were impossible to detect amongst all the blonde. Would I look as good at her age? Probably not. With black hair, gray would shine like a lit jack-o'-lantern on a dark night. "Why didn't you tell me this yesterday?"

I tried to shrug.

"Is there anything else?"

Should I tell her?

"What is it?"

Seriously, could she read my mind? Or was this a supernatural mom ability? "I feel like I'm bathing in evil."

Cataleen yanked her hand away as if she might get infected and straightened.

A breeze brought our attention to the door.

Kai stepped through. "I found blankets." He dropped two on my mother's belongings and unfolded one.

My mother stood to help cover me with the blanket. "Goodness, child, you should have had more than that thin blanket last night. The nights are growing colder."

"I was fine."

"Mmmhmm. Kai, will you please find Sully?"

Searing pain shot behind my eyes, and my vision went white as my body convulsed.

"Fallon!" Kai called.

Hands gripped me, someone sat on me, holding my arms as my legs flopped. Someone else gripped my head, keeping it from slamming against the ground. Finally, I stilled.

Kai touched my cheek. The earlier concern had grown into full-blown terror.

"Please," Cataleen begged. "Get Sully. Now!"

Kai lowered me back down and threw me one last look. "I'll be right back." He dashed away.

I MUST'VE DOZED OFF. A rattling cough woke me. Sully was sitting cross-legged on my mother's bedding beside me, pocketing a handkerchief, speaking in hushed tones with my mother. My head didn't hurt at all. All my aches were gone. But I was warm. Too warm.

"It may be our only choice." Sully's voice was raspier than normal.

"But how can we—"

"What's going on?" I asked, pushing the blankets off me. How many were there? Three. No wonder I was so warm.

"So—" Sully coughed, then cleared his throat. He reached across the divide toward me. "Sorry we woke you, child."

I helped him along by grabbing his hand.

His liver-spotted hands clasped mine in his. They were cold. "Your mother told me about your sickness—the temporary blindness, the headache, and the fever. But what is this evil sensation? Can you explain that?"

I looked into his gray eyes, no longer disgusted or unnerved by their appearance. Now, I saw Sully and felt nothing but love for this unusual man. His presence calmed me. I needed him. I shivered. "I can't explain it."

My mother gathered a blanket I'd shoved aside and placed it back over me. "Try. Anything you say may help."

I searched my mind for foreign thoughts and feelings. "I think it's gone now. Whatever it was."

Sully and Cataleen exchanged glances, even though Sully can't see. Their shoulders relaxed, and they deflated as if they'd been holding their breath. Though their faces weren't as tense, worry lines still crinkled their foreheads. "Can you remember what it felt like?"

I released Sully's hand and pushed myself up to sit, wrapping the blanket around my shoulders. "It was like something else was in my mind with me. Something evil."

Sully touched Cataleen's arm. "You say she convulsed at the mention of my name?"

When my mother nodded, he gave a noisy exhale and folded his hands in his lap. "I guess we now know Morrigan's plan."

Again, she nodded. "In part."

"Hmm." Sully tugged on his beard.

"What?" I must be misunderstanding. "Is Morrigan taking over my mind?"

My mother wrapped an arm around me. "I'm afraid so. That's likely why she needed strands of your hair. It seems she's found the secret to the mind-link between Aodan and me."

I pushed away. "But that can't be."

"'Tis true, child." Sully patted my knee. "This is a spelled version of the mind-link as opposed to the not-so-natural link the twins had...or the weaker versions you had with your uncle and brother in your dreams, so there are differences from what you experienced with them." He sat back, a deep, rattling breath vibrating in his chest. "This explains why there was no army met us along the shore. And why the fasgadair picked off our watchmen last night."

"So, it's my fault? Those men died because of me?" Morrigan was using me as a spy? Stacking events in her favor to do the most damage *and* enslave me in the process? My stomach twisted like a contortionist. I pulled myself up, ready to—ready to what? Launch myself off a bridge so I couldn't do any more damage?

"Did you kill those men?" His gray, sightless eyes seemed to stare into my soul. "Morrigan ordered those men killed. Morrigan is infesting your mind. This is Morrigan's doing. Not yours."

Always the voice of reason. I crisscrossed my legs. "What do you mean not so natural? Do you know what caused the mind-links to begin with?"

"Dear one, the mind-links, the ability to start fires... Fasgadair blood caused them."

"What?" The man must be getting batty in his old age. "That's not possible. I was never a fasgadair." I motioned to my mother. "Neither was she. Right?"

"Right." She squeezed my hand. "Nonetheless, fasgadair blood courses through our veins."

I yanked my hand away. "No. It's not possible."

"My father, your grandfather, was bitten. The demon tried to turn him, forcing him to drink fasgadair blood. He miraculously escaped the fasgadair and spat out most of the blood. But not all. We assume the incomplete transformation into a fasgadair both kept him alive temporarily and slowly killed him. He died about a year later."

"Your mother and Aodan were conceived during that time." Sully straightened his back with a groan.

I hugged my legs. "So, you mean to tell me, my grandfather was somewhere in between a human and a fasgadair? All this time, I've had *demon* blood in me? Then how does it redeem fasgadair? Why didn't Aodan's? Or Declan's? Or Alastar's? How did they become fasgadair if they share my blood?"

"That will always be a mystery. All I can say to that is because God willed it to be so." Sully's voice sounded like he had another frog in it.

"I thought the fire-starting ability was a gift." The ships I'd burned pervaded my mind. "Am I cursed?" Cursed sounded more accurate than gifted. It would explain my life.

"We're all cursed." Sully coughed. He retrieved a handkerchief from his pocket as he continued, each cough deeper with more rattling than the last.

"Are you okay?" I asked.

He nodded and wiped his mouth. Folding and pocketing the cloth, he cleared his throat. "We live in a broken world that suffers from sin. But God has a plan, and He uses it all for good for His children. You, dear one, are one of His children. Fear not."

"Fear not? How can you even suggest that at a time like this? Morrigan has access to my mind. Is she gone now? Will she return? Can she take it over whenever she wants?"

"Morrigan probably disconnected when she heard I was being summoned." The creases around Sully's eyes deepened. "She isn't fond of me."

"That's an understatement." My mother puffed air out her nose.

I gawked at these two. How could they laugh at a time like this? Morrigan was using me like a pawn. I'd already lost our weapons, and now, I'd become a tool for the enemy like the time I'd scored a touchdown for the opposing team in gym class, but worse. Way worse. "Will Morrigan take over my mind again when you leave? What will happen to us? What will happen to me?"

Sully's face grew somber. A much more appropriate expression given the circumstances. "I'm sure she'll attempt to control you again."

"Should I go back to my realm? Isn't that why my mother went there in the first place? To hide from Aodan?"

"Not this time, child. Now is the time to stay and fight. Things always get worse before they get better. And if we're to eliminate Morrigan, we'll need you. We must be more careful." He pursed his lips. "We may need to blindfold you to keep her from knowing where we are. And you must learn to block your thoughts."

Block my thoughts? That's like asking me to stop breathing. My mind did its own thing. "That's impossible."

"It requires diligence, but it's possible. Think of someone you care about. Keep their image in your mind. Recall a pleasant time with them."

"How can I focus when I have Morrigan in my head distracting me?"

"Pray and trust. I will stay close. But an even better protection would be to ensure you're connected to God."

"How?"

"Talk to Him. Sing songs praising Him, reminding you He's with you." Sully's little chuckle hacked into another cough. "And Morrigan won't be able to tolerate it. It might push her out of your mind."

That sounded more doable. Keep a song in my head. Too bad I didn't have my cell phone. "There's one more problem."

"What's that?" Cataleen rubbed my back.

"Those fasgadair knew where to find us... and not to bite anyone. I think I've already given Morrigan all the information she needs."

CHAPTER TWENTY-FOUR

I wished I had never confessed to being possessed. Well, not possessed exactly. Spelled? In any case, it had the same effect. Word spread around the camp. Everyone avoided me as we packed up. Suspicious glances drifted my way, mouths silenced, and people shifted away, out of hearing.

But Morrigan wasn't with me now. At least, I hoped. If only I could transform into a falcon and take to the sky. But that might tempt her to join me. And the view I would have as a bird would give away far too much.

Or were we being paranoid? What more information could I offer? Fasgadair attacked. And it wasn't a rogue pod. They were strategic. And, with Morrigan connected to them, she undoubtedly knew our location. She was behind the attack. As long as the fasgadair follow us, she'd always know.

But I couldn't blame them for treating me like a pariah. It wasn't me they feared. I would avoid someone possessed by Morrigan, too, and insist they didn't come with us. I should be grateful they didn't plan to leave me behind. Or did they?

Would it be better for everyone if I left?

My headache was gone. No chills. No evil thoughts. Well, no Morrigan-sized evil thoughts.

We loaded up and headed out, traipsing through the forest, surrounded by selkie. But today I had a much wider girth around me. My mother stayed close. Kai stuck to me like a lamprey on a fish. Alastar and Declan hovered in case we needed the triplet fire. Did Morrigan know about that too? Probably.

A selkie flanking me in the woods caught my eye and averted his gaze as if I might ignite him. I hated being so disconnected. Worse, I hated not knowing if they were right to shun me. What if Morrigan had merely been experimenting before? What if she'd perfected the mind-link? Was that why I no longer sensed her? Was she planning to use me as an unwitting spy?

No. That made no sense. She had her fasgadair minions. Morrigan had heinous plans. She must.

God, protect me from whatever she is planning.

Since we'd gotten a late start, we kept marching straight through lunch. The earthy scent of damp soil hung in the air, suppressing my appetite. Deep woods surrounded us, making it seem as if traveled in circles. But no, we followed the setting sun, jumping roots and felled trees. And it was wet here as if it had rained though we hadn't seen so much as a drop, just the darkened sky looming in the distance.

"Water!" the crowd shouted as we neared a brook.

We paused to drink and refill our leather canteens, then continued.

My stomach had stopped grumbling hours before the group halted and dropped their loads. When we prepared to make camp, my mother, my brothers, Kai, Sully, and I had our own little camp separate from everyone else. Rowan, Maili, and Ji Ah had abandoned me. Not that I minded Ji Ah distancing herself from me...and Kai. At least this quarantine brought some benefits.

Rowan's laughter wafted my way. I glimpsed her packing her

things through the trees with Evan. My old roommate. Her avoidance stung. At one time, she wanted me near for friendship and protection. But now... I understood the princess's concern that I might subject her to an evil spy with supernatural powers and witchcraft.

But I missed her. She and Evan seemed to be friendlier with one another. My curiosity begged for information. If nothing had changed, I'd be pumping her every chance I got. She liked Evan. Now that he would be king when he returned to the selkie lands, did that open the possibility of a relationship for them? Would she have a chance to marry for love *and* her country? Or was Evan sticking around because she understood what it was like to take a position for which she felt unworthy? Was she just helping him become a king?

But I couldn't find out without asking someone else to pry. Not until I somehow cleansed myself of this evil being and convinced everyone else Morrigan was gone.

The wind carried more laughter our way. I wanted to be present and happy with those I had near. Instead, the temptation to feel like a leper and give in to my self-pity tendencies overwhelmed me. Was this part of Morrigan's diabolical plan? Divide and conquer? Pick us off as we approached?

Once the smaller tent my mother and I shared was erected, I retreated to my solitude. I lay on my bedroll watching the shadows dancing from the fire outside, listening to the merriment, feeling sorry for myself. Morrigan wasn't here, but she'd probably accomplished what she hoped. She'd built a wall between me and my friends. And, by focusing on them and not being happy and present with those who remained, I was allowing her to sever all my relationships.

I mustn't let that happen. I had to be content with those who stuck by me. They deserved my loyalty.

SHOUTS AND THUNDERING feet pounding the dirt and cracking twigs woke me. I jumped off my bedding. "What's happening?"

"Probably more fasgadair." Cataleen threw me a cloak. "Put this on and come with me." She covered herself, peeked out the tent, motioned me to follow, and slipped into the night. Alastar and Declan met us at the fire.

"Where are they?" I asked.

"We don't know, but you're coming with us for a perimeter check. Stay close." They took off past my tent, and I hurried to keep up.

We came upon a soldier cradling a wounded man's head. He watched us with vacant eyes. "He'd dead." No emotion inflected his voice. He must be in shock.

"A fasgadair?" Declan asked.

Life returned to the man's eyes—no, horror. His mouth opened into a giant O. "Get her out of here!"

"She's here to help," Alastar growled, glaring as if he might pick a fight with this poor guy holding his dead friend.

"She's the reason for all this." He let his friend's head slide off his lap as he stood. Crouching, he donned his weapon and aimed it at me. "If it weren't for her, he wouldn't be dead." He waved the dagger at his friend, then poised it, ready to strike me should I step closer. "I'm warning you. Back away."

I raised my hands and took a step back.

Declan pushed Alastar back, then grabbed my hand and tugged me away. "She's not your enemy."

Alastar followed in a huff. "Why'd you let him talk to her that way?"

"What do you want me to say to a grieving man, Alastar? There's no point."

Alastar snorted and hurried along to stay within arm's reach. I agreed with Declan, but I appreciated Alastar's desire to protect me. The man's words stung, but he wasn't in his right mind. Or wrong.

We continued our search. I sniffed. No electric fasgadair scent. Perhaps they were aware of their unique scent and retreated downwind after their attacks. Assuming they'd followed the same MO and killed all the men standing watch.

"I don't get it." I kicked a pebble in my path. "Why do they just keep killing our watchmen? Why don't they attack our camp?"

"In Morrigan's mind it makes perfect sense." Alastar scoffed. "She already depleted her army by sending so many to Bandia, then to the selkie lands. She doesn't have enough warriors to spare. I guarantee she's keeping them close by to defend her. And she loves mental warfare. Instilling fear and causing division. Picking us off night-by-night accomplishes that goal."

My stomach churned. What else had such a devious mind planned? "I wonder what she's planning for me." I lowered my voice to a mumble. "*If* I arrive."

"Don't worry." Alastar patted my shoulder. "She wouldn't do such things if she weren't afraid. And we have God on our side."

With the loss of Turas and the element of surprise with our blood and the triplet fire, that was all we had going for us. *God, I know You're all we need. Help me truly believe it.*

My foot caught on something, and I pitched forward. Pots and pans clanged, disturbing the quiet. A troop of selkie came running, weapons poised.

"It's just us." Declan held his hands up. "Fallon tripped on an alarm. We're checking the perimeter."

A selkie with menacing eyes threw us a murderous look. "Be more careful."

Grumbling, the group returned to camp.

Declan helped me stand.

I brushed dirt from my pants and stepped over the taut string between the trees. "Sorry, guys. I know I'm not privy to the plans anymore, but someone could've warned me the woods are booby-trapped."

"Booby-trap?" Declan's lips matched his words. "Oh. You mean the alarms."

"I told you they were useless against fasgadair," Alastar said.

"We had to try." Declan huffed.

After circling the entire border, we didn't find much except dead bodies and a clear message—no one wanted me around. They all saw me as the reason they were getting picked off each night. They looked at me as if I were Morrigan herself. Twelve had died tonight. They must've doubled the night watch.

CHAPTER TWENTY-FIVE

The next day we walked in silence. As much as I wanted to focus on the loved ones who remained, I hyper-focused on those I'd lost. The lost camaraderie. The trust.

"What are you thinking?" Kai adjusted the pack on his back and stepped over a felled tree.

"Nothing much." I followed him over the trunk.

"We're nearly there."

I put a finger to my lips. "Don't tell me anything about where we are."

He laughed. "Even if Morrigan showed up, knowing we're nearly there isn't saying much."

"But *I* know where we're going. I wish I didn't, but we planned this before we left. And we've known all along." I didn't dare say the words *Somalta Caverns*, but the more I tried to avoid them, the more they begged to come to mind. "How am I going to keep my thoughts from Morrigan?"

"Who says she'll try to take over your mind again?"

"Oh, she will. I'm sure."

The giant army kept cutting through the woods. She didn't need to now. She knew our whereabouts. And our weaknesses.

THAT NIGHT, I stood near the same shore I always visited in my dreams. But the beach where my mother first stood, then Declan, was now empty. The popping lights swirled, forming a window into someone's mind on my left. It had to be Morrigan. What was she up to? I turned toward it. No. Wait. If I looked into the mirror, would that allow her complete access to my mind? Sully had warned me about this last year when I told him about the dreams with Aodan. He'd warned me to run.

So I ran, keeping the beach to my left and the window behind me. The scenery never changed. I wasn't gaining traction. I dared look behind me. The window was inches away. A hand with pale splayed fingers stretched through the window.

Terror seized my heart. Like a spooked horse, I bolted, but the probing hand grasped me. Then the other hand. They tugged as I tried to run. Morrigan's face emerged, a sick smile crinkling the corners of her dead eyes. She writhed free from the window.

Without someone to wake me, would I remain in this maddening dream forever? Would Morrigan occupy my body while I remained trapped here?

Morrigan twisted me around. Her smile making me want to projectile vomit onto her face. Her evil glee filled the space, mingling and clashing with my fear. She held my collar, bared her fangs, and went in for the bite.

I woke with a start and yanked my legs, clutching them close as if Morrigan might grab my feet.

My mother sprang from her blankets and grabbed me. "Are you all right?"

"I'm okay. I just—"

"Had a nightmare."

I nodded.

"About Morrigan?" She touched my forehead.

Nodding again, I gave way to tears. My mother hugged me close and smoothed my hair.

"Get away from me." I pushed her with surprising force. My tone was unrecognizable, even to myself. I'd never sounded so malevolent.

Her eyes widened and filled with horror. She crab-walked away. "I'm sorry. I—"

"I'm getting Sully. Don't move." She stood and threw a cloak around her shoulders. Then dashed through the exit.

I flopped back onto my bedding. What happened? Had I brought Morrigan with me through the mind-link? Was she with me now? I didn't sense her evil. Just that one rush of anger at my mother and the sudden burst of strength that didn't seem to be my own.

Was I possessed?

If that were true, if Morrigan was stowed away in my mind, I'd have to be careful what I thought. I mustn't think of—No. Kai. Yes. Think about Kai. I pictured his smile, his dimply smile, and my heart eased.

But something else squirmed.

Cataleen returned with Sully. He stumbled in his haste to reach me and held his hand up to my cheek. His hand felt cold. Ice cold. I stared into his gray eyes as he seemed to peer into mine. His blind eyes saw into the spiritual realm. Could he see my soul? Could he see Morrigan within me?

Something inside writhed like a snake dipped in acid. Such torturous agony emerged from the pit of my being, rising to the surface. "Aaaaagh." My body twitched, then convulsed. Sully grabbed my head. My mother helped hold me. My vision failed me, but my mind was all too aware that my body, though it felt as if encased in concrete, flailed out of control.

"Sing your song, Fallon." His voice held a power I'd never heard from him.

What song was he talking about? Oh yeah.

Standing on the promises that cannot fail,
When the howling storms of doubt and fear assail,
By the living Word of God I shall prevail,
Standing on the promises of God.

The convulsing stopped. The thing within me slithered away, but not entirely. It—*she*—had burrowed someplace deep within my flesh. She was still there.

"Praise God. Thank You, Lord," Sully said, his eyes heavenward.

I shivered. My body weighed a ton, and I desperately needed a nap. "She's not gone." My jaw didn't want to cooperate, slowing my words.

My mother wrinkled her nose as if she'd caught a whiff of something unpleasant and placed a blanket on me.

"No." He frowned. "It's not that simple. But she's deterred. That's enough for now."

"What was that? Was that a seizure?" I tried to prop myself up on my elbows, but flopped back to the bedding.

"It appears your body is attempting to reject Morrigan's presence. You are a child of the One True God. Evil can't live in a transformed spirit that God occupies. She'll never gain complete control. But she's trying."

He tapped his chin and tipped his face skyward. Then squinting, he returned his sightless gaze my way. "This isn't a perfect illustration, but perhaps it will help." He shifted his body on the floor, settling in. "Imagine a cup of oil and water. You're familiar with how they respond to one another, correct?"

"They don't mix." I smacked my lips. My tongue tasted like chalk.

"Correct. Envision your flesh as oil and your spirit as water. Your spirit is occupied by God. No evil thing can penetrate it. But your flesh can be manipulated. Other oils can come in and intermingle. Envision Morrigan as another oil."

"She's trying to mix with me?"

"Aye. She wants to gain full control, but she can't. She can't mix with the water—the Living Water. So, she's infusing herself in your flesh. She retreated to avoid touching the water—God. This is why you're not sensing her as you had before."

"But what made me freak out?"

He cocked his head. "You mean convulse?"

"Yeah." I so wished they understood my lingo.

"I believe that was caused by contact with your spirit and their rejection of each other."

"And that's why she doesn't like when you're near or when I sing a song for God?" My eyes felt heavy. But I fought sleep. I needed to hear this. And I needed Sully to stay as long as possible.

"Or pray." He nodded. "When you do those things...and, apparently when I'm near, you're closer to God, you're more connected with your God-filled spirit than your flesh. Let's say it floods your body with more water, more of God. The contact causes her torment. And when you're full of God, she has less room. It squeezes her in. She had no choice but to retreat. But you're right. She's still there. You must continue to resist her."

I spotted my brothers by the doorway. How long had they been there?

"Everything all right?" Declan tiptoed closer, Alastar at his heels.

"As right as it can be." I fought the exhaustion and dragged myself up to sit.

"We heard the commotion and thought there was another fasgadair attack." He gave me a sheepish grin. "I hope you don't mind—"

"You overheard everything?"

He quirked his lips and held up his hands, palms outward.

I sighed. "Doesn't matter. If everyone fears me, they might as well have a good reason, right?"

My brothers huddled beside me. Each put an arm around me, yet the fire didn't ignite. Perhaps we were gaining control. Or I was too tired. No, they weren't connected to each other. Duh.

"How am I supposed to do anything? We haven't even arrived

yet, and Morrigan has already whisked Turas away, isolated me, and uncovered all our secret weapons. And now, she's taken up residence within me." I fought the urge to tear apart my flesh to purge her from my system.

Shouting came from the night.

Not again.

Alastar hopped up and dashed outside. Declan ushered me to follow, half carrying me.

What the death toll was this time?

CHAPTER TWENTY-SIX

I clutched Kai's arm as he led me, blindfolded, through the woods. Everything was being taken away from me—my friends, my sanity, and now, my eyesight. Not to mention the respect of the army.

How did Sully function like this? But he had said he sees in his own way. And he'd shown me the angels in the spiritual realm before I'd gone to Alastar as Na'Rycha. So, it was different for him. That's why he didn't stumble when he walked and looked at people when they spoke.

Other than last night. That was the first time I'd seen him stumble. Why did something about that nag me so? That and his ice-cold hands.

No. He'd stumbled because he was rushing to me, and I probably had a fever. That's why his hands felt so colder. They probably weren't actually cold.

In any case, I didn't have the ability to see here or in the spiritual realm. But at least my condition wasn't permanent.

"Watch your step," Kai said.

"I can't watch my step," I grumbled, fighting to control the urge to rip the blindfold from my eyes and throw Kai to the ground. Morrigan's presence heightened my irritation a gazillion times. An inner rage boiled, ready to blow. My flesh, full of its own irritations and desires, had received a nitro boost.

Kai lifted me over something. I almost thanked him. But just as I controlled Morrigan's desire to be nasty, she controlled my desire to be nice.

He is something to look at. Remove the veil and give us both an eyeful.

I shuddered at Morrigan's words. They disturbed me on so many levels. But I couldn't engage with her. I had to control my thoughts. I envisioned Kai's face to protect myself from falling into any of her traps.

Wouldn't you prefer to see his face? Touch it?

Don't talk to her, Fallon. Focus on walking. On Kai. Focus on following his lead.

Sully's words came flying back to me, "You must continue to resist her."

Standing on the promises that cannot fail...

Agh!

I laughed at Morrigan's discomfort and continued my song as she seethed and retreated. It took all my senses and effort to trudge through the woods without vision. How did Sully manage it? Kai would pick me up occasionally, and I'd hear sloshing. Or he'd jump over something.

I tripped over a root. "For Pete's sake, why do I have to wear this blindfold? If Morrigan wanted to, she'd just rip the thing off. You're only making things more difficult for *me*."

"Could she?" Kai sounded scared. He huffed. "It's not me, Fallon. I'm not the one making you wear that thing."

"Sorry, I'm just complaining."

"As your mother said, it's only to make everyone else more comfortable."

"I know. I know." But it wouldn't stop me from complaining. "Have we fallen behind? I can't hear the others."

"A little. Here." He stopped, and I lurched forward. "Get on my back."

I reached out for his shoulders. "Are you sure?"

"Of course."

I hopped on, his sweet pine aroma calming me. *Thank You, God, for Kai. Sully, my mother, and my brothers too.*

Morrigan recoiled, slithering away to a deeper recess.

Even though we trudged through the thicket in silence, I sensed the others nearby. Especially Sully. Morrigan must sense him too. It kept her at bay. As did the songs that played in my head.

Kai adjusted me on his back. I wanted to ask how many people died last night. But there was no use. No one would tell me.

Those poor men. Their demise reminded me of the time Stacy's mom bought a fish tank. She knew nothing about caring for fish. But that didn't stop her. She bought a school of little neon fish because they looked pretty and she liked seeing so many. She later brought home two bigger ones.

We never saw them fight or even nip at each other. But every morning, Stacy would wake up and find one or two smaller fish missing. One day she found a floating head. But most mornings, no evidence of foul play existed.

I never understood how the bigger fish acted so docile during the day. The tank must've become something from a Stephen King novel every night when the murderer became active. After ten days, the little fish were no more. Once the bigger fish died, Stacy's mom made the entire tank disappear.

We lived in that tank of horror.

Morrigan seemed to enjoy my reliving the tale. Sicko.

Standing on the promises of God.

Curses!

We stopped to make camp. No one allowed me to light fires or help. Or see. Kai delivered me to a log and left to help, abandoning me on the sidelines, blindfolded, waiting to eat, sleep, wait more, and repeat.

The waiting was the hardest part. When I had nothing else to concentrate on, my mind wandered... dwelling on my current situation. I had to fight my tendency to overthink. Morrigan's presence lingered.

How did Morrigan do this? Did she sit in meditation, doing nothing else but watching me? She had to take a break sometimes. Right? She wasn't God. She couldn't be in two places at once...even mentally. Could she?

She was quiet. Still, I couldn't risk letting my guard down. It took so much concentration not to allow certain thoughts that might give away our location or grant her an upper hand.

How I wish I didn't know our destination. My brain needed a break from fighting. How much easier it would be to say it.

An undercurrent of eager anticipation surged through me.

Morrigan. She was there. Biding her time. Waiting for me to slip.

God, please help me.

I peeled the bark from the log beneath me and focused on the sounds the army made as they set up camp. Metal clanging metal as men hammered stakes into the ground. Feet crunching twigs and debris. Fires crackling. Shouts breaking out. Indiscernible conversations coming to an end as they neared my perch.

A smoky breeze swept past, and I coughed. I tapped my feet. Somehow, a rock had gotten into my right shoe. I removed it, knocked the shoe against the log, and then reached inside it to ensure the irritant was gone. My fingers touched something on the bottom of my shoe near where the ball of my foot had worn a small hole in the rubber. Great.

Someone sat beside me, bringing a pine scent.

"Kai." My mind eased. Though it was easier to ignore my problem with others around, in other ways, it was more challenging. Talking to people put my guard down. I'd have to be diligent not to accidentally say, or think, the wrong thing.

As much as I wanted to know how much further we had to go, I couldn't ask. I hated being in the dark. And now, I was always in the dark, both literally and figuratively.

"Your tent is ready." He stood and led me through the entrance.

The minute I stepped inside, I yanked the blindfold off. Although my eyes had been covered, not my mouth, I breathed easier. Dropping on my bedroll, I blew in frustration, sending a tuft of hair into my face. Aggravated, I pushed it behind my ear. "I'm getting so tired of this."

Kai held my hand. "You'll get through it. I'll help you."

I gazed at my hand in his. His comforting touch soothed me. But I couldn't allow him to lull me into passivity. I had to stay alert. To fight. I pulled my hand away. "You can't help me. No one can. My brain is occupied by a demon. It takes every ounce of energy to keep her out."

"Not to worry, Fallon." Kai knelt before me and grasped my hands. "I've no doubt you'll succeed."

"Don't you know how exhausting it is?" I fell back on the bedding, fighting tears.

"Fallon." My mother's voice. She sounded like she'd caught me doing something wrong.

"What?"

"What did I say about you and Kai being alone in the tent?"

I bolted up and glared at her. Anger rose within me, laced with an evil that took great joy in my rage. I glared at Cataleen. "He is trying to help me." I seethed, chest heaving. Who did she think she was? She met me when I was seventeen. Too late to act like a mom.

Kai stepped back.

"What are *you* doing for me? Huh?" I spoke through clenched teeth as my fingers dug into my knees. "You know what it's like to have your mind taken over by a demon. I'm fighting not give her any information, and it's driving me crazy. Do you think your ridiculous accusations are helpful?"

Folding her hands, she took a deep breath. "I don't know exactly what you're experiencing. I never had information Aodan needed.

160

He wanted to get me out of the way, drive me to kill myself so the prophesied child"—she motioned toward me—"would never exist. He never gave me a moment's peace." She scoffed. "It almost worked. I tried to kill myself."

I softened as a shudder quaked over her and Morrigan delighted in her pain. Which was worse? Having a malevolent being wait for you to slipup or aggressively attack? Probably the aggressive attack.

She sat next to me. "I trust you, Fallon. You're a good girl." She smiled at Kai. "And you seem like a nice boy. That is not my concern with you being alone. Although, even under normal circumstances, it's better not to put yourselves in that position."

Nice girl? Boy? I fought the urge to smack her. Instead, I peeked at Kai. His tan cheeks rosier, he watched his shuffling feet. "What is it, then?"

"Well..." She stretched her arms, then refolded her hands in her lap. "When my brother occupied my mind, he drove me to do things. Like I said, I tried to kill myself, but not as an attempt to escape his torture. He had gained enough control to make me act. His command was a continual, growing thing. You have Morrigan in your mind. With her magic, we don't know what she's capable of or at what rate she'll progress."

"You think she'd get me to harm Kai?"

A solemn nod. "She might. She will want to cause as much damage as possible. There's no telling what she might do through you to unsuspecting people." She clasped Kai's hand. "No offense?"

Kai shrugged. "None taken."

"But what about you? You sleep in my tent. Alone. Aren't you in danger?"

"I'm willing to take that risk."

"But if Morrigan is so powerful within me, why doesn't she tear off the blindfold and figure out where we are?" The idea amused Morrigan.

I stared at Cataleen, waiting for a response. But we both knew the answer to that. Morrigan already had all the information she needed at the moment. Our dying watchmen were evidence enough. Still, I voiced what we both knew. "She doesn't need to. The blindfold is useless."

"She doesn't seem to have enough control over you to cause direct physical harm. But that doesn't mean she won't gain strength. Remember what Sully said. It's different with this magic-made version of the mind-link." My mother sighed. "And I'm sure she's thought of that. She probably has other plans."

"That's what I'm afraid of."

CHAPTER TWENTY-SEVEN

That night I dreamed of the beach again. Like before, no one occupied the shore. I didn't dare turn to my left. I sensed Morrigan. But my body itched to know for sure. I craned my neck, twisting my body as my feet remained planted. Sure enough, Morrigan stood behind me. I tried to run, but my feet wouldn't budge.

A slow smile slithered across her face, failing to reach her soulless eyes—twin black holes that sucked the life from anything good. Her hand clutched my throat. I hadn't seen her move.

My hands hung, useless stumps at my side. Why couldn't I move? I coughed as her fingers cut off the air to my lungs.

"Fallon!" Something gripped me. "Fallon, wake up!"

My hands rushed to my throat, ripping out of Cataleen's grip while I thrashed on my bedding. She backed away as I remembered where I was. "I'm sorry. She—she—"

"Morrigan was choking you?"

I probed my throat for evidence. Leaning forward, I bared my neck to my mother. "Did she leave a mark?"

"Oh, child." Cataleen shook her head, pity softening her purple eyes. I resisted the urge to smack it from her face. "There wouldn't be a mark. She wasn't here."

"Why would she attack me in my dreams?" I slumped and rubbed my throat.

"I can't pretend to understand a demon's reasoning." She quirked her lips. "She's probably attempting to weaken you. Creatures like that dominate through isolation and fear. She's slowly cutting you off from all but a few. And if she can keep you afraid, she'll keep you complacent. But that's good. It means *she's* afraid."

"If she's so scared, why doesn't she kill me?" I almost wished she'd take me out of this game. I didn't want to play anymore.

"She's tried that. Look how well it's worked out for her. The first time she killed Aodan instead. The second time she sent Alastar and Declan after you. Both are no longer fasgadair. She's lost so much of her army. And they can't use their instincts to kill anyone, or she'll lose more. Once we infiltrate these lands, we'll have contaminated their food source. They have no way of knowing which food is clean to eat. But the biggest reason is likely that she knows God is protecting you." She chuckled. "No wonder she's afraid."

Everything my mother said made sense. But Morrigan was more powerful than I was. And her presence exhausted me. And now I wouldn't be able to find relief in sleep? Isolated, exhausted, possessed.

I'd go insane. My mind was not my own. If this got much worse, would there be anything left of me? By the time we reached her, I'd be useless.

AFTER A WEEK OF WALKING, I grew more tense. Constant pressure and lack of sleep had wound me tighter than a frayed guitar string, ready to snap. I struggled to distinguish between Morrigan and me. Was the constant anger bubbling under the surface all me?

My new reality was a continual tension between giving in to violence and dissolving to tears. Nothing about me felt familiar. Never had I been so unbalanced, even at my most bitter, before I had God, when I despised my life to the point of cutting myself, with no family except Fiona and only one friend. I wanted to rip myself open and relieve myself of Morrigan's burden, even if it meant ending my life.

Intermingled with all this anger threatening violence and bitterness taking root was a perverted happiness that clearly wasn't me. The mixture of evil and happiness made me sick to my soul. That's why I hated horror movies with clowns or that sicko with the lollipops in *Chitty-Chitty Bang-Bang*. Watching those things filled me with that same feeling... Only this was infinitely worse.

Why didn't Morrigan attack us already?

"Ow!" I stumbled over something. Kai's grip on my arm tightened, holding me upright. "Are you trying to kill me?" It would be nice if he let me hitch a ride on his back, but he was probably afraid I'd choke him. He kept me at a greater distance now—not that I blamed him.

"Sorry, Fallon. I didn't see that root under the grass." His voice sounded remorseful...and scared. Gone was the Kai who joked in most every situation. His confidence seemed to be waning. He must be tiring. The journey was hard enough without having to guide a blindfolded demon-possessed freak who might bite your head off. Or who's head might spin around and projectile vomit split-pea soup.

I opened my mouth to apologize.

No. It was his fault. He should be more careful.

Agh! At this rate, my sanity would be gone far before we ever reached the battlefield.

Fulfilling Morrigan's plan, I'm sure. I was more than useless. I was a liability.

Each night, the fasgadair picked off our men. Like the big fish, they appeared in the night, taking out more watchmen. And we were helpless to stop it. Or so they said.

"Why don't we travel at night and camp during the day? That's how Cahal made us travel last year." I asked whoever listened and dared speak with me. "We wouldn't be losing men every night."

"There's a good chance we'd lose more men each night if we traveled that way." Alastar's voice came up from behind me.

"You know we can't discuss strategy with you." My mother's voice came from my left. "Just trust that we're doing the best we can."

"I know." Did I, though? Or did I think I'd come up with a better plan? I'm sure they had their reasons for every choice they've made along the way. But I hated not knowing...not being included.

Wasn't that the story of my life? Being on the outside? Never included in anything? Most people at least had a family that loved them.

No. I would not allow myself to throw another pity party.

I recalled several songs from church. They jumbled together into mash-ups, but they were becoming my lifeline—the only thing allowing me to keep a grip on reality.

"Step this way." Kai pulled me to the right. "Duck your head."

Following his directions, I made it past whatever he maneuvered me through. He did a good job leading me. I couldn't see the terrain, but it wasn't smooth. Guiding me through it couldn't be easy. If we got through this, we could get through anything.

An evil rumble of disgust coursed through me.

We came to a stop and set up camp. I continued to sit idle, waiting. Once my tent was ready, I ducked inside and peeled off the blindfold. I blinked a few times and exhaled lungs full of pent-up tension once my vision returned. My shoulders tensed. I'd hopped from one cage to another.

I stooped to my pack and unrolled my bedroll, then moved to unpack my mother's.

"What do you mean, I can't see her?" Pepin's voice floated through the tent.

Oh no. If I heard Pepin that meant...

Standing on the promises of God.

I plugged my ears, dropped my mother's bedding, and paced, repeating a jumble of hymns.

CHAPTER TWENTY-EIGHT

My mother poked her head into the tent. Then, seeing me with my fingers in my ears, pacing, she grasped my arms and tore my hands from my ears. "What are you doing?"

Dare I say it? It was already in my mind. If I knew, Morrigan knew. "I heard Pepin."

Cataleen's wide eyes grew wider still. She stood and threw on her cloak. "Stay here." She dashed from the tent.

I resumed pacing and singing, even if it was a wasted effort.

My mother returned. "Pack up. We're moving out."

"But we—Isn't it too dangerous to travel at this hour?" My stomach growled. "I haven't even eaten."

"I have dried lamb." Her eyes wild, she rolled up her bedding and shoved it in her pack.

"Wait." I dropped to the ground and pulled her to sit. She seemed like a spooked horse, fleeing without thinking. "How does running away help Pepin's people? If I know where I am, Morrigan does too. Her men are following us. They've been following us all along. And the pech are with us now to join the quest. Or are you

168

afraid Morrigan will kill the pech who remain behind once we leave?" Where had all this calm reasoning come from?

She shook her head. "It might be beneficial for Morrigan to know, the only pech here are soldiers aiding us in battle. The others are elsewhere. The pech will join forces against a common enemy, but they still don't trust us. Thank God. Their distrust may have saved lives regardless."

"Then why are we running?"

Every muscle in her body tensed. Then she sagged. "I don't know what to do." Tears welled up in her eyes. She ran her fingers along the bottom of her lids, wiping them away.

"Did anyone tell you to take me?"

"It breaks my heart to see you suffer." Tears brimmed her eyes once more, and she pointed to herself. "I'm the only one here who has any comprehension of what you're going through. I understand the torture of having someone toy with your mind."

Sucking in a breath, I asked, "What were you going to do?"

She let the tears fall as she stared at me. "Return you to your realm."

I shifted, putting distance between us. What would make her do such a thing?

"Not forever." She grabbed my hand. "Only to give your mind a break. You need a break."

I hugged her. Part of me, the real me, was grateful she cared enough to do something stupid. Another part, the Morrigan part, urged me to shove her. I released Cataleen before the desire became strong enough to succeed. "I can't tell you what it means to have someone understand and try to do something."

"We all want to do something."

Yeah, like snuff me out. I'm sure the selkie who blame me for their fallen comrades would prefer me dead. I scoffed at myself, wishing I could forever bury my negativity. Truthfully, I was grateful she cared. "Not enough to do something extreme like returning me to my realm to help me." The words *thank you* formed on my tongue, but my lips refused to breathe them to life.

She patted my knee. "You're right. It was extreme. A desperate attempt. I need to trust God and help you stand strong, not succumb to doubt and fear. Forgive me." She wiped her wet cheeks. "Perhaps I can convince the others to allow you to continue without the blind-fold. Morrigan knows where we are. Keeping you blindfolded seems like unnecessary cruelty on top of all you're already going through."

But it made people more comfortable. And it was a blessing in disguise, forcing me to draw nearer to God. But again, the words refused to come. And I wouldn't dissuade her from convincing the others to allow me to see.

"I'll talk to King Abracham about it." She sighed. "There are those who'd prefer you not travel with us. They don't understand the prophecy. The blindfold was an attempt to placate them."

"I get it."

"You can't be part of the strategic planning for obvious reasons. I'm sorry to keep you in the dark, but—"

"I understand. Really."

She drew her lips into a thin line. "I'll get your brothers to sit with you while I speak with the king."

DECLAN, Alastar, and Kai sat in my tent, playing tic-tac-toe in the dirt. Though the game was unwinnable and boring, it distracted me. Everyone was more relaxed than I'd seen them in a long time. Perhaps because I was getting better at keeping Morrigan at a distance.

"What is that song you keep humming?" Kai started a new game by drawing an X in the center square.

Had playing songs in my mind become so ingrained that I hummed aloud unaware? "It's a hymn I learned from church called 'Standing on the Promises.'" I placed an O in the square below the X.

"Standing on promises." He scoffed and drew an *X* in the upper right-hand corner.

"It's figurative, not literal." I drew an *O* in the bottom left, blocking him. "The chorus goes like this—

" 'Standing on the promises that cannot fail,

When the howling storms of doubt and fear assail,

By the living Word of God I shall prevail,

Standing on the promises of God.' "

Smiling, he drew an *X* in the bottom right to block me. "You have a nice voice."

"For me, it's a good reminder that God is with me. If I keep my eye on Him and His promises, I can't fail." I placed an *O* in the upper left.

Kai marked an *X* in the middle right and drew a line through his three *X*s in a row. He released his stick and threw his fists in the air in triumph. "I won!"

I stared at the squares. How had he won? What did I miss?

Alastar and Declan hooted for Kai. Winning an unwinnable game was quite a big deal involving lots of fanfare.

I jumped at the sight of Pepin in the corner of my eye. Was Morrigan now making me see things? "Pepin?"

The others simmered down. They all looked in the same direction, so they must see him too.

He walked toward me, dropped to his knees, and hugged me. He backed away, his amber eyes searching me. "Your mother told me what happened. With—with—"

"Morrigan."

"Right." He sat on the ground with us. "I wish they'd allow me to tell you what's happened, but—" He glanced at my mother behind him.

"It's okay. I'm just glad to see you."

"I have something for you." He reached into his pocket and pulled out an amulet. It was plain compared to Drochaid. A small diamond figure took up the center, outlined by another diamond with symmetrical lines jutting out in angular swirls. "It's an interrealm transport amulet and a language translator." He pointed to the center. "The diamond shape symbolizes the megalith and the continuity between both worlds." His chubby finger traced a line. "These lines represent the different languages. They mirror each other to symbolize the ability to understand the languages as the same. And look." He held it up by two cords. "You can wear it while you fly, by putting these cords over your wings." He placed it in my hand and wrapped my fingers around it.

"You're giving this to me?"

He nodded. "My teacher, Annar, made it for you."

"Why?"

"Because you require a language translator." He lowered his gaze. "And we need Drochaid."

My hand flew to the amulet, covering it. Give up Drochaid?

"I hate to take it back, Fallon." Bushy brows waggled over gleaming amber eyes. The amber swirled, liquid and imploring. "But it's a one-of-a-kind. It's the only one we can use for Turas. My people want it returned. As a show of goodwill between our races. Besides, you no longer need it."

"How do you know I don't need it?" I clutched Drochaid. "Did Sully say so?"

"He doesn't have to."

"Yes, he does."

"Fal—"

"No," I cut him off. "Look. Drochaid is more than an amulet. It's my guide. It led me to Notirr, past the fasgadair in Gnuatthara, to Aodan, to Turas. If not for Drochaid, I wouldn't know about my brothers."

"When was the last time it lit up?"

"Not since facing Alastar. I mean, Na'Rycha. But I'm about to face Morrigan. I can't do that without Drochaid."

"You can and you must."

"What do you need it for? Can't you wait until I defeat Morrigan?" Assuming I do. "You won't need it until you can travel back overseas to selkie land."

Pepin shuddered at the word *overseas*.

"See? You won't go back. Wait until this war ends. If I survive, I'll bring it back to Turas for you." As much as I hated the idea of getting on a ship again, I'd agree to almost anything to hang onto Drochaid.

"Fal—"

My mother stepped forward. "The pech won't join us unless we give them Drochaid."

"What?" I must've misheard her. "They won't join us? Over Drochaid? That's the most ridiculous thing I've ever heard. If I don't give them Drochaid, they're going to step aside and let Morrigan destroy what's left of their people and control Ariboslia?"

"No." Pepin shook his head. "They'll go into battle on their own. They'll—"

"Shhh." My mother held her fingers to her lips.

How many secrets were they keeping from me? They risked exposing as much as they had because they needed Drochaid. No, they didn't need it. I needed it. But what was I supposed to do? "Let me talk to Sully."

Everyone in the room adopted the same deer-in-the-headlights look and eyed each other. I was the only one missing out on a secret. I stood up and placed my hands on my hips. "What's going on?"

CHAPTER TWENTY-NINE

After what seemed like hours, my mother led me to Sully's tent. As soon as I entered, I yanked the blindfold off. My eyes took a few seconds to adjust. Sully lay on some kind of a makeshift stretcher. I ran to his side and fell to my knees.

The man was already pale, but he appeared ghostly gray, like his eyes. His cheeks were sunken. Every wrinkle more pronounced.

"Sully, what's happening? Are you okay?" What was I saying? Look at him. Of course, he wasn't okay. When was the last time I'd spoken to him? I couldn't see during the day. We didn't share a tent at night. How long since I'd sensed his presence? It must've been days.

He patted my hand. "I'm old, child." What was this? He was still comforting me as he lay... No. My heart twisted, and I held my breath. He couldn't be...

I snatched his icy hand, wrapping it in both of mine, and brought it to my lips. A tear slipped onto his hand. "This is just an illness, right? You'll be all right."

Sully coughed, and his chest rattled. That sounded bad. Very bad. "God is calling me home."

"No!" Tears streamed down my face as I pressed Sully's hand to my cheek. "You can't know that. Only God knows. You can't know."

"I know what God chooses to reveal." He gave my hand another weak pat, then coughed again.

"Did He—did He say—"

"My time has come. Today, I will be in paradise." He smiled such an angelic smile it squelched the lifelessness in his face until he shone. "And you, dear one, will be well cared for in God's hands. Without Drochaid."

I fell on him, wrapping my arms across his middle as I sobbed.

His weak hand smoothed my hair. Even in his death, he comforted me? "All will be well, dear one. You are loved." He took a deep breath. The rattle echoed in his chest under my ear. Then he stilled and breathed no more.

THE MINUTE we returned to my tent, I tore off the blindfold and aimed a death stare at my mother. "What? Were you going to let him die and tell me in a few months? Were you planning to mention it *ever*?"

"I wanted to tell you." She reached for me.

I stepped back, swatting at her. "Let me guess? They—whoever *they* are—didn't want Morrigan to know. They only told me to make me to give up Drochaid. Here." I pulled the amulet off my neck and flung it at her feet. "Take it. Take it and get away from me." My chest heaved as I turned my back on her.

I heard her pick up the amulet. She walked past me, discarded the new amulet on my pack, and left the tent.

I TOSSED and turned on my blanket. Sleep wasn't happening. I was raging. How much anger belonged to me? It felt like me. All me. And

I longed to wrap myself up in it, bathe in it. I rocked my body, slamming my fists and feet like a toddler in the middle of a tantrum.

I stood and kicked my mother's empty bedding. Where was she?

What did I care? As long as she didn't come anywhere near me.

But they wouldn't have left me alone. My brothers must be watching outside my tent. They all had even more reason to fear me now. Even I no longer perceived where I ended and Morrigan began. And Sully wasn't here to save me. And Drochaid wasn't here to guide me.

Hoping I didn't draw their attention, I snatched my rolled-up clothes acting as my pillow and screamed into them. "What do You want from me?" I whisper-yelled to the roof. "Why are You taking everything away from me?"

Drochaid's replacement lay on my pack, taunting me. I seized it. Stupid thing. Did it even have a name? Probably not. It was one of many generic amulets. It would never light up and tell me where to go. My feet itched to run from these people. Now. So what if Morrigan killed me? I wanted off this crazy ride.

Who would calm me now? Sully was the only one. And Kai. But Kai didn't know God like Sully did. Sully made me feel safe in a way Kai wasn't able. Kai seemed to believe in God. Not that I could judge someone else's beliefs.

It didn't matter. I needed Sully. I needed Drochaid. I needed connection. I needed to stop being pushed aside, treated like a liability. I needed Morrigan purged from my mind.

Why was God allowing all this? He'd taken the only person capable of shedding light on all I was going through and comforting me.

I wanted to rage—to tear my clothes, throw my things, burn the whole stinkin' camp.

Yes!

No!

I had to get out of here. But where would I run? I couldn't escape myself or the beast within me.

Stop fighting me. I'll help you exact revenge.
I don't think so. I hate you most of all!
Hahaha.

I screamed as loud as my lungs would allow as if the ferocity of my rage could push Morrigan out through my mouth.

My brothers and Kai, wild eyed, seemed to search for the beast murdering me. But I was alone—destroying myself. With or without Morrigan's help.

"What happened?" Kai moved toward me as if to wrap me in his protective arms, then caught sight of me and changed his mind. He stopped out of arm's reach.

I dropped onto my rumpled blanket, covered my face in my hands, and sobbed. They crowded around me. Kai heroically wrapped an arm over my shoulder.

"What am I going to do now?" My hands muffled my voice.

"Without Sully?" Declan asked.

I lifted my face, no longer caring what I looked like. "Who will tell me what to do? Without Drochaid or Sully..."

"God will tell you." Declan patted my knee.

"Aye," Alastar agreed.

"How? He always used Drochaid or Sully." No. That wasn't true.

"Perhaps 'tis time you stop relying on others and trust God Himself. You don't need trinkets and people to lead you. Just Him." Declan crossed his arms.

I hiccupped, peeked at Declan then the others. "That sounds like something Sully would say."

He smiled. "Perhaps because 'tis something God might say."

"So, what should I do?"

"Talk to Him. Give all your anger and grief to Him. He can handle it. He knows anyway. Nothing is hidden from Him. But whatever you do, don't give way to those emotions and allow Morrigan to control you. Let God guide you. And, as tempting as it might be to run and face this on your own"—he eyed Kai as if he'd promised to convince me not to run—"as you seem wont to do, don't. Talk to God

177

about it first and wait until He leads you. Don't go off on your own." Head down, he peered up into my eyes. "Agreed?"

"Technically, I was following Drochaid and Sully when I ran to Aodan and you." I pointed to Alastar. "You know, when you were an evil vampire overlord."

They all threw me unimpressed looks as I laughed at my joke.

"Okay. Okay. I'll let you know before I run to Morrigan."

"In all seriousness, Fallon." Declan stared me down. "We must stick together. We may need the triplet fire."

"Okay. I got it. I won't leave without you."

"Or me." Kai squeezed my shoulder.

"Or you."

But what if God told me to go alone?

CHAPTER THIRTY

W e held a combined service for Sully and the fallen watchmen. My mother, Kai, and my brothers stood by me. I tried to ignore the freshly dug holes and the suspicious glances as I surveyed the landscape. The somber atmosphere contrasted with the surrounding beauty and the crisp air. I inhaled a deep, exhilarating breath, allowing it to refresh me like a tall glass of water.

Cahal, Wolf, and Pepin joined us, and we exchanged consolatory hugs. Their presence comforted me.

The foliage had turned color. With the blindfold, I'd missed the slow change. The transformation was stunning. But leaves were darker here than at home with more reds and purples than yellows and oranges.

Dispersed among the trees with dying leaves were others that appeared to have already lost their foliage. But green and white covered the trunk and branches of these barren trees, like snow-covered moss. "Are those fur trees?"

"Aye." Declan nodded. "Their fur is growing back in. Beautiful, aren't they? You might see them in winter with their full coats. Some have fur that grows so long it drops to the earth, creating a perfect tent—camouflaged and warm."

"I'd like to see that." Anything other than the sight before me. But my gaze drifted to Sully's sunken form, wrapped in his cloak, in the hole in the ground. He looked peaceful.

Even so, I hated to see him there. Lifeless. I almost wished for the blindfold. But I was grateful they conceded and let me continue without it. It really was unnecessary. I wasn't Morrigan's only source.

But, judging from the glares coming my way, many didn't care.

A minty breeze swept through, clearing my sinuses. I tugged my sweatshirt sleeves over my hands. Good thing I packed warmer clothes.

Several graves surrounded Sully's with men I didn't recognize. Were these more from last night? They wouldn't carry our dead with us, would they? No. There weren't enough gravesites for that. Had they been holding funerals each day while I waited in my tent?

It shouldn't be such a nice day. It should be dark and stormy.

Evan emerged from the woods with Rowan, Maili, and Ji Ah. His blue eyes saddened when they spotted me. He quirked his lips and embraced me. "He will be missed."

Kai came to my side, and Evan released me.

"Aye." Declan drummed his fingers on his legs. "But I have to admit, as nice a day as this is, I envy Sully's scenery right now."

Wolf loosed a low whistle. "I can't imagine what he must be seeing."

The thought of Sully seeing anything brought a smile that nothing, not even Ji Ah's adorable pout could thwart.

Rowan gave me a quick hug. "I wish I could see you more. But, under the circumstances..."

"I get it. But what I don't understand is why you're talking to me now."

"I wanted you to know that I still support and care about you, particularly on this day." She waved toward the open graves.

King Abracham arrived, head down. He threw me a sad smile as he passed, then stopped beside Sully's grave. Once everyone settled in among the graves, he cleared his throat. "I must admit, I'm tired of funerals. I don't want to keep mourning losses. But each of these men understood the risks. Each one sacrificed himself for a greater cause. And they will be remembered for their sacrifice."

He droned on, taking time to talk about each man lying in his grave. And I should have focused on his speech, to appreciate each one. But my gaze kept drifting toward Sully. And I kept reliving moments with him, from the first moment I saw him and his gray eyes scared me, to the conversation before I flew off to fight Alastar, to all the times in between. He'd been like another grandfather. A wise old man. No, he was way more than that. He was a prophet. He'd been my connection to God on earth.

Now prayer would have to suffice. Would that be enough?

My ears perked up at Sully's name.

"A mighty man of God who guided us to this point. With the power God bestowed upon him, he restored King Aleksander's health. It warms my heart that we should remember Sully and put his body in its resting place on such a day. For this is just his earthly host. His soul is shining in a more beautiful, perfect place God prepared for him in his real, forever home. His eyesight is better than ever. He has no pain, no sorrow, and no regret. The true King has welcomed Sully into His arms." He bowed his head.

"God. Thank You for all these men. Thank You for their sacrifice. You brought them into this world. You determined their steps. You knew their final day when they took their first breath. Thank You for giving them to us at such a time to see us into this final battle against Morrigan. Go before us and bless this mission, I pray, amen."

Morrigan seemed subdued. Or she left. Either way, I no longer felt rage. Hers or mine. Exhaustion and sorrow had settled into my bones, rendering me incapable of anger.

A gust of wind swirled through, sending leaves dancing. I gripped the ends of my sleeves, shutting off airflow, and hugged myself, then took my turn beside Sully's grave. No worry lines creased his face. He was at peace. "We'll be together again, Sully." Possibly soon. I wiped tears with my sleeve.

God, I don't know what Your plans are. Forgive me for depending on others and not enough on You. I know You have a plan. You told Sully about me long before my birth. You brought me here. You led me to my family. You restored Declan and Alastar and so many others. Forgive me for failing to trust You after all You've done. You've proven yourself time and again. Help me trust You.

The leaves danced, a refreshing minty scent cleansed my lungs, and peace washed over me. Morrigan still had access to my mind. But her abilities had limits. There would be difficulties to come. But God never promised there would be no difficulties. And, though I hated to admit it, those problems brought me closer to Him.

"Goodbye, Sully. I'll see you in paradise." I followed the procession, then broke off to return to my tent.

Kai stood outside the entrance, his arms tight across his chest.

I smiled.

"A smile?" He threw an arm over my shoulder. "That's something I haven't seen in a while."

"Something I wouldn't have thought possible while Morrigan is still haunting my head."

"What's different? You seem different."

I breathed in the fresh air. "God. Even though things have gotten worse and they'll get even worse still, He'll see me through. Somehow."

Kai squeezed me. "I need to get to know this God of yours."

"He can be yours too. If you let Him."

"How? Do I need to become a fasgadair and have you bring me back?"

I laughed, then stopped when I saw his face. He was serious. Then again, I suppose it was confusing. I'd come to God through His Son in Saltinat, in person. Not something most people experience. The redeemed came to God through their transformation. Again, only made possible through His Son. But what did it take for people in this realm?

Valter's face flashed in my mind. Duh! Why was I overthinking things? I hadn't given it a second thought when Valter lay dying. So, I told Kai about man's fall, their need for redemption, and God's plan to save them, all the while wondering how much I butchered the story.

"So, what do I do?"

"Do you believe Jesus can save you?"

His arm no longer around me, he nodded.

"You can ask Him to save you now. Or later if you'd prefer to be alone."

"No. I want you with me. What do I do?"

"Just talk to God. Don't overthink it." Like I tend to.

Jerking back a step, he looked around. "Where is He? Will He hear me?"

"He's everywhere. You can always talk to Him, and He'll hear you. You can even talk to Him in your mind."

"Like thinking?"

"Yup. He knows your thoughts."

Kai raised an eyebrow. "What do I say?"

"Whatever comes to your heart."

He glanced at me out of the corner of his eye and gave me a sheepish grin, showing off his dimple. "God, I want to know You. I've made mistakes. Please forgive me. Fallon says Your Son can help me, and I believe her. So, please save me. Give me what Fallon has. Fill me with Your Spirit." He peeked at me. "Is that all?"

My heart exploded with joy, and tears streamed down my face. "That's all." I gave him a big hug. "Welcome to the family, brother."

"Brother?" He stiffened.

"Spiritually. We're both God's children now. That makes you my brother."

"As long as we can still get married, that's fine."

Married?

He blushed, then planted a kiss on my cheek.

Seriously, though...married? How did these things work in Ariboslia? Or among the selkie? Did he plan on *asking* me? I was only eighteen. Way too young to get married. And marriage was the last thing I needed to concern myself with now.

He flashed me a wide smile, his dimples deeper than ever. Why'd he have to be so cute?

CHAPTER THIRTY-ONE

The council let me continue our journey without a blindfold, but I had to remain separate from the others, particularly leaders like Rowan. And they still kept me out of the loop. But anything was better than carrying on without my sight. And, since Ji Ah and Maili were her tentmates, it kept Ji Ah away from Kai. That was a plus. But the ache in my heart over losing Sully followed me like a shark on a blood trail. Nothing would shake it.

If naysayers who wanted me blindfolded existed, I saw why they lost the fight. "Are we heading into that?" I pointed to the jagged-sided mountain. Had someone split it in two? Steep walls flanked either side of the river.

"Aye." Declan forged on ahead. "'Tis easier to walk through the canyon than scale the mountain."

Kai and I eyed each other with uncertainty, then followed Declan and Alastar across the grassy valley to rocky terrain and steep inclines I wouldn't have been able to scale without my sight. The path turned into a ledge, requiring us to walk single file. The river raged two feet below, splashing my feet when we rounded a bend. I slipped on a spot slick with algae. Kai caught my pack from behind. My heart raced as I paused in the backward position and gulped at the white-water rapids. Kai's wide eyes looming over my head, we both exhaled, and he nudged me to stand.

I'd fallen behind Declan, but I didn't hurry to catch up. That slip was a wake-up call. I'd rather fall behind than into the river. The ledge narrowed, forcing me to turn and hug the mountainside and shimmy sideways. My pack felt heavier than usual, threatening to pull me backward. My knuckles whitened in a death grip on the rocks as I forced myself not to look down. Just keep going. Inch by inch.

How much longer would this nightmare hike last? No amount of blazing the safe trails in Bandia prepared me for this. Why hadn't I at least attempted the more challenging courses? Sweat beaded along my brow. A drop dripped by my eye, begging me to wipe it away. But I didn't dare. One slipup on this ridge, and I'd topple into the turbulent water with a pack that would likely sink me.

God, help us through this.

I navigated the shelf for another fifteen minutes or so, at points having little more than my toes with a foothold. Then shelf expanded and dropped to a pebbled beach. I found an empty spot, discarded my pack, and wiped the sweat that had been driving me insane. Normally so many people packed together on a beach would bother me, but I was too relieved that I could move somewhat freely. I drank, emptying my canteen, then plunged it into the rushing river, letting the icy water chill and redden my hand.

I wiped my dripping hand on my jeans and returned to my pack and flopped down, taking the burden off my aching feet. I removed my shoes and knocked them free of the debris hitching a ride. If only I'd brought another pair of shoes. My toes poked through the canvas. And the soles at the ball of my feet wore thin. I rubbed my feet.

A selkie approached. He looked familiar. Right. He'd accused me of killing his friend. My breath caught and held while I tried to read him as he neared. His lack of facial expression told me nothing.

He knelt beside me, and I stiffened, braced for some sort of attack. But none came. He picked up one of my shoes and put something inside. "This leather will help until you get new shoes." He grasped my other shoe and did the same.

My mouth moved, but words wouldn't come. As he stood and started away, I choked out, "Th–thank you."

He turned, nodded, and continued on his way.

I wiped a tear away. Why would he help me? Did this mean he didn't blame me anymore?

I put my shoes back on. The leather padding he'd tucked in there rounded from the soles of my feet over my toes, providing plenty of protection. I fought the urge to cry. Why had his kind gesture made me so emotional?

THE SKY DARKENED, and we stopped to make camp. With no firewood or meat, we went without fires. So, we drank, refreshed our flasks, and ate jerky and biscuits. My stomach rumbled for more.

We laid out our bedding in a single file beside the stream. I pulled a few stones out from underneath only to find more rocks. Giving up, I rolled up my T-shirts underneath my head and tried to adjust myself into the most comfortable position possible.

The moon peeked out from the mountain ridge above. An owl hooted. My heart leapt. Was there a fasgadair among us? No. It wouldn't make its presence known by being vocal. Unless it was a ruse to keep us from suspecting. I scanned the darkness in the direction the sound had come from, then laughed at myself. It was just an owl. I hoped.

Sheer exhaustion, cool air on my face, and the calming sound of water racing through the river must've put me right to sleep. It seemed I no sooner rested my head, than I found myself on the shore in my dreams. But something aside from the empty shore differed. Where was the dazzling light that always blinded me? Clouds choked the sun, painting the sky gray. And the swirling lights were already open. Wasn't she already in here, with me? Or was that evidence of an open connection? Was there a way to close it?

I inspected the empty shore and surrounding fields. Where was she? Had she retreated to her own mind? Was that why I hadn't sensed her presence as I had earlier? I fought the urge to peer into the window. If that was a portal to her mind, and I somehow invited her into my mine by peeking... I couldn't take that chance. Instead, I watched the sea and sang my songs.

I woke the next day more refreshed than ever. A rare breeze swept through, and I threw on a hoodie. A shadow clung to much of the gorge, but a break in the mountains to the east allowed dawn's light to shine through. I washed one of my shirts in the stream, wrung it out, and hung it from a protruding rock in the cliff to dry, humming as I went.

Kai braced his back and stretched. "You seem happy this morning."

I glanced over my shoulder. Something about him seemed lighter, less weighed down. "So do you." My good mood surprised even me. How sad. I hoped that would change someday, and my attitude this morning would be the norm.

We sat with my brothers, waited for the signal to move out.

My mother returned from the waterline, capping her flask. She gave me a once-over. "You look much better today."

Part of me cringed that a good mood would be such a shocking thing. But I refused to let it bring me down. "Surprisingly, I slept well." A hawk screeched, making me itch to savor the moment fully by shedding my flesh and taking to the skies. "I had my dream, but Morrigan wasn't there."

"Really?" My mother's eyes narrowed with suspicion.

Kai cocked an eyebrow at me. "Is that possible?"

"I don't know what's possible and what's impossible. I mean, how'd she end up in my mind in the first place?"

188

"Good question." Kai locked his hands behind his head and stretched out his legs. "But I'm glad you're feeling better."

"I am too. So please don't think I'm trying to ruin your day when I say this." My mother leaned in, her purple eyes boring into mine. "But she might be trying to lower your defenses. Whatever you do, don't let your guard down."

CHAPTER THIRTY-TWO

W e traversed mountains for three more days, winding our way through the twisting canyon. The rock walls caging us receded, revealing a stunning view. The mountain yielded to lush greens spotted with a variety of boulders fanning out on either side of the river. I paused to soak up the sun and inhale the sweet air before beginning the continual downward slope, my arms swinging at my sides with the trek's easy and fast momentum.

Without the mountains, we were exposed. But, unlike the woods, this didn't offer anywhere to hide. Even a fasgadair wouldn't be fast enough to approach us unaware.

It had been a week since we left the Somalta Caverns. The hill plateaued, then stopped, leaving nothing but blue skies with miles of treetops before us. As the land fell away, the river pitched over the side. "I hope that's not a long drop."

The people traveling ahead of us disappeared over the edge without screaming as they plummeted into the abyss. I breathed easier. There must be a path.

Rushing water tumbled over the edge of the world. Once we arrived at the edge, I peeked over at the waterfall. It was a long drop.

The bottom wasn't visible through the trees. My vision swam and my surroundings faltered. I lost my balance and fell into Kai.

He grasped my arms, studying my face until only one clear version of him stood before me. "It's all right, Fallon. Look." He pointed down. "There's a path."

I dared peek over the edge at the steep, skinny trail. That was the path? My view wavered once more, and I covered my eyes, hoping to halt the rising nausea. People came up behind me, and Kai pushed me aside to let them pass.

The path cleared, but another group of selkie would be upon us within minutes. Kai descended before me, his feet skidding on the stones, making my feet tingle as if I were sliding. He offered his hand. "I'll help you."

Now or never. I clutched his hand and jumped. My feet slid, but Kai caught me. We stared wide eyed at each other for a moment too long. He released me, and I backed up as much as possible.

"Hold on to me."

Clinging to his tunic, I followed in his footsteps, avoiding eye contact with the ledge. The air cooled as we descended. A swift breeze wetted us with mist. The sun abandoned us to the cliff's shadow. After about an hour, we dipped below the thick tree line. The waterfall was no longer visible. But I heard it thundering ahead.

We reached level ground, and I released Kai's tunic and rubbed my sore fingers. The trees gave way to a crystal-clear, sandy-bottomed lagoon. The waterfall plunged into the water, sending up a mist.

Men scattered throughout the trees dropped their loads. Time to make camp.

THE SOUND of the falls and the cool air on my face lulled me into a deep sleep. I arrived in my usual dream space without Morrigan. The sky seemed gloomier than it had before as if fog filled the entire space. How long had it been growing dim? An apprehensive chill swept over me, and I scrubbed away the goosebumps covering my arms.

I woke the next morning, and apprehension coursed through me, setting me on edge. Though an entire army surrounded me, I felt alone.

My mind tumbled to its typical state of overthinking things I had no control over. How would I kill Morrigan? Had she resurrected her sisters? Would I have to kill them too? How?

Kai threw me a smile. I tried to return it, but couldn't. What was my problem? Why did I keep him at arm's length? Was I concerned about Ji Ah? Or that either one of us might die? Or that, once he knew the real me, he'd run screaming for the hills?

"What are you thinking?" He took a swig from his canteen and shoved it in his satchel.

"Oh, nothing important." I picked up my bag and got ready for another day of walking. "Any idea how much further?"

"I overheard a soldier say Nica is only a week's walk from here."

"Oh good." All I had to do was force my wrought muscles to continue for one more week, then deliver myself into the hands of my enemy completely exhausted and incapable of fighting back. "Can't wait."

Kai met my sarcasm with his head tilt I'm-not-impressed look.

THE DAYS BLURRED TOGETHER. With no path, we trudged through the woods in silence for almost a week. My shirtsleeves were torn from protecting my face as we forged a torturous route, like walking through an endless tunnel with junk in our way. But we had air, and the sun peeked through in places.

Murmurs of the forest's edge reached my ears.

My mother, her hair disheveled from invading branches, returned from the frontline. "We're making camp."

"But it's daylight." I glanced at the sun nearing its zenith and smoothed my hair, hoping it didn't look like hers.

"I can't give you the specifics. But they want you to rest up."

"But I just slept." I trembled. No way was I returning to that infested dreamland.

"Sleep more." Her no-nonsense stare caused me to pause. Better to just back down and do as she asked. "Okay, okay."

We rolled our bedding out, and I lay back, hands folded over my chest, watching the birds in the sky. Were they fasgadair? We must be close to Nica. And they must know we're here. Would Morrigan be there? Or was she still in Ceas Croi? Was she still in my mind? I hadn't sensed her since Sully's death. I would've thought she'd be thrilled with him out of the way.

Or was God keeping her at bay?

I stared in the sky and watched the birds, suspicious, and not tired in the least. They seemed to multiply as they flitted, twittering to each other. Their tweets of answer and reply morphed into a rhythmic song. I closed my eyes and hummed along until a creepy sensation swept over me.

I opened my eyes. The birds must've lulled me to sleep. I was back in the place in my dreams. Yet again, it was empty, and the fog had thickened. I sat, and the ocean waves lapped up on the beach. Black tendrils swirling like smoke came up behind me, curling and thickening, blocking out the sun. The black stuff kept streaming from the window, enveloping me in despair. I brought my knees to my chest and wept as self-pity and depression rocked me to my core.

Your mind is mine.

I should stand up and fight. Do something. Anything. But I didn't have the will to move. Instead, I curled up in a fetal position and cried.

"FALLON." A prick of light penetrated the darkness, streaming from the sky at me like a laser beam.

What was that? Had someone spoken? Or had I imagined it?

The glow swirled around me, surrounding my torso in a spiral. But it didn't bind me. I touched it, but my hand slipped right through as if nothing were there. But a pinprick of hope pierced my heart.

I allowed the rope light to pick me up and guide me to the window. Cringing, I peeked. Declan's profile came into view on the left, then disappeared. The view turned to the right. Kai. He threw me a sideways smile. It was as if I were walking with him.

Wait.

Kai wouldn't smile at Morrigan like that. And Morrigan wouldn't be walking with my friends. Was this just a dream?

Or was Morrigan manipulating my body?

I dropped to my knees. This couldn't be real.

But what if this was all I had left of myself, a view through a window and nothing more? Could I somehow regain control? I had to. What would happen if I didn't? Would Morrigan use me to sabotage the attack, even if I wasn't privy to the plans?

"No!" I screamed. "Get me out of here!"

Nothing changed. Darkness shrouded the entire place.

Morrigan had entered through the window. What if I went through? Would I leave my body and enter hers? A full body shudder racked me.

But what else could I do?

With the caution of one stealing honey from a sleeping bear's claws, I touched the window. My touch sent multicolored flashes rippling like a stone in water. I rubbed my fingertip with my thumb as if I expected to find a burn or residue. The surface smoothed over once more. Dare I stick and arm through? What if something snatched it on the other side? Should I peek inside?

My hands and feet tingled with anxiety as I fought to determine my next move. If only I had Drochaid to point me in the right direction. Or Sully to tell me what to do.

Sully would tell me to go to God. Could I reach God here? The light surrounding me had to be from Him. How else had I stood, fighting the crippling despair?

"God! Where are You? Are You here?"

"I am." A voice thundered from the space in the sky where the glow began. The blackness billowed with His words, light filtering through the gaps. Then the sky stilled and darkened but for the string wrapped around me. I sucked in my breath and trembled at such awesome power.

What should I say? Was He here?

A glowing figure emerged from the blackness, growing in size and definition as it neared. I shielded my eyes. Whoever it was wore a white robe cinched with a gold rope. An angel?

No. Not an angel. I recognized His kind face and Santa-Claus eyes. "It's you!" The Man from Saltinat! My fear melted as a surge of pure love emanated from the Man.

He smiled the most genuine smile in existence. "I knew you'd prefer me in this form."

I wanted to run into His arms. But should I? Dare I approach Him?

He opened His arms to welcome me, and I stopped fighting. I rushed into His embrace as every negative emotion suffocated in His love.

He touched my cheek with such tenderness.

I wanted nothing more than to stay where He was, in His presence. His loved bathed me, washing my impurities. What I wouldn't give to stay this way forever. "Have You come to take me away?"

He shook His head. "Your time hasn't yet come. There's much for you to do."

"But I'm trapped. Morrigan has taken over." Somehow, in His presence, that realization didn't fill me with misery.

"My child, she can't control you. You're Mine."

"Then how—"

"You're allowing her to do this to you. Somehow, you're not

aware of the power within you. My power. It's been there for you to use anytime you choose."

"How do I do that?"

"By letting go."

"Huh? I don't understand. Should I roll over and let whatever happens, happen? Isn't that what I'm doing now?"

"No, you're trying to control things as if you had the power. Give up and seek Me. Tap into My power."

But I had no control over anything? What could He mean? Then, as if His thoughts penetrated my soul, I saw my reactions to —everything. All this time, I could have basked in His power, trusting Him, and experiencing His peace even in the face of losing Turas, my eyesight, and Sully. And Morrigan wouldn't have been able to control my mind. I allowed it. I should have trusted God— asked Him to show me what to do. But I didn't. I fought for control. My guilt warred with the love emanating from Him. "But how?"

"Keep moving forward, knowing I'm in control. Trust Me to guide you." He took my hand. "Come." He led me to the window. "What do you see?"

Alastar and Declan faced the window, their eyes wide. A city loomed in the background. That must be Nica. They were so close already? It had only felt like a few minutes had passed. Did time move slower in here?

"Why isn't it working?" Alastar asked.

I turned to Jesus. "Are they trying to start the fire?"

Peace radiated from Him. "Without you, it won't work. Morrigan wouldn't let it if she could. There are aspects of your mind she can't penetrate."

"But she crawled in here."

The glow surrounding Him flashed. "She gave you an image of her crawling in. But she's not here. She can't be where I am."

"But the darkness—"

"Those are the lies she's filling you with. The lies you're believing. She's suffocating you with them to push Me aside so she can control you."

"And the Light is You?"

He nodded to the sky. "Up there, beyond the gloom. And here." He patted his chest. "And here." He pointed to my heart. "I will always be with you." He grasped the thin cord surrounding me and tugged. "This is your faith. It need not be this small. That part is up to you."

More pinpricks of light shot through the gloom.

He smiled. "See? You're already trusting the Truth. Keep believing, and you will obliterate the lies and with it—the darkness."

"What lies? Can You show me?"

"That's something you should always remember to ask. It pleases Me to shed My Light on such deception." He wrapped an arm around me. "The biggest lie you tell yourself is that you're not worthy of love." A tear dripped down His cheek.

He cried? My feeling unworthy brought Him to tears?

"I created you, dear child. Shouldn't it hurt me when you don't value yourself as I do?"

Was He reading my mind again?

"I know your innermost thoughts. There is nothing you can hide from Me. I know you better than you know yourself. Which is why it's important you ask Me to reveal your heart to you, so I can show you and help you grow closer to Me."

"But I can't. I'm not worthy of such love. No one has—"

"Stop feeding yourself lies. You think, because your grandmother couldn't love you, you're not worthy?"

I nodded. Tears slipped down my cheeks.

"She had no love to give. She didn't know Me. She couldn't love herself. How could she love anyone else? Do not judge your worth by the opinions of those around you. Come to Me. Ask Me. I will tell you how loved you are."

"How loved am I?" His image blurred though my tears.

He held up His hands to show me the piercings. "This much."

I slumped into His arms and wept.

He whispered in my ear. "If it had only been you, I still would have done it."

Sobs racked my body. He was right. Every lie I bought hinged on me feeling unworthy of love. Every judgement I passed onto others stemmed from my own insecurities based on that lie. All the little lies branched from that giant lie. How different would I be if I trusted the truth? He held me while I ugly cried until my eyes were dry and I had nothing left but shuddering breaths.

When I calmed, I pulled back, still clinging to His robe. A light more dazzling than before replaced the darkness.

"That's better." He held my face in both hands and peered into my eyes. Such gentle strength and fierce love met me there. "I've shown you before how much I love you. When you forget, come to Me, and I will remind you."

"What do I do now?"

"Go show Morrigan she can't manipulate you. And you take My love and share it with others. Although I would give it to you alone, it's not meant for you alone. It's for all who choose to believe."

CHAPTER THIRTY-THREE

The copper scent of blood assaulted my nose. Fallen men were strewn throughout the courtyard. Fasgadair appeared and vanished like swift ghosts, slitting throats. Where were Alastar and Declan?

God, show me where they are.

I ran through the city gate and found Alastar lying in a pool of blood. "No, no, no! Please! I can't be too late." I slipped in the blood and righted myself before I fell. "Alastar!" I shook him. His eyes opened. "Are you hurt?"

He grasped the back of his head, winced, and sat up. "A fasgadair threw me. Must've knocked me out." He eyed me with suspicion. "What happened to you?"

"Uh." How could I explain how I acted here when I wasn't present? "I'm okay now."

"Fallon! Alastar!" Declan came running up behind. He gave me the same look Alastar had, only a little more wild eyed and impatient. "You all right?"

I reached for his hand. "We need to stop this."

Declan pulled away. "But the fire won't work."

"It will now." I clasped his hand. We each grabbed Alastar to pull him up. The moment we all linked hands, the fire ignited. We ran through the mayhem like a wrecking ball, incinerating all the fasgadair who crossed our path. Anything to stop them from slaughtering more of our people.

The fasgadair took notice, surprise masking their demonic faces. They must've thought Morrigan still possessed me.

"Fasgadair, listen and heed my words! Salvation is here!" I shouted to the crouching fasgadair. "God will save you, shed you of your demon flesh, if you surrender to Him." Where were these words coming from? Was I making this up as I went along? How was I going to save these creatures when most didn't want to be rescued?

Wrong question. How was *God* going to do that?

God, You want to save these people more than I do. Show me how.

Maili appeared in my periphery. "If you want salvation, Maili will show you how."

She watched me like I'd lost my last marble.

"But I warn you—one wrong move, and my brothers and I won't hesitate to kill you."

Several fasgadair dropped their weapons and approached Maili, while others sneered and skulked away.

Though I hated the idea, I had to set them on fire. Never had I started fires with such swift accuracy. I somehow sensed their speed and direction. It could only have come from God. Further confirmation that their temporary pain was for their greater good...if they were redeemable. "Cut them!" I yelled to our men with blood-dipped weapons. One way or another, we would test them.

Sure enough, they had made their choice. Each fasgadair who tried to leave turned to dust, while all those who sought out Maili, allowing her to cut them, lived. Yet I was grateful God gave me the chance to know for sure and not leave me with the guilt of their death as misplaced as that may be. He gave me the opportunity to try.

Something within me clicked. This was why God allowed difficulties into our lives. Such challenges forced us to pick a side. And, if we picked Him, difficulties brought us closer to Him, making us more dependent upon Him. Only then could we truly live—when our circumstances no longer dictated our attitudes. Instead, God's love made us content in any circumstance.

"Fallon?" A strange voice pulled me from my thoughts.

A man in a brown robe, a redeemed fasgadair, walked toward me, head low. He lifted his gaze and lowered his hood, revealing an eye patch.

"Uh. Yes?" What did he want? To praise me? "If you're here to—"

"I'm here to seek your forgiveness." His fingers fidgeted by his side, then clasped together in front of his robe.

"Forgiveness? For wh—" No. It couldn't be. A fasgadair missing an eye? Was this—

"My pod came upon you in the woods last year. I—" He lowered his gaze, watching his twisting fingers. "I killed one in your company."

Ryann. My jaw clenched as my fists shook. I fought the urge to rush at the man and take back the redemption he didn't deserve. If only I had such power.

But what of God's power? What would God's power afford me in this moment? What would He have me do?

God, please show me what to—

Forgive.

The word came on so fast and strong it knocked me back a step. My nose and chest tingled with the urge to cry, but I fought it as I scanned the man cowering before me, full of true remorse. Wasn't God's redemption—His love and forgiveness—for everyone? I didn't deserve it either. How could I claim it for myself and not offer it as well?

I stuffed down the part that resisted what I was about to say. "I forgive you." My heart softened and grew, like the Grinch's, so that it might burst from my chest. I'd only half-felt the words before I uttered them, but now I meant them wholeheartedly. I'd truly forgiven this man, and I felt lighter.

He rushed to close the gap between us and latched onto my hand. "Thank you." His eye misted.

"Sorry about your eye." I pointed to his patch. The image of his grapelike eyeball skewered onto my talon turned my stomach. "Why didn't it regenerate?"

All this time, I'd pictured it regrown.

He released me. "Apparently, eyes plucked from the socket can't come back from nothing." He loosed a hearty laugh. "'Tis better to lose an eye and save my soul."

KAI CHARGED THROUGH THE CROWD, heading straight for me. He slowed as he neared. "Are you back?"

I crossed my arms and scowled. "I hate to think what Morrigan might've done or said while I..." While I what? Detained?

"It is you." He gripped my face and kissed my forehead. "I thought I'd lost you." He kissed my head again. Then seized me, pulling me to his chest, and smoothed my hair.

"What happened?" Not sure I wanted the answer. "What did she do?"

"She tried to pretend to be you. But I knew something was wrong. And then, when the fire didn't start, she laughed. Then the fasgadair attacked."

King Abracham stood at the castle entrance. "The castle is clear, but we need to be careful. There may be more. Morrigan might send others to attack before we invade Diabalta or Ceas Croi. And we've lost four hundred and twenty-three men. Go nowhere alone. Stay together in groups. And await further instruction as we assess the situation."

He bowed his head. "God, thank You for restoring the city of Nica. Please bestow Your blessing upon this kingdom and me as its ruler for a time. We pray for the souls lost in this war and entrust them into Your hands. Most of all, I pray we will never again lose sight of You and Your authority over us all, amen."

Everyone gathered repeated the word and moved into the castle.

Never had prayer had such meaning for me.

"You are not leaving my side again." Kai snagged my hand as we headed into the study where the leaders gathered. Everyone present eyed me as I passed. King Abracham approached me. "I understand Morrigan has left you. Is that correct?"

"Yes. She's gone, and she's not coming back." And I meant it. I still didn't know how I'd eliminate her. But she would never ooze her lies into my mind again.

"That's a relief." He placed his hands on my shoulders. "If it hadn't been for you, we would have lost this war."

The old me wanted to say, "If it hadn't been for me, so many wouldn't have died." But I couldn't go there. Not anymore. God allowed what God allowed, and I needed to do my part to keep my eye on Him. And stop belittling myself. It was an offense to Him.

He tugged his Merlin beard. "There is much to do and to discuss. We must clean up and take time to regroup before we consider moving on to Diabalta, then Ceas Croi." He turned to Evan.

Evan! I hadn't seen him in so long. He was alive. *Thank You, God!* And Rowan. Both were grungy and disheveled, but alive.

"Do you have a headcount of those who survived?"

"We'll take a census to be sure." Evan wiped his dagger on his tunic and sheathed it. "But we're close to two thousand five hundred gachen and selkie."

"Thank you, Evan. Does that number include the redeemed?"

"No, Your Highness. I'll check with the infirmary."

"Very well. And what of the pech?"

"Pepin is collecting their numbers."

"Roughly nine thousand," came a gruff voice from the door. A pech. Not Pepin.

"I'm sure it pales compared to the number of fasgadair Morrigan has left standing, but God has shown that He is with us. We must prayerfully consider our next steps. In the meantime, we have wounded to tend to in the great hall. We need to take stock of food supplies and prepare something for everyone to eat. Set up camp in the valley to ensure everyone has a place to rest."

Someone grabbed me from behind, lifting me. Once my feet hit the ground, I turned. "Wolf!" I flung my arms around him. "I've missed you."

He choked. Sorrow filled his eyes. "And I've missed ye, lass."

"It's okay. I get it."

Cahal appeared over his shoulder. I released Wolf, and Cahal smothered me in a bear hug. This must be what it was like for Mowgli to hug Baloo. If they existed.

"It is so good to see you guys."

"Guys?" Rowan stepped up behind me with Evan. Then Maili. I gave hugs all around.

"I'm so glad to have you back." Evan put an arm around me and squeezed.

We weren't through the woods yet, but rather than focus on the losses and the difficulties ahead, I saw God's hand in it all. He was putting things right.

CHAPTER THIRTY-FOUR

Nica was a beautiful city on a hill. From the main entrance, where we'd arrived when I was unaware under Morrigan's spell, the city seemed to sprout from the grassy mound with random patches of trees before it. Its ideal location provided an amazing three-sixty view. Kai and I stood in the tower at the tallest point, offering the best vantage point without morphing into my bird form. We could see for miles in every direction.

"I love this place." I sighed as I peered out at the lake. The backside of the hill sloped into it, its greens blending with where the mountains reflected on its smooth surface.

"It reminds me of home." Kai shivered. "But it's much colder."

"It's winter." I pulled my sweatshirt sleeves over my hands. "Doesn't it get cold where you live?"

"It gets cool at night. But not like this. This is the first time I've seen snow. It's like God covered the world with a sparkly blanket to protect it from the cold." His chest filled as he breathed deep. "Smells minty."

I returned his smile and took in the view with new eyes. In

Maine, I'd seen more than my fair share of snow. Enough to be thoroughly sick of it, particularly since Fiona wasn't one to shovel. That backbreaking work was left to me.

Snow certainly didn't impress me. But the dusting of snow covering the trees and circular dwellings built into the mountainside opposite the lake shimmered—magical. I inhaled the sweet, invigorating, eucalyptus scent. Each cleansing breath replenishing my soul.

Yet an undercurrent of impatience to complete our quest kept me itching to move on.

Huffing and puffing accompanied heavy footfalls from the tower stairwell. Pepin's chubby hand appeared on the rail, then his bent body, gasping for breath. "That... is... a lot... of steps." He reached the top and grasped his sides. His face red, cheeks puffing with each exaggerated breath.

Kai and I stared as Pepin collected himself.

"Maili... is looking... for you." Pepin straightened and gave a final puff, then eyed the window and approached, standing on tiptoes. "Wow. Is this what it feels like to be a bird?" He stepped away, rubbing his eyes. "Other than the lake. I could do without the lake."

I laughed. "We're aware." How often had I heard him complain about water? Countless times.

"Maili is in the training room, ready for your lesson."

I searched for an excuse to delay my lessons with Maili. But it was no use. There was no way to escape her. Better to get it over with. That was the only thing I didn't like about Nica—the training room.

"READY?" Her hand hovered over the switch.

I wanted to say no, but Maili would turn the contraption on anyway. And she never waited for my response. She flipped the switch, and the beast roared to life. The beam I stood upon spun. The only way across was to run. Anything else resulted in falling onto the mat below. Which I had. Many, many times. My body still felt the bruises from the not-so-soft landings. But Maili was relentless, forcing me back with no choice but to attempt not to fall.

I ran across the log onto the platform and ducked in time to miss the beam swinging at my head. I stayed low for two counts, waiting for the beam's return swing before standing and running across another spinning beam. Though it seemed safe, I'd learned not to stay put too long. A floor would fall away, or something would knock me over, sending me tumbling to the padding. So, I jumped to the lowest rung before me and climbed. The ground no longer swayed below me. Two months of this torture was curing me of my fear of heights.

The rung at my feet collapsed. Legs dangling over the mats far below, I pulled myself along the monkey bars to the next platform. I swung my body until I had enough momentum to make the leap and released, landing on the platform. Three beams swung at differing times, with no space to rest in between. I counted their swings until the timing was right, then ran along another spinning log to the finish line.

"Ha!" I thrust my arms into the sky. "I did it!"

Maili clapped. "I guess it's time for a new configuration."

What? No congratulations? No well done? She was always ready to move the pieces to ensure I didn't memorize the course, forcing me to think quick and react according to ever-changing obstacles.

I'd never admit it to Maili, but nothing I'd done before had instilled me with such confidence. Her training strengthened me.

"That's all for today. King Abracham has called a meeting in the auditorium." She gave me a once-over from the corner of her eye. Her nose wrinkled. "You have an hour to clean up."

After I'd cleaned and rubbed Maili's salve on my bruises, which meant basically everywhere, I found my friends. We sat on a bench near the front of the auditorium. I picked at the callused blisters on my palm as the surrounding seats filled. King Abracham sat on the stage with Evan, Rowan, and General Seung.

King Abracham stood and tugged his beard. Once everyone had

settled and quieted, he clasped his hands behind him. "I know many of you are as eager as I to move out and reclaim my father's kingdom, Diabalta. After seeing what devastation, the fasgadair have caused here...the slaves they kept in captivity for labor and," he lowered his shaking head and mumbled, "a food source."

Then he raised his head and projected his voice once more. "I'm sure you understand our need for delay to help these wonderful people. Thank you for your patience and assistance as we restored order in the City of Nica. But now it is time to do the same for Diabalta. King Evan and Princess Rowan will remain with a regiment to assist with the rebuilding efforts. Once permanent leadership is established, they will return to their kingdoms in the selkie lands and Bandia. In the morn, I will lead our forces into Diabalta." King Abracham turned to Evan. "King Evan, would you say a word?"

Evan stood. "Uh. Eh-hem." He bowed to King Abracham, then the audience. "Yes, thank you, King Abracham."

He looked green. Good thing he had a chance to practice being king here with Rowan before returning to his permanent kingdom.

"Thank you for the honor of allowing Princess Rowan and me to aid you in this war. Though it pains us to remain behind for this final battle, we know this is where God would have us. Our prayers, and God, are with you." The green subsided a bit as he surveyed the room, building confidence. He faced me, and a warm smile emerged. "Fallon, we've been through so much together. You are a dear friend. Though we've been through many difficulties, we've come through them stronger. I have no doubt God will see you through to the end."

Evan's eyes roamed the crowd once more. "God is for us. None is powerful enough to stand against us. The battle is already won!"

The crowd cheered.

"Thank you, King Evan." King Abracham patted Evan's back. "Everyone should know what their role is. Please confirm with your regiment and advise me tonight if there are any changes. The total number joining the war in Diabalta is shy of twelve thousand."

King Abracham bowed his head. "God, we thank You again for reestablishing this kingdom under Your sovereign rule. We ask that You go before this army and defeat the enemy that seeks to undermine Your authority. Protect our people and bless this mission, amen." He lifted his head. "Rest up. We move out in the morn."

CHAPTER THIRTY-FIVE

At first light, we loaded up our packs and started toward Diabalta. Marching along with so many men, silent but for their clanking armor and resolute footfalls, their jaws set in firm determination, filled me with inexplicable overwhelming emotion. I swallowed a lump in my throat, blinking back tears as I set my jaw and focused on keeping step.

I wasn't eager for the walk ahead. But it should only take three days to reach Diabalta. That was nothing compared with what we've already been through. And I needed to keep close to my brothers. Just in case we required the triplet fire.

The ground felt soft thanks to my new shoes. No more rocks poking through. I'd never had tailor-made shoes before. They seemed good so far. The soles provided ample padding yet moved with my feet better than sneakers. They laced up over my jeans and the thick, wool socks Declan scavenged for me. But, with the cushy grass and melted snow, the ground was softer. The true test would come should we travel a rockier path.

We hadn't walked far, and I was already growing warm under my coat. I'd need it for the winter months. But what would I do with it while I walked and overheated? I unbuttoned it and fanned the flaps to cool myself down.

"Here." Kai slid my pack off my shoulder as men circumvented us. He motioned for me to give him my coat.

I removed it, and he tucked it through the strap, draping it over my pack.

"Put it back on."

I pushed, but it would only flatten so much. Oh well. A little bulky, but it worked. "Thanks." I sighed. "Is it bad I'm tired of walking already?"

"No. It's like getting on another ship." He cringed. "And I love the sea. But I never want to set sail again."

"Same." I kicked a pebble in my path. "If only we hadn't lost Turas. I wonder how difficult it will be to seize Diabalta without it."

"We'll find out in a few days."

"But last time Morrigan thought she could take me out of the game. Now she knows she's lost that battle. She'll be prepared for me. Somehow."

"If she's there. She may be at Ceas Croi."

"I almost wish she'd be there, just to get it over with. Having to deal with all these battles before getting to her is like being that last in line to give a presentation."

"Huh?" He gave me his tilted I-have-no-earthly-idea-what-you're-talking-about face.

"Trust me. It's bad. Very bad."

He shrugged. "Just remember. She's no match for God. No one is."

True. *I trust You, God. Help me trust You more.*

AFTER A DAY'S WALK, the trees thinned, and civilization emerged. At least, there were buildings. But no signs of life. The place reeked of death. Something creaked, banged, and creaked again. I jumped, facing the sound, ready to act. But it was only a door blowing in the wind. Bent fences choked cadaverous houses like shackles with rotting or missing links. The thatched roofs sank inward, gaping holes visible. Windows like gouged-out eyes gawked beyond absent or crooked shutters.

Nothing had survived here.

I passed a filthy teddy bear with one eye. Stuffing escaped where an arm should be. My heart broke as I imagined the bear's owner being carted off in a cage like Alastar had been, reaching through the bars for the fallen bear, crying. Was he or she still alive somewhere?

I was letting this place depress me like Atreyu's horse in the swamp of sadness.

God, I feel as if I'm walking the last mile to my death. Don't let me forget, no matter what's ahead, You are with me. If You are for me, nothing can stand against me.

As we journeyed the next day, the houses grew closer together. Stone buildings replaced the rotting wooden structures. Crumbling and half decimated, they lay like skeletons on an old battlefield, chilling me to my core. I hated to think what happened to all the people.

If Diabalta was another day's walk—though the scouts clearing the way slowed our progress—this must've been an impressive city. Still, Nica and Bandia didn't compare in size. The stone structures elevated into multiple stories with alleyways, staircases, and balconies. The castle towers jutted above and beyond vacant dwellings and storefronts, reminding me of the goblin king's castle beyond the labyrinth. Snow-capped mountains loomed like malevolent leaders, protecting its inhabitants with a heavy hand.

If this was Morrigan's kingdom, why was she rarely here? Each time I'd seen her through Turas, she'd been in Ceas Croi—her lair hoarding all her witchcraft. She seemed to prefer to lurk on the sidelines, allowing others to take front stage, such as Aodan and Alastar.

And where was everyone? Her bloodsucking minions or their captives?

I prayed our plan would work, whatever it was. Although they were trusting me more, they weren't telling me much. Conversations still hushed when I neared. Not that I blamed them. I wouldn't trust that Morrigan was gone either. *I* didn't even have any way of knowing for sure.

At least, I hoped they had a plan.

My heart grew anxious as we neared the skeletal towers ahead. It was third-grade science class all over again. I had an incomplete project. And it was almost my turn to present.

With no room for our tents, many took shelter in the abandoned buildings. I didn't believe in ghosts. But I still couldn't bring myself to sleep inside one of those places.

We found what might've been a park. Dead gardens lined a crumbling brick path. An area of patchy, overgrown grass and weeds overtook the center.

"How's this?" Declan asked.

It wasn't ideal, but nothing here was. "It'll do."

We put down our things, claiming the spot.

"Is this smart?" I asked Kai as I tore dead branches from vines along the wall for the fire. "Won't they come out here and attack us when night falls?"

"That depends on whether their plan is successful or not."

I dropped my tinder. "Plan? What plan?" Since when was Kai privy to the plans?

With a fake smile curving his face, worry lines crept across his forehead. "Ah..."

"It's okay. It's okay. Don't tell me." I stooped to pick up the kindling and discarded it in a pit in the middle of the park and set it on fire.

Hooting and hollering emerged from the edge of the camp and made its way to us. Declan came running. "It worked! The castle it ours!"

"What?" What had I missed?

Everyone whooped and gave each other congratulatory back pats. Had they all gone mad? I huffed at them, placing my hands on my hips. Their excitement and my cluelessness frustrated me.

"Will someone *pleeeeease* tell me what's happening?"

"Remember Le'Corenci?" Declan bounced as if he'd downed a case of energy drinks.

Why did that name sound familiar? Then it clicked. "The fasgadair Wolf led to us and everyone thought he was a traitor? The one who told me to go to Ceas Croi last year?"

"Right. He said an angel led him to guide you. And he was right. Because you followed his instructions, you fulfilled the prophecy and killed Aodan."

"I didn't kill Aodan."

He held up his hands and blew out an aggravated breath. "Right. Morrigan killed him. But it was because of you and all part of the prophecy."

"Yeah, so?" What was he getting at? "What does that have to do with anything?"

"He was in Nica when we seized it. He was one of the fasgadair who approached Maili."

"Who was?"

"Le'Corenci."

"So?"

He grabbed my shoulders and shook me. "Don't you see?"

"No." I peeled his fingers off me and planted my hands on my hips once more. "Tell me."

"Because of what had happened before, we trusted him. Though he was desperate for redemption, he agreed to remain a fasgadair to fulfill a mission. We sent him ahead to Diabalta with a flask of redeemed blood."

"To do what—single-handedly cut every bloodsucker?"

Declan laughed. "He contaminated their water supply, then laid low until they had their daily ration. Only the redeemed remained."

"The fasgadair drink water?"

Declan's shoulders twitched in silent laughter. "That's the best part. They've been watering down their blood supply to make it last since we've been squeezing in on them."

"What?" I sucked in my breath. "That's incredible." All that worrying for nothing?

"That's what I'm telling you."

"This is crazy. How didn't Morrigan know? They're connected."

Alastar stepped up. "Le'Corenci had denied his thirst for so long he was nearly desiccated, making Morrigan's connection to him weak. It also made his mission a long shot. But he was the only one we could trust to accomplish the task."

"Does Morrigan know this? Should you be telling me?"

Declan narrowed his eyes. "Are you concerned she might still have access to your head?"

I hoped not.

"Whether through you or her own connection"—he eyed me with renewed suspicion—"she knows they're dead or no longer fasgadair."

CHAPTER THIRTY-SIX

A skeletal man with loose skin spotted me. Joy leapt to his eyes as he straightened. Then his spine settled back into its hunched position as he approached, keeping his eyes trained on me. He reached out a spindly hand. Did he expect me to shake it? I'd never shaken hands with anyone in Ariboslia. Did they do that? I raised my hand, tentative. He seized it in both his. I relaxed, glad I didn't shake it.

"Fallon." He smiled, revealing a big gap in his teeth.

Something was familiar about this man. No, I would've remembered him with his curved spine and gap teeth.

"It isss so good to see you."

No way. That lisp. It had sounded more sinister as a fasgadair. More snake-hiss like. But this had to be him. "Le'Corenci?"

"No." He spat on the ground. "That wasss my fasgadair name. My real name isss Ennisss." He pumped my hand. "I held on to the hope that the angel would keep hisss promisss. After waiting more than a year, I thought I must've done something wrong. But look." His overjoyed eyes crinkled, and he shook my hand with renewed vigor. "Here you are. And here I am." He loosed a hearty laugh. "No

216

longer a fasgadair. Just asss the angel promised. I've been waiting for you to arrive to thank you." He released me.

I folded my hands. "I should thank you. We came expecting a fight. Or, at least, I did. But, thanks to you, there's no fight. No losses."

"Only the gainsss of the redeemed. Myself included." His smile widened further, taking over half his face. "God may not be on my schedule, but He keepsss Hisss promisesss and He'sss alwaysss right on time. Imagine if God had redeemed me when I had wanted? Who would've been able to get into Diabalta with the redeemed blood?" He cupped his mouth and chuckled. "Oh, and whatever you do..."

He leaned in and whispered in a not-so-hushed voice, "Don't drink the water." He gave my shoulder two firm pats and shuffled off giggling.

WE HELD A CELEBRATION THAT NIGHT. King Abracham retrieved wine from the cellar and filled glasses for everyone in the great hall. He raised his glass. "Brothers and sisters, we have overcome great odds. We traveled to the lands to the east, endured shipwreck and heartache, and raised our weapons against our foe. But it was a worthwhile journey. Look what God has done! He's restored the gachen's relations with the selkie. He's freed the pech out from the underground and united us. He's reunited the clans and returned our kingdoms. Most of all, He's restoring us to Himself."

The king took a deep, satisfied breath. "All we've lost, He is setting right as we follow Him. We must not allow those losses to dampen our victory. God is with us. He is restoring what we lost due to our faithlessness. We will rebuild with His blessing. And, although we must refuse to allow the ghosts of the past to taint our futures, we must never forget where we've come from or repeat the mistakes. From this day forward, my friends, let us remember to praise our God, to keep Him first, above all else, on His rightful throne. And let us love each other."

He thrust his drink in the air, sloshing some over the edge. "To God be the glory!"

"To God be the glory!" the crowd shouted.

Everyone drank their wine, and cheerful notes of a flute floated through the air. Drums and a stringed instrument soon joined the refrain. I grabbed Kai's hand to go outside. The merriment continued throughout the hall, into the foyer, and out into the courtyard where a gangly man juggled flaming sticks. A group danced in an organized fashion like in a Shakespearian play. Alastar scooped me up and swung me into the mix. I didn't know the dance, but everyone else seemed to, except Kai. My mother had roped him in. They swung us around, whisking us away in the general direction we should go. Others gathered us, keeping us in line. I watched their feet to mimic their steps and fell into the rhythm and came face-to-face with Kai. A broad smile brightened his face. We clasped hands, stepped on each other's toes, and twirled in the wrong direction, laughing every step of the way. Others swooped in to bring us back in step.

Why had I always been so afraid of dancing?

THE NEXT MORNING, my brothers, Kai, and I delivered porridge in carts to the courtyard. The whole way, I tried not to worry about the unknowns encroaching on me.

I needed to trust God with this. And I did. For the most part. But it was so much easier said than done. I mean, an undead demon skilled in witchcraft who had likely resurrected her evil sisters loomed in my obscure future. Facing her was inevitable. I didn't have to fear. I shouldn't fear. But how could I not?

We met a crowd gathering in the courtyard. They started at Alastar's cart for a bowl, then scooted to Kai, Declan, or me to scoop porridge for them. They smiled at me and said thanks. Amazing to see how many people had taken part in this journey, and now I got to serve them. The honor filled me with an inexplicable joy.

Once the crowd dissipated and our tureens were almost empty, we ladled a portion for ourselves and sat on a low wall surrounding a garden. I scooped a spoonful and took a bite. It was cold and lumpy but tasted wonderful. I scoffed it down and set my dish aside.

I chewed a chunk of porridge as my thoughts returned to the imminent final quest. "When are we leaving?"

My mother collected our bowls and set the stack beside her. "I think we should take time to reestablish this kingdom as we did with Nica."

"But Nica was further away. I hear it only takes a day to walk to Ceas Croi."

"Aye." My mother nodded. "But people still need time to rest. We need to pray and await God's timing. The people here need us, as with Nica. Whatever their experience, all were enslaved...many since birth. That's not easily overcome."

It made sense. Still, I felt sicker and sicker each moment I thought of what lay ahead. Better to face it now than wait.

I SHIMMIED through the tunnel on my belly. Where was the end of this thing? And why did Maili love torturing me so? She knew I was claustrophobic. My breaths came in tight gasps as I rounded the dark corner. The floor dropped out from under me several feet above the mat. Panicked, I reached for a bar as I fell. My fingers nearly slipped, but I adjusted my grip and spotted a platform. I swung myself back and forth, gaining momentum. One more swing, and I should make it. But I had to be quick or the bar supporting me might disconnect. Maili did everything she could to make me move fast.

After the third swing, I landed on the platform, arms windmilling to keep me from falling backward onto the mat. I stepped forward, and the platform collapsed, sending me down a chute on my butt. I rolled at the bottom and landed on my feet in a crouch, arms spread, ready for whatever surprise Maili prepared for me. Sure enough, a log swung from my left. I pitched forward, splayed out on the mat. The log swept past with a whoosh, blowing my hair.

Maili jumped into the pit, landing with a soft thud. She clapped as she approached.

Was that it? Was the torture over?

"Well done, Fallon."

I glanced around, watching the log, then slid forward and stood a safe distance away. "You really do enjoy torturing me."

She laughed. "Look how far you've come." She threw a towel at me.

"How is this supposed to help me fight Morrigan?" I wiped the sweat from my forehead and the back of my neck. "I can't outmaneuver her."

"For one"—she jutted her thumb—"you're overcoming your own demons before contending with the ultimate one. Look how well you're dealing with your fear of heights and confined spaces? Second"—she aimed her pointer finger, forming a gun trained on me —"you're much more agile. And third"—she added another finger— "you're learning to be on the alert and react quickly." She patted a beam of the torture device, gazing upon it as if it were a long-lost friend. "The trees offer great natural courses. But I might have to construct a course in Kylemore when we return. This one is even better than Nica's." She touched her lips and studied the thing. "I'll have to make a sketch."

"Great! I'll leave you alone with your beloved torture device." I'd almost made it to the exit when my mother appeared in the doorway.

"Done training for the day?" she asked.

"Yes." I peeked at Maili as I slid close to the exit.

Maili gave an absent nod and continued scrutinizing her pride and joy.

"Good." My mother stepped out into the hall, allowing me to pass. "Eat a decent meal and rest up. We leave for Ceas Croi in the morn."

CHAPTER THIRTY-SEVEN

If she wanted me to sleep, she shouldn't have said that. I tossed and turned all night. If we leave in the morning, will we camp outside Ceas Croi for the night? Though it was a mountain without windows, Morrigan must be expecting us. Whether she still had access to my mind or not, she had spies. And we were so close. She'd see us coming.

Wait. Evan wasn't with us. How could we go without him? Wasn't he the only one who knew the secret tunnels? Without him, we never would've escaped.

The pech? They created Ceas Croi. Pepin led me to the secret entrance near the peak. He said there were other "surprises" too. But they'd abandoned Ceas Croi to the gachen generations ago. Unless they had a record or blueprints, how would they know where the tunnels were? And what surprises was Pepin referring to?

I flopped to my side and faced my mother's bed. She lay on her back, hands folded across her chest. A slight snore escaped her lips. How could she sleep so peacefully? She'd been held captive there and only escaped a little over a year ago. Wasn't she as anxious as I was?

I huffed, half wishing to wake her. But no. She responded with another snore.

The early rays of dawn streamed into the window.

My mother stretched. "How'd you sleep?"

"Not at all."

"Oh." She eyed me as if afraid I might bite. "I shouldn't have told you we were leaving."

"You think?" I couldn't contain the sarcasm. Not after that sleepless night.

"My apologies." She peeled the covers off her and put on her traveling clothes. "I'm going to wash up. See you at breakfast."

I nodded, hoping I'd enjoy what might be my last meal.

AFTER BREAKFAST, we donned our things and headed out. This time, since it was our last seize and only a day away, we traveled lighter. I sidled next to Pepin. "Are we going enter through the tunnels?"

"That's my guess."

"You don't know?"

"Given our relationship, they didn't want to tell me." He wrinkled his nose like he smelled something foul and eyed me. "Not to mention, I'm not familiar with Ceas Croi."

"But you told me about the entrance at the top of the mountain."

"I said that?"

"Yes, right before I left to confront Aodan. You don't remember?"

Pepin narrowed his eyes. "How could I tell you something I don't know?"

"I don't know how you did it, but you did." I racked my brain to conjure the conversation. It was so long ago, and I couldn't even remember what I ate yesterday. But I recalled him acting strange, absentminded, and repeating himself.

"Morrigan killed the pech in Ceas Croi hundreds of years ago.

There's not a pech alive who has ever seen the inside. We've only heard legends."

My hands shook. I folded them to keep them still. "Then how are we to get inside? Should I fly in like last year?"

Pepin stopped and grabbed my arm. He stared at me and growled. "Do *not* do that."

"But it sounds like you're not prepared. We need a plan."

"We have one. I just don't know what it is. And you don't need to either." His grip tightened. "Do not run into this alone."

"Okay. Okay." I tried to shake his arm loose, but his sausage fingers gripped tighter.

"I mean it, Fallon. Don't take this into your own hands. Trust God. Otherwise, you'll ruin everything."

"Oookaaay." I drew out the vowels and bugged my eyes out as if that might somehow convince him.

He pointed to Kai and my brothers. "Watch her. See she doesn't leave on her own."

"What?" I raised my free hand in defense. "I said I wouldn't."

"And I know you too well." He looked to the boys again. "Watch her." He waddled off.

Great. Why did I have to feel like a prisoner before I'd even approached the enemy?

I'D NEVER OBSERVED Ceas Croi from the outside. Last time, I'd flown to the summit as a bird. Clouds had hidden the landscape. When we escaped through the backside tunnels, we were running for our lives. Or, in my case, carried away. I never glanced back. Plus, I'd lost a lot of blood from three bites courtesy of Aodan, Evan, and Evan's brother, and I was out of it.

The mountain loomed in the distance, the tip obscured by clouds, and I wanted nothing more than to change into a falcon, ditch my captors, and sneak in as I had last year. But then what?

Somehow, God made everything work out before. He'd do it again. Right? I wish He'd let me in on His plans. But no. I'd have to swallow bitter pills of nervous energy—energy tempting me to avoid waiting, prompting me to fly into danger to get it over with—and trust Him.

God, You have a plan. Help me keep putting one foot in front of the other, trusting You.

We avoided the road heading to the main entrance. Someone had to know where a secret passageway was. Right?

The question was, did Morrigan know?

CHAPTER THIRTY-EIGHT

Thousands of us trudged through the dark woods, following those in front, like an army of ants to a picnic lunch. We moved slowly, keeping to a broad column rather than fanning out. Considering our numbers, we were surprisingly silent. Crouched with weapons ready as if they might actually sneak up on Morrigan. But there was no way she didn't know we were coming.

The entire trip, I didn't come upon any living things. Little wonder there were no land-dwelling critters. They'd probably scampered away at our approach. But no birds? Not one scattered as our troop neared. Nothing.

Did every living thing keep a safe distance away? Perhaps they sensed the evil residing within. Other than the unnatural quiet, nothing seemed out of the ordinary. No electric smell. Yet every hair stood on end as if attempting to incite me to turn in the opposite direction, away from the malevolent beings. My heart pounded harder, thumping like the grim reaper knocking at my door, persistent, banging louder with each blow. I clenched my shaking hands and fought to still my feet itching to run...anywhere but where I headed.

Where was Morrigan's army? Where were her guards?

Alastar. He'd know. I spotted him with Wolf and rushed to his side. "Where are Morrigan's guards?"

"We've never needed them before. Morrigan owns the entire area and nearby cities." He scoffed. "At least, she did."

"But she knows Nica and Diabalta no longer belong to her. Right?"

He kept his gaze dead ahead, focused on his mission. "Aye."

"And that we're on our way?"

"Aye."

"Then don't you think she'd station vampires out here to intercept us?"

His fingers tightened around his dagger. "I've never known what to expect from Morrigan. But she knows she's lost minions. She doesn't need you for that. Her connection with hundreds of fasgadair severed when Nica and Diabalta fell. There's no way she didn't notice."

"Does she know where the secret tunnels are?" It unnerved me that he didn't glance my way, not even once. If I didn't know better, I might've thought he was angry with me.

"I wasn't aware of them. But that doesn't mean much. Morrigan kidnaped me and raised me as a so-called son which means she tormented me to make me mean and barely tolerated me as a human, isolating me to protect me from her bloodthirsty minions until I had grown enough to transform into a fasgadair." His nostrils flared as he blew out air like an angry bull. "Then she trained me and gave me control of her armies. In all that time in her presence, I never understood her. I never knew what she would do next. If she's anything, she's unpredictable. If you're hoping anything you might've learned about her will help you fight her, you're wrong."

Wow. I'd never seen him so uptight. Aside from when he was a fasgadair. Then again, he headed to face someone who was a much bigger demon to him in a deeper way than I could fathom. My blood rushed faster with each step lurching me closer to her. How much worse must it be for him? My heart aching for him, I placed a hand on his shoulder, wanting to fill him with peace through my touch.

He finally made eye contact, for a second. But the crooked smile he gave me didn't reach his frightened eyes. "All *I* know for certain is that she's evil. I'm not eager to see her or meet her sisters." He kicked a stone in his path. "I will say this, though—the fact that there aren't guards surrounding this mountain terrifies me."

"Why?" I held my breath, barely uttering the word.

He grimaced, looking like he wanted to puke. "It means she wants us to come inside."

WE REACHED AN ESCARPMENT, stretching into the forest. Cataleen waved others forward. She'd escaped with me last year. She must've remembered the general location. A crowd felt along the cliff side while soldiers ringed us, eyes darting in every direction.

"Oh!" A pech almost fell through the rock. He jumped up as if he'd intended for that to happen and waved us forward. His bushy beard covered his smile, but the deep crinkles and his sparkling amber eyes made it clear.

Was he unaware of what lay ahead beyond those tunnels? Or was he that excited to enter Ceas Croi, eager to reclaim it? Probably a mixture of both.

I'd barely been conscious when I escaped last year. But I remembered the windy staircase. Last time, we descended. But going up? For a mile? Assuming this was the same entrance and the same staircase, this would be an exhausting climb.

I crossed through the stone façade behind Alastar with Kai by my side. A familiar musty odor hit me, transporting me back to these tunnels last year. My foot slipped on something greasy coating the stairs. The same stuff slicked the sides. Yuck.

Torches lining the wall lit the way. The pech must be lighting them. If I'd been in front, I could've made their job easier for them and quickened our pace.

At least we were in better shape. Last time we'd been escorting decrepit prisoners, and I'd suffered the loss of three bites. We made it then—we could make it now.

We'd barely progressed, yet I was already growing dizzy and panicky from the constant upward spiral. My thighs and calves burned. I wanted nothing more than to transition, fly to the top, and wait for everyone there. But what would I do with my clothes?

People's backs blocked my view. My chest constricted. I peeked down the stairwell. Nothing but a sea of heads coming up from behind, I tensed. My heart pounded to the marching steps echoing in the stairwell. No. Not now. Don't panic.

Standing on the promises...

Kai put an arm around me, steadying me. "Are you all right? You look green."

"I'll be okay." I kept my gaze low, focused on the steps before me, fighting the urge to push the people in front out of my way. Warm bodies squeezed in from every side. I lifted my gaze to the low ceiling. How much air was in this place?

Air. I gulped, needing more air. My breath came in gasps.

"Oh no." Kai caught me as my feet gave way.

People shuffled aside as much as possible, giving us room. He picked me up. Those in front saw my struggle and pushed aside, allowing us to pass. My head and feet bumped multiple people as he maneuvered us to the front of the line. Declan and Alastar stayed close behind.

My breathing came easier with the clear path before us.

"Feeling better?" Kai frowned at me, concern wrinkling his tan forehead.

I took a deep breath. "I can walk now." So much for Maili's training. I wasn't doing as well with the claustrophobia as she thought.

He glanced at the pech falling behind, then jogged a few more quick steps, and put me down.

Alastar and Declan bumped into us.

Kai lugged me ahead of the coming crowd. "Since we're in front, we need to keep the pace to stay ahead." He flashed a dimple at me. "If you can't, I can try carrying you on my back."

"I'll tell you if I need it." I smiled back. "Thanks for getting me out of there. You always come to my rescue."

His dimple deepened as he viewed me askance, his dark eyes gleaming.

Our progress slowed. The pechs' did too. A faint shuffle sounded from below. Thank God for their short legs.

"Can we take a break for a second?" I doubled over to catch my breath and rubbed my sore quads, then my calves.

Grunts, heavy footfalls, and clanging armor of oncoming pech rounded the corner. Great. Here we go again. This was like filming a workout session/horror film. Good thing such things don't exist. Though they would be highly motivating. I could see the tagline now —Keep up the pace...or die trying.

When I thought my legs would buckle underneath me and I'd never walk again, gray bricks blocked our path. "Is this it?" What if people heard us through the façade? I lowered my voice to a whisper. "The fake wall?" My aching body was grateful to reach the end, but I'd prefer to remain on this side, safe from Morrigan's clutches.

"It must be." He brought his hand up as if to test it, then thought better of it. "There's nowhere else to go."

Sweat wetting his sideburns, Alastar scratched his head. "I wish I knew this was here. Perhaps I could've escaped Morrigan. I wonder where it leads?"

Declan shrugged. "This is my first time in Ceas Croi."

"I was too out of it to remember," I said. "All I remember is passing through a bunch of fake walls."

The pech had lagged behind again. But nervous energy made me bounce despite my aches, shaking my hands while Kai looked at me as if I were an alien—albeit a cute alien, judging from his face.

Our short friends neared. Kai descended a step and tugged me with him. Declan and Alastar flanked him on either side, making a barricade so the pech didn't crowd us. Still, the moldy stink of whatever lined the stairwell combined with musky body odor to produce a new offensive smell.

A pech in front came to a halt, faced the oncoming troop, and raised his hand. A mass of red hair dangled from his chin, blanketing his chain mail. Metallic beads gleamed where they'd been interwoven into braided sections of his beard. Gleaming, angry brown eyes peered out from his helmet.

The oncoming pech lurched. Some bumped into those in front before realizing the seemingly endless staircase had come to a stop.

Bead Beard puffed out his chest. "It is time. We've awaited this day for centuries. Pech will speak of it for generations to come. Are you ready?"

The pech nearby shouted and waved their weapons in the air. An echo of their enthusiasm reverberated down the stairwell.

"Are you ready to reclaim our ancestors' honor?"

They shouted louder. Determination steeled their faces.

"Are you ready to reclaim what's rightfully ours?"

I covered my ears. How would anyone within a mile radius not hear this?

"Let's go!" He thrust his fist toward the fake wall.

Kai hauled me up against the bricks as screaming pech ran through the façade like Super Bowl hopefuls storming the football field.

I sucked in my gut for fear of a weapon coming too close as they streamed past. Was this the plan? To make sure everyone heard us coming and had ample time to warn others?

Two pech stormed into the wall and bounced off. Others caught them and stopped. Had the wall solidified? Or had the pech on the other side gotten backed up, causing a traffic jam?

The standstill continued. Too long. We were trapped. The room closed in on me, and my chest squeezed. No. No. No. No. Not now. I can't have another panic attack.

God, help me!

CHAPTER THIRTY-NINE

The pech waiting to exit froze. One moment they'd been
roaring, ready for a fight. Now they stood motionless. Their
faces calm. Their eyes vacant. They'd fallen into a vegetative state.

Oh no! "Are they—" I caught a whiff of fasgadair.

Alastar and Declan grabbed hands and reached for mine.

"Give us room!" Alastar yelled.

"They're under the fasgadairs' power." Declan shoved them
aside. "Help me move them."

They shoved the pech away, clearing a path to the façade.

I nudged Kai behind me. He backed away until he bumped into
someone.

Once my brothers and I had a wide enough girth, we ignited the
fire. Despite our efforts, the flame touched a pech. But it didn't burn
him. That was Alastar's doing. Somehow. He probably didn't understand how he protected people from the flame any more than I understood how I started fires. I thought about starting a fire, and it
happened. But when I connected with my brothers, it seemed something that happened without thought.

"Stay here," I told Kai.

"But—" He stepped forward.

"Wait until the pech are no longer in entranced. Then you'll know the area is free from fasgadair."

He huffed. His dark eyes narrowed as he clenched his jaw. But he stayed put.

We broke through the fake wall into a dim hallway strewn with bodies. Vampires stood over some of them, blood dripping from their chins.

We rushed at them.

The first fasgadair leapt at our approach but failed to get out of our way. It disintegrated on impact. The next bloodsucker seemed confused and slipped in a pool of blood in his hasty retreat. We caught up to him, and he melted too. Two other fasgadair fled.

I glanced down the hallway to the right of the façade. It was empty. Had the pech split up in two directions? Or had they only come this way?

Declan disengaged to touch one of the fallen. The moment the fire disappeared, the coppery blood stench assaulted me. I poised my arm over my nose.

"What were they thinking barging in here like this?" My heart squeezed at the lost lives filling the hall. "As unbelievers, they're unprotected."

Alastar shrugged. "I wasn't part of the planning."

"Neither of us were. It was the only way to stay by your side." Declan brushed off his hands. "He's dead." He glanced at the other bodies. "We should check them all."

Kai and some dazed pech emerged from the stairwell. Wolf, Cahal, Maili, and my mother followed, eyes wide.

Wolf surveyed the dead bodies. "They must not have received the message in time."

"Who?" I asked. "What message?"

"Hmph." Cahal readied his battle-axe.

My mother stepped over the bodies. "We need someone with redeemed blood to guard this passageway."

Did I speak? Why was everyone ignoring me?

"I'll do it." Wolf stationed himself against the wall opposite the façade.

I sniffed the air. Still no fasgadair, but they had to be coming. Where were the other pech? Far more than this had rushed through the wall.

My brothers and I rounded the corner with Kai close behind. A stream of pech, gachen, and selkie decked out in chain mail followed.

The eerie halls were vacant. Flickering lights illuminated sections in a dancing glow, leaving other spaces pitch black. Several rats scurried along the corridor from one shadow to another as we neared.

We passed the last of the fallen pech. Some must've made it through to somewhere...or they went in another direction. Either way, once any unbelievers came upon fasgadair, they'd fall into their trance, waiting to become their next meal. Whose dumb plan was that? Stupid.

We rounded many corners, climbing and descending stairs through a perpetual maze. This was as I remembered Ceas Croi, but I'd come from the top. And how many secret passageways had we missed? Evan had taken us through some to escape. Why hadn't we recruited him for this mission? He and his brother had mapped out the place.

The electric fasgadair scent blasted my nose. I stopped, holding my arms up to keep my brothers and everyone else back.

My brothers wrinkled their noses. They must smell it too. We crept along the wall with Declan in the lead. He peeked around a corner, then ducked back, waving at us to back up.

He drove us back around another corner before uttering a word. "There's a huge cavern full of fasgadair. It seems they're gathered for something."

"And so we have." Malevolent voices rang out around me, sending an icy shock pulsating along my spine. I bolted toward the cavern, but arms I never saw coming held me firm. My brothers struck their hands out to ignite the fire, but Morrigan doppelgangers materialized and captured them. One grasped my brothers. The other grabbed Kai. They fought Morrigan's sisters' grips.

Kai reached for me, but I was swept away. My feet didn't touch the ground as Morrigan pulled me at an incomprehensible speed through blurry halls.

CHAPTER FORTY

Morrigan delivered me to the lair I'd seen through Turas. But she'd moved the table with whatever potion or spell she was working on to the side, in front of shelves built into the wall to make room for a red pentagram. The heinous thing took over much of the floor. Was that blood? It had to be. The coppery scent filled the space.

The witch's look-alikes appeared in the entryway with my brothers and Kai. What did they want with them?

As my brain attempted to process what was happening, Morrigan pushed me toward the pentagram. I tripped and fell near the center, landing on my butt. A sharp sting radiated from my hand. Blood covered my palm.

"Fallon!" All three of my would-be rescuers called out in unison. Their voices mimicking the fear and desperation in my heart.

I inspected my hand. The blood wasn't mine. I'd caught myself on the pentagram. It wasn't a drawing. Someone had carved it into the stone floor. Blood pooled inside the indentation. My stomach squeezed as my last meal threatened to reappear.

Please, God, please tell me they're not planning to use them to force me to do something they want.

After everything I'd been through, I'd grown stronger. I could handle a lot. But not that. Not Kai. Not my brothers. I'd fold like a loser in a card game before I'd allow them to get hurt because of me. I had to do something. Anything. God wouldn't have brought us here without giving us a way out.

Would He?

I ran toward Kai and slammed into an invisible wall and bounced off it onto my rear. Panic welled up as I stood, touching the air before me. My fingers found the unseen obstruction. Like a mime pretending to be in a box, I felt along the sides. The wall ringed the pentagram. I was trapped.

"Set her free, ye hag!" Alastar yelled.

Morrigan raised an eyebrow at her former ward. The next second, she stood before him, her hand wrapped around his throat. "Such vulgar words from one who should be grateful, son." She said *son* as if the word repulsed her.

Alastar's face turned purple as gurgling sounds struggled to escape him.

"Leave him alone!" I banged on the wall. It made no noise and had no give, but I persisted. My chest heaved as I raged at her. "Why are you doing this?"

She released him and glided around my cage. He sucked in breaths, and his normal color returned as Declan and Kai fought against their captors.

"Why am I doing this?" Her head cocked to one side, reminding me of the face I'd first seen in my dreams, masked in eerie calm, right before the attack. "You are aware of the depth of human cruelty, are you not? Your own grandmother treated you with contempt. Human beings are fickle creatures who feign love for others as long as it suits them. But truly, they care only for themselves. They are a plague upon the planet, and I made it my mission to wipe them out."

"You're insane!" I braced myself against the invisible wall.

"Perhaps," she jeered. "But I didn't make myself this way, did I? The lord of Hades gifted me with the ability to create a race of fasgadair under my control. He saw my heart and showed me a better way."

I sucked in my breath. "You work for Satan?" Of course, she did. Why did that surprise me? There are only two choices—follow God or follow Satan. Perhaps the surprising part is that she did so knowingly.

"I spent an eternity in Hades. How would I not know its master? Why would I not serve the one who offered me freedom and power?" She looked at me as though her gaze alone could suck all hope through my pores and disintegrate it on contact. "All he asked in return was to do what I already wanted to do."

I wasn't Morrigan's prisoner. Satan himself had bound me here. Every muscle in my body tensed, begging for release.

Declan reached for Alastar's hand, and their demon captor laughed. "You're useless without her fire."

The rage and agony welling up within me threatened to push my heart from my chest. My fists shook while my hatred formed as fire aimed at the laughing witch. A spark lit the concealed barrier between us, then fizzled.

"The only thing you'll be able to set on fire is yourself." Morrigan grinned like the Cheshire cat as she circled my cage.

An insidious dread and hopelessness seeped in, diluting my anger. I pressed my hands against the wall, looking to my brothers and Kai as if they might offer a solution.

But they were equally desperate, their faces plastered in determination and fear. Veins bulged at their temples and in their necks. But their efforts were in vain. The witches didn't even twitch. My friends were no match for their inhuman strength.

I fought the self-pity threatening to drop me to my knees, weeping. The complete depression I'd experienced at Turas in the demon's presence surrounded and filled me here. I choked on it. But I couldn't give up.

God, help us!

Morrigan's self-satisfied smile remained fixed but didn't touch her eyes. They were dead. As dead as her soul. "How is it that such a weak little thing has countered my every move?" She circled my cage counterclockwise. "No matter. Your resourcefulness has helped me become more..." She glanced at her doppelgangers who snickered.

"Creative." All three spoke this last word in unison.

She stopped between Kai and me, blocking my view. "And with my sisters' help, we will be unstoppable."

"What do you want with us?"

"Us?" She closed her hideous eyes and snuffed, stepping aside, allowing me to see Kai again.

The look in his eyes pained me more than anything Morrigan could do to me physically.

"I only need you." She circled my cage again. "With you under my control, threat to my rule will be abolished. My sisters and I will combine powers and become unstoppable." Her eyes darted toward her other prisoners. "I don't need them. Though they might help speed up the process."

"Not that it matters." The sister holding Declan and Alastar looked identical to Morrigan. Were they really her sisters? Or clones? "We have all the time in the world."

"But, if this takes too long, we may need a snack." The third sister bared her fangs and hovered over Kai's neck.

"No!" I slammed my shoulder against the invisible barricade.

Kai's captor's eyes widened, still nothing but black. "This one's blood must be untainted." A snaky smile slithered across her demon face.

Morrigan approached Kai and slipped a finger across his cheek. He yanked away and glared at her with such ferocity, had I not known him, he would have scared me. Instead, my entire being wanted to turn into the Tasmanian devil, destroying everything in my path to rescue him.

"This one is clean. But these two..." Morrigan motioned toward

Declan as she passed him, then stopped before Alastar and ran a finger under his chin.

He jerked his head away and threw Morrigan a death stare as savage as Kai's.

"I will tear these traitors apart should Fallon fail to give us what we desire." She pulled her hand away and leaned into his personal space. "Starting with my son."

"I'm not your son." Venom lacing his words, Alastar spat in her face.

"Why don't we just take it from her?" Kai's captor asked.

"We need a willing sacrifice." With the back of her hand, Morrigan wiped the spittle clinging to her cheek.

"Sacrifice?" Kai yelped.

"No!" my brothers shouted.

They renewed their fight, but the doppelgangers didn't budge.

Morrigan pointed near me. "Pick up the knife."

I turned to the most hideous knife I'd ever seen. The blade was rough and translucent as if made of stone and glass rather than metal. The handle was a mosaic worshiper in the prone position. I crept toward it. Evil emanated from it like vapor, growing stronger as I neared. My fingers recoiled, refusing to grasp it.

"Pick. It. Up." Morrigan clipped her icy words.

I made my fingers obey. The repulsive object dangled between my pinched fingers like a dead animal.

"Cut your wrist." Morrigan didn't show emotion, but eager anticipation seeped from her pores. How dare she enjoy this? She wanted to see me cut myself? That was a whole new level of sadistic.

"Don't do it!" The anguish in Kai's voice tore my insides to shreds and twisted them like a maypole.

"But she's done it before," Morrigan sneered.

I almost shouted, "Not my wrist!" But then Kai would know what she said was true. Declan already knew. But it was one thing to share your darkest secret in confidence and another to be exposed. And how did she know that? I'd never thought about it. Had I? What else had she reaped from my mind?

She skimmed across the floor to her witchy objects table and selected a hand mirror. "I no longer require this trinket. Mere child's play compared to what I have planned."

She moved next to Kai. "Cut your wrist and allow the blood to flow through the pentagram, or Macha will get her meal."

Macha grinned, revealing her fangs.

I repositioned the knife in my hand, grasping the blade.

"Don't do it." Kai's voice nearly killed me. But not as much as witnessing him become Macha's lunch.

I held up my wrist. When I'd cut myself in the past, I'd done it to escape emotional pain. To have control. And it was always superficial. Still, I cringed at the thought of ever having mutilated myself that way. It was an offense to God. And I never wanted to return to that.

As awful as cutting myself had been, this was worse. I had no control. And she wanted me to slice a vein? People rarely die from slicing their wrists sideways, right? Unless she left me to bleed out. It would be a slow death.

But it was my only choice.

Please, God, let this somehow save them.

I steeled myself to do it quick and dragged the utensil of torture across my skin. It stung.

Kai's gut-wrenching howl sliced me deeper than the blade. I fought my instinct to wrap my wrist and instead poised it above the chiseled floor. My blood dripped into the canal, roiling through the channel, writhing as if fighting intermingling with the stagnant gore.

"Keep your wrist over the pentagram and lay down."

Kai was sobbing. His reaction hurt more than what Morrigan forced me to do. And I understood why people in great distress tore their clothes. But I was already lightheaded, losing the energy to fight.

Please, God. Save them.

I laid down.

"Are you ready to become one, sisters?"

They nodded, and all three chanted something incomprehensible. It was as if my amulet refused to translate the horrid words. The witches released my brothers, and they struggled against unseen bonds, trapped where they stood.

Their voices deepened, growing more malevolent, with any trace of femininity stripped away. A demonic echo from the pits of hell mimicked their cadence. The sound pricked every nerve, sending them jumping as if attempting to escape the evil sensation gorging on my mind. The infernal sisters clasped hands. And, whether it was their spell or my blood loss, my vision blurred.

CHAPTER FORTY-ONE

Black smoke billowed from the window in my dreamspace, choking out the sun. I imagined Morrigan crawling through the window, and every nerve in my body tingled, urging me to run. My body lurched forward, but my legs were stuck as if my lower half was encased in cement. I tried picking up my legs as if to pluck them free of some invisible confines, but they wouldn't give. My heart skittered, begging me to move.

Darkness overtook the space as smoke plumes converged. Were those lies I believed? If I focused on God and not the lies, the darkness would abate. Right?

"God, where are You?" Listening, I searched the horizon. *Please, please, please, be here.* Nothing appeared. The gloom fogged in until the window offered the only light. I peered into it. Whoever's mind I saw through glanced at my body on the floor.

Three hands appeared. Each cut their palm and held it over the channel rushing like a bloody river through the pentagram. The vision showed each of Morrigan's sisters in turn. So, this window belonged to Morrigan's mind.

I briefly glimpsed my brothers and Kai—but, oh, their anguished faces!

"Your God isn't here." Morrigan's malevolent voice reverberated through the space. "Your body and mind belong to me and my sisters now. We are one." Evil glee pulsed in the surrounding darkness...victorious.

"No!" There's no way. God wouldn't allow this. Evil couldn't win. This wasn't what He promised.

What had He promised? *Think, Fallon, think!*

He'd said Morrigan couldn't control me. But she seemed to control me now. Perhaps Morrigan couldn't do it alone. What about three of them combined?

No! Lies! Don't believe the lies. God said I needed to do something, right? What was it?

Give up control.

Was I fighting too hard? Trying to control the situation? Even in following her orders, I was attempting to control things with a weak hope God would show up and save the day.

But He'd said His power was within me. Where was it now?

I needed to give up control and trust Him. How do I do that?

"God, I refuse to believe the lies. I know You're still here. You are with me...inside me. I don't know what Your plans are. But You have one. I trust You." I took a deep breath and stared into the ebony sky. He was there. I didn't have to see Him to trust His promise. He was there.

I imagined myself as a falcon, flying up through this darkness to Him, and I ascended. Not in falcon form, but in human form. My soul? I wanted to glance down, sure I'd find I'd shed my flesh and left it behind, but I refused to take my eyes off the goal. With my renewed determination and hope, I increased speed until my head poked out of the blackness. My entire body emerged from the smoke until the light's warmth bathed every part of me.

The sun. Or...what I'd always assumed to be the sun, flickered.

"God? Is that You?"

"It is."

Relief washed over me anew.

"I am glad you've come to Me. Well done. My good and faithful servant."

Tears of joy flowed at such words.

"Am I to stay with You?"

"Your time has not yet come." The light pulsed as He spoke.

"Then why am I here?"

"Why did you come?"

"There was nothing left for me to do. You're my last hope."

The energy pulsing from the light seemed amused, yet sad. "Make Me your first hope. I created you. I knit you together in your mother's womb. I know every hair upon your head. I am your strength and your refuge. Your *only* hope."

I laughed and cried as I dangled, mysteriously suspended midair. The love and energy emanating from Him filled me to overflowing. The vessel that housed my soul couldn't contain the emotion. The pain and agony I'd felt earlier was a faint memory. But I wanted to go back and save my friends if that was God's will. If it wasn't, we'd meet again. He'd saved us all. Whatever difficulties or separations we endured weren't permanent. We'd be together again, better than before, free from pain and trouble.

"Ah." God sighed, and a warm wind rushed into me. "That is what I want you to hold on to. Real hope only comes from Me."

As much as I wanted to stay with Him, I would do whatever He wanted me to do. And if that meant rescuing my family and friends and eliminating Morrigan, even better. "What *do* You want me to do?"

"Go through the window."

"Into Morrigan's mind?"

"Yes." The light flared. "Now that they're connected, you can eliminate them all."

"But how? Don't I need the zpět? Sully said I did." How is Sully, by the way? But I held back my question.

The light quivered as if laughing. "My servant did well. He eagerly awaits your reunion. And yes, Sully advised you rightly."

"How can I get the zpět when I'm in here?"

"The zpět is where their souls meet. Remove it and bring it to Me."

I sank, my body dropping into the cloud. "But how will I find it?"

My head submerged, plunged once more into the gloom. The weight of it threatened to pull me into despair. But I wouldn't let it. A glimmer penetrated the darkness. I lifted my hands. They were glowing. Did my face glow too? Was this from being in God's presence?

Back on solid ground, I tried lifting my foot. It moved!

I walked to the window and pulled myself through.

CHAPTER FORTY-TWO

M orrigan's mind was pitch black. As I expected. But it was worse than what she'd done to me. This place seethed with every kind of evil. Billowing smoke assaulted me, pushing me. The glow surrounding me waned.

No. God had filled me with truth, with light. For this purpose. I couldn't allow the sadistic thoughts and emotions to affect me. I stood, steeling myself for another attack. But none came.

My glowing hands pulsed, then brightened.

Three little girls with snarly, black locks ran past without glancing my way. They wore tattered skirts and grimy frocks. Dirt caked their bare feet.

Were these Morrigan's memories? The scene unfolded like a movie in a dark theater, but I'd become part of the film.

"Badb, Macha, Morrigan!" a woman's voice with a thick Scottish brogue called.

"Coming, ma!" the tallest girl responded.

The two older girls ran while the littlest crossed her arms and scowled.

The tallest looked back and stopped. "Come along, Morrigan."

Morrigan was the youngest? She'd struck me as the oldest.

"No, I donnae wanna go home." She tightened her arms, deepened her scowl, and stomped a foot for good measure.

"Ye best come now if ye know whot's good fer ya."

Morrigan remained unmoved.

The middle girl rolled her eyes and groaned. "Morrigan, if we—"

The oldest held a hand to quiet her sister and approached Morrigan.

"Please, Badb," Morrigan whined. She grabbed her sister's hand and tugged. "We can make do on our own. We donnae need that beastly man."

Badb shook herself free and raised an eyebrow at Morrigan. "Ma needs us, Morg. Come with us now. Donnae make Ma fetch ye, or yer'll be smartin' in the morn."

The older girls turned and walked at a fast clip away from Morrigan.

"Fine." Morrigan stomped her feet as she trailed her sisters in a dramatic display of reluctant obedience. "But I'll not be callin' him Da!" she yelled after them, quickening her pace as the distance between them grew.

The girls traversed the dirt path to a thatched-roof hut. The meager wooden door slammed behind them. I reached out to ease the door open, but my hand slipped as if the door didn't exist, so I stepped through to the other side.

Inside the hut, the sisters morphed and sat taller in their seats. They had aged and appeared to be in their teens. Morrigan looked more like a preteen. A haggard version of the girls with hair gathered into a bun and a wisp of gray hair forming a skunk line sat at the rustic table.

The girls slurped porridge, sliding their spoons away from them to gather the gruel, opposite of how I ate. Their mother reached for a bowl covered in a linen cloth. She pulled out two rolls, broke them in half, and distributed them to the sisters. She tucked the last portion inside the basket.

"Why aren't ye eatin'?" Badb asked through a mouthful tucked into her cheek.

"I'm nae hungry, lass." She stood and pushed in her chair. "Better save it for another meal."

Badb eyed her mother with suspicion and took another bite before swallowing the bit still in her mouth.

"Girls." With their mother's voice so soft, it took a moment to realize she'd spoken.

As each girl paused chewing, a tear slipped down their mother's face. "I've failed ye."

"No, Ma." Badb reached out for her mother's hand.

"I have." More tears followed. "I dinnae protect ye. But I shan't fail now. Finish yer meal, then pack yer things. I've arranged transport to my sister's. We'll stay with her."

Morrigan swallowed her bite and rose with such force she knocked her chair over. "Honest, Ma? Ye mean it? We're leaving this place? And *him*?"

"Aye." She nodded. "Whilst he's away. As I should have years ago."

Screams rang through the well-ventilated home from outside. The girls rushed to the window and pushed open the shutters to see what was happening.

"What fog rollin' in," said Macha.

"'Tis no fog. 'Tis smoke. Look." Badb pointed at the harbor. "Our ships be ablaze."

"'Tis the Fir Bolg." Their mother wrapped a ratty shawl around her shoulders. "Keep to the house." She dashed out the door where she met other adults rushing toward the wharf.

The scene blurred, swirling as everything fell away, replaced by gravestones upon a hill. The two older girls clung to each other and to Morrigan between them, dressed in black, standing in the shadow of a beast of a man with a puffy red beard and a silver hand. Grief masked the older girls' faces, but the littlest clenched her fists. Jaw set, her chest heaved. She stared at the open grave as though she didn't see her mother's coffin—only vengeance.

The scene roiled away in a billowy fog. The giant man with the silver hand lay on the floor. His flesh hand covered a gushing wound in his gut. The silver hand raised against an older Morrigan. "Please." He begged with a gasping breath.

"I warned ye to stay away from me and my sisters." A young Morrigan held a dripping knife poised over the man. "Ye failed to protect me ma, then dare harm her children? She trusted ye!" Morrigan screamed, cursing the man as she thrust the weapon down. I shielded my eyes but couldn't block out the sickening slasher sounds of Morrigan stabbing him far more than necessary to kill him.

Billowy smoke stole the scene away. Rather than allow it to solidify and show me more, I ran through it. Was I happening upon random memories? Or were these set up to gain my empathy? I couldn't allow myself to become distracted. The last thing I needed was to remain locked in with Morrigan's memories forever. I needed to keep to my quest—find the zpět.

As I ran blind, faces and objects materialized and vanished in the fog like the tornado in the *Wizard of Oz*. Strong emotions accompanied them. An image of the zpět appeared, bathed in a fierce desire. The freaky knife I'd used to cut myself manifested before me with an intense hatred. Alastar's face flew by accompanying a mixture of betrayal and anger. Aodan produced longing and regret. Many other faces whirled by, carrying jealousy, hatred, rage, and lust. Each image and emotion pulsed like a heartbeat, then vanished as I rushed past.

Morrigan's sisters brought the only source of comfort and belonging. But none brought love. No love existed in this place.

I continued racing through the endless cavern of Morrigan's memories and emotions, collected over thousands of years. How would I find a small amulet in such a place? What if I got trapped in here? Forever?

CHAPTER FORTY-THREE

Burning ships. Fallen bodies in pools of blood. A large man with an enormous stomach and a Viking helmet, laughing like he'd just witnessed his nemesis's demise made me pause. A beautiful woman with a pregnant belly emerged behind him. A trail of many women with pregnant bellies followed.

Was I supposed to learn something from this? Or were they distractions keeping me from my quest?

Nothing solid, no points of reference helped me navigate. Was I walking in a straight line or circles? Death and destruction followed wherever I went, bringing a sick satisfaction. No. Worse. A sadistic joy and an insatiable hunger for revenge that made me want to puke.

The only source of light came from the glow pulsing from my hands, threatening to fade. Did Morrigan sense my presence? She had to.

A picture of Morrigan emerged from the cloud, and the sensations shifted as if someone else's emotions intermingled with hers. Was I nearing the place where the witches merged?

God, how will I find the zpět?

The space recoiled with rage, lifting me on a billowy cloud, tossing me, as if wanting to purge me. I flew through the void and tucked into a roll as I landed. Whatever made up this space, gravity didn't work the same here. It was like being harnessed on a trampoline. A whirlwind swept me up again, then dropped me. I fell with a soft thud.

A stream of smoke came at me. As if realizing tossing me didn't work, the space switched tactics. I ducked. Another came at me, then a series of strikes. I scampered away from each one.

I stood, arms splayed, eyes darting, ready for another onslaught. Who knew the torture I'd endured from Maili's beloved contraptions would come in handy? I hoped I'd have a chance to thank her.

Until then, I had to figure out what was happening. Why the sudden assault? Whatever it was attacked when I first arrived. Could that be because Morrigan wanted to reject the light I brought with me? But then it left me alone. Why barrage me now? Was I getting close to the zpět? Or was it because I prayed?

I should test it.

God, please lead me to the zpět.

Again, the swirling cloud of memories acted like a tormented bull, desperate to purge itself of the rider clinging to its back. It hoisted me into the air and threw me, but it was a wasted effort. I landed safely. And it needn't disorient me. There was no point of reference in which to get my bearings. This was the ideal place to get lost.

I moved forward. Whether in a circle or a straight line, well, I had no way of knowing. But something shimmered up ahead. Like a moth to a light, it drew me in, taking shape as I neared. A window, like the one in my dreams. I closed in with caution. Could this be where their minds merged, where God had said I'd find the zpět?

I searched around the portal, groping the floor with my glowing hands. But I didn't find anything. Either this wasn't the place or...

If this was it, I only had one option—crawl through the window. I gulped.

I inched toward the thing and poked my head through. Black, like this one. Should I enter? What if it wasn't the right place? What if it was another level of Morrigan's consciousness and I fell deeper and deeper into her warped mind?

My glow dimmed.

No, God wouldn't steer me wrong. This had to be it. The glow pulsed, strengthening with my faith. I'd have to trust God brought me here for a reason and jump in.

I took several deep breaths, calming my mind, and stepped through the portal into the blackness.

Three windows surrounded me. Though they were bright, they couldn't penetrate the darkness. I'd come through the closest one, but I didn't dare move from the spot. If I searched the darkness or tried another window, I'd lose track of which I'd come through. There was nothing to orient myself. What if I needed to return this way?

If only I had something to mark the correct exit! But I had nothing.

Taking another deep breath and willing my dulled hands to reignite, I let go and padded to the center. God would see me through... somehow.

I shuffled forward, groping the darkness. My elbow bumped into something rough. I used my glowing hands to see the pillar and ran my fingers along the cold stone until I reached the top. I bumped something. It clanged on top of the pedestal. Could it be? I held my breath. Something circular lay on its surface. My heart squealed, daring to hope this was the zpět. It had to be. Isn't this where God said it would be?

I snatched it up, and a cord dangled, hitting the back of my hand. Yes, this was it. I put it around my neck, and it clanged against Drochaid's replacement, making me feel like an Olympic athlete with a collection of medals.

The floor quaked, and I fell. I fought to stand in the dark. The windows pulsed and faded as if warning me to get out. Which one had I come through?

The ground pitched again.

God, help me choose the right one.

The lights of the furthest window stopped swirling and dripped and faded like the aftereffect of raining fireworks. The whole thing melted and disappeared. My heart squeezed into my throat, choking me. The window to the right of the one that had disappeared gave a final pulse before dissolving like the first.

I jumped up to the last window before it vanished. Then I clamored through, dropping over the other side. I pulled my legs over the edge and lay there panting as the window evaporated. Smoky memories whirled around me. This had better be Morrigan's head.

The bitterness and anger stuffing the cavern intensified. A scream tore through the clouds. I covered my ears and ducked as it swooped near. Visions of me being murdered in various ways squelched the sadness and images of Morrigan's sisters. So, these things weren't just memories, but imagination as well. Desires.

If Morrigan didn't want me dead before, she did now.

I had to get back to where I belonged. But how? What if *that* window dissolved like the others?

The hazy thoughts seemed to understand my predicament. They swelled and slithered together like a serpent. The head hurled itself at me. I sidestepped it, and the thing dissipated.

Did she know I invaded her conscience? Was she looking for a way to exterminate me?

I ran through the nebula, creating a foggy wake.

God, You got me here. With Your help, I found the zpět. I trust You to get me out.

I glanced at the additional amulet just to be sure it was the zpět. Either that or it was a carbon copy. The thing lit up. A beam of light shot out, like a super-focused flashlight into the fog. I ran, only able to see a few feet at a time, but with each step, I saw just enough to take the next steps, keeping my eyes on the light and avoiding the violence attempting to take shape.

The foundation shook as it had where I'd found the zpět, and I faltered, regained my footing, and kept going. Another quake threw me. I tried to get up, but the ground rose, ballooning into an ever-steepening hill. On my hands and knees now, I tried to crawl, but I kept sliding.

I had to keep going, focusing on the light. But I couldn't scale the mounting slope. Smooth with no footholds. I slid a few more feet. This was worse than Maili's ever-changing so-called *training* contraption. I gritted my teeth and lunged up the incline, then fell on my face and slid to the bottom.

"Agh!" I smacked the floor, then peeled myself up to stand on the level ground behind me. The zpět's light aimed upward, over the hill. I raised my glowing hand. Everything just looked black. There was no way to tell if the mound had any scalable nooks. Could I go around? Images of myself in various stages of death hedged me in on both sides. Disturbingly creative means. *Nice work, Morrigan, you sick freak.* Bile rose in my throat.

Take hold.

Was that God? Even in here? Take hold? Of what?

I reached for the zpět. The blaze streaming from it was solid, like a glowing rope. I latched on, and it retracted as if attached to a winch. It pulled me up over the hill, through the smoke, toward a crumbling window.

Oh no! Don't disappear!

I clutched the glowing rope as it dragged me across the expanse. My gut wrenched at the agonizingly slow pace. Had I taken too long? My fingers tingled, tempting me to let go and run. But no. Something told me to hold on even as I watched the window dissolve.

The beam delivered me to the window and extinguished. I scrambled to my feet and dove headfirst through the melting portal onto the field by the shore.

I caught my fall and turned to see the last of the dripping light. The swirling lights that had once been a gateway to Aodan, then Alastar, and finally to Morrigan disintegrated like the others. I dropped onto my back. "Phew!" That was close. Too close. I placed a hand on my heart, expecting to feel it racing. In this place, I didn't need to catch my breath. Still, I needed to rest from the mind trip. Smoky tendrils of Morrigan's negative energy, cut off from their source, recoiled above me and burst into tiny puffs that rained and evaporated midair.

It was gone.

The sun shone once again. Hope permeated the space. Sparkles shimmered on the water. I took a deep breath. It was over.

Thank You, God.

The bright sky pulsed. *Well done, my good and faithful servant.*

CHAPTER FORTY-FOUR

I woke in the center of the pentagram. As if little time had passed while I was fighting Morrigan's demons. Had I died?

I touched the amulet. Both were there, Drochaid's replacement and the zpět.

The witchy sisters gawked. Their eyes wide, mouths open yet rendered mute.

Morrigan found her voice. "Noooo!" She rushed my enclosure, both fists poised in the air, ready to strike. But she slipped past the barrier onto the pentagram. I crab-walked from her, then scurried to stand, keeping as much distance as possible before she strangled me.

The two sisters dashed to her side.

I backed away, right out of the circle. Whatever I did in Morrigan's mind must've affected her spell here. The barrier had broken. I continued my retreat as the sisters skulked closer, caging me in. Their sinister eyes bent only on evil. And their gnarled fingers ready to mutilate me.

My brothers writhed against their invisible bonds. Too bad whatever I'd done hadn't eliminated that spell too. How would I escape these witches now? I had the zpět. Wasn't that enough?

Wait. Hadn't God told me to give it to Him? I'd left the dream space too soon. Now what should I do? My heart squeezed, and air stilled in my lungs as the sisters closed in.

"Back away from her!" Pepin materialized between us. Where had he come from?

The witches paused, startled by the small man stepping between them and their revenge.

Morrigan's black eyes narrowed. "Kill him."

The pech showed no fear. He widened his stance as if expecting them. He reached out to something. "Grab them!"

Who was he talking to?

Pepin latched on to Macha and disappeared. Morrigan and Badb disappeared too.

I turned to my brothers and Kai. "What happened?"

They shook their heads and fought their binds. Then, as if the bonds magically fell away, Kai pitched forward, catching himself before toppling.

He dashed to my side, grabbed my arm, and inspected my wrist. The wound had stopped bleeding. I must not have cut myself as deep as I thought.

"I'll fetch a bandage." Alastar rummaged around the shelves, toppling things in his mad hunt. "This will work."

Fingers tender, Kai touched my face. "Are you all right?"

"I think so. But—"

He grasped my chin and kissed my lips. Whatever I was going to say a distant memory as his soft lips lit everything within me on fire.

He released me, his soulful eyes peering into mine. Pink coloring his cheeks, his dimples deepened.

Alastar and Declan stood frozen, eyes wide. Cheesecloth dangled from Alastar's hand. He glanced down. Then, as if remembering what he'd been doing, he stepped up to wrap my wound, stifling a smile as he tied the bandage.

Higher-level brain functioning returned. "What happened? Where did Pepin come from? And where'd he go with the witches?"

"I don't know." Alastar tied the bandage on my wrist. "But his timing was ideal."

"A little late if you ask me." Kai held my arm in a tender grip. "Can you stand?"

"I think so."

Kai and Declan helped me to a chair.

"Where'd you get that?" Kai pointed to the zpět. "Is that—?"

"The zpět. Yes."

Alastar, Declan, and Kai exchanged glances, mouths agape.

"How'd you find it?" Alastar asked.

"You'd never believe me if I told you."

"Try us."

As I opened my mouth, Pepin reappeared and reached for me. "Come with us."

Declan stepped forward, hands on his hips. "What do you need her for? She's lost a lot of blood."

Despite that fact, I wasn't woozy.

"We need her to finish this." Pepin wagged his sausage fingers in the air, impatient for me to grab hold, his amber eyes pleading. "Come with us if you want. But everyone needs to link hands."

Were the pech using Turas?

Once my brothers, Kai, and me linked hands, Pepin snagged mine. The moment we connected, more pech stood in our midst with Drochaid hovering in the air before one. He brought us to April 24, 1521 BC, when Stonehenge was whole and unplugged Drochaid from the stone.

"What are you doing?" Fear crept into my throat, choking me as I searched beyond the outer circle for demons, waiting for despair to overtake me. "We can't stay here."

"It's safe for the time being." Pepin moved to the edge of the inner circle. "To finish God's work."

"What are you talking about?" I followed him, keeping my eyes peeled for danger.

"The angels are waging war with the demons, holding them back.

Morrigan and her sisters are being contained until you return the zpět." Pepin spun around, eyes wide. "Where are they?"

My heart sank. "But I missed my chance. I was supposed to give it to God."

Pepin paused his frantic search. "You haven't missed anything. You're to give it to the angel, as he instructed." He continued his hurried pace along the inner circle.

"What if it's a trick?" I chased after him. "What if the demons disguise themselves to get the zpět back?"

"Bah." Pepin waved me off with a flick of his wrist. "That's not—"

Bright light flashed before us, flickering. An angel took shape within the light.

Pepin stopped short, and I ran into him, catching myself on his shoulders. He dropped to his knees before the celestial being, and I did the same, keeping Pepin between us. If he'd been about to say it wasn't possible for a demon to disguise himself as an angel, he was right. There was something dangerous that instilled fear, but beyond that, a hope no demon could fake.

"Fear not. You have done well. The demons are secure, but we'll need the zpět to ensure their eternal imprisonment." The angel closed the gap, his light brightening and dimming as if a kid played with the dimmer switch. "Have you brought it with you?"

"Yes." Pepin bowed. "Fallon has it."

"Do not worship me." He stepped closer. "I'm only an angel. God's messenger."

Pepin cleared his throat. His posture shifted from a worshipful bow to a cower.

I understood why he bowed. This creature wasn't God, but his persona commanded respect. He shone as if he basked in God's presence regularly. What must it be like to stand before God? I shied from him as he neared.

"Do not be afraid, Fallon." He reached out. "I've come to destroy the zpět and return Morrigan, Macha, and Badb to Hades for eternity."

I removed the zpět from my neck and handed it to him. Our hands touched for a moment. Power and love surged from him to me, erasing the fear. The reality of heaven and everything God promised pulsed through me.

The angel left the circle. "Remember to use Turas with caution. And only for God's glory." He leveled his gaze at me. The light surrounding him intensified and enlarged, then disappeared with the angel.

CHAPTER FORTY-FIVE

I turned to Pepin. "What was that? How did you get Turas back?"

A slow smile lifted the edges of Pepin's beard and crinkled his eyes. "That's why we needed Drochaid."

"You mean it wasn't just a gesture of good faith toward your people?" I placed my hands on my hips.

"Well, it was." Pepin shrugged. "While the armies marched this way to face Morrigan, a remnant returned the way we'd come, across the seas to the selkie lands."

"But not you."

"Of course not." A scoff accompanied his crossed arms. "We were concerned my disappearance might rouse your suspicion." He wagged a finger at me. "You're not one to let things go. If you wondered where I'd gone and connected it with my taking Drochaid, you might suspect I'd gone for Turas. Then Morrigan would know, and we'd lose the surprise. We couldn't chance her intercepting our plans. The selkie knew the way, and I gave instructions how to work Turas once they arrived. Many of them had seen it in action when we reclaimed Bandia."

"And you got out of having to travel overseas," I said.

"Yes, well. That did work out in my favor, didn't it?" His smile returning, he flourished a chunky bow.

"Thank God." I dropped onto a rock as if I'd lost the energy to keep standing. "If you hadn't shown up when you did..." A shudder ran through me.

He placed a hand on my shoulder. "But we did. Everything worked out according to God's plan. The witches have returned to the underworld, and the angels will destroy the zpĕt, never to resurrect a soul from the afterlife again."

I motioned toward Kai and my brothers. "Their restraints fell after you took Morrigan. Does that mean all her spells will break?"

Pudgy fingers lifted to scratch his red hair, even as his forehead crinkled. "I imagine so."

"What about the fasgadair? Will they return to their old forms?"

He shook his head, his eyes sad. "I'm afraid not. A spell didn't cause their damnation. It was the demon blood they ingested."

"So, we could still run into fasgadair." It wasn't a question. More of a sad fact.

"Yes, but we have weapons to use against them and salvation to offer."

"But the fight isn't over." I deflated. Then again, how realistic was it of me to think the battle in this world would ever end? There would always be trouble as long as evil existed.

"For now. But not forever. God will prevail." Pepin braced a warm hand on my forearm. Such comfort in his touch. Such truth in his statement.

"I hate to interrupt." Alastar latched onto my shoulders and leaned, pressing me forward. "But there's still one thing we must do."

I shoved him off me. Yup, he was adapting to his little brother role quite well. "Right now?" I was exhausted. What else could we possibly have to do?

Alastar's Adam's apple bobbed, and he wrinkled his nose like he swallowed something foul. "We need to rescue Morrigan's king collection."

"We should get Abracham." Declan drummed his fingers on his leg. "In case his father is there."

Pepin delivered us to the bowels of Ceas Croi. Blackness surrounded me. Mold and death assaulted my nose in the still, thin air. Though I didn't want to inhale, I sucked in only what I needed to survive.

Something touched me, and I jerked, brushing off whatever had invaded.

"It's me." Alastar's voice echoed. "Here. Light this." He thrust what I assumed was a torch into my hand.

I grasped the stick and felt my way to the tip and ignited it. Flickering light illuminated a few feet around us. I half expected to find something else standing in our midst. I turned around, casting the light as far as possible to ensure we were alone.

Alastar grabbed a couple more torches and lit them from mine. "Follow me. I think it's this way."

We followed him among the muck-ridden halls. This must be what it's like to be a miner. How could they work in a place like this day after day? I fought rising panic.

You're okay, Fallon. You've been through much worse. God will see you through.

We reached a room nothing like the hall we'd left. I lit the sconces along the wall to brighten the place. Bats scattered from the tall ceiling, forming a black cloud and whooshing past us into the hall. Torches illuminated a mock throne room with golden tiles, ornate pillars, and a high ceiling painted to resemble the heavens. Thrones lined the walls.

Within most of the thrones sat a withered, emaciated body.

I latched onto Kai, waiting for them to rise and attack.

Abracham had stilled beside me. His hand, which tended to stroke his Merlin beard, now kept a firm grip as if about to rip it off.

Was his father here? Could he recognize him? He'd only been a boy when their kingdom had been torn away. And these gray bodies lacked recognizable features. To me, anyway.

Alastar pulled his dagger from its sheath and pivoted to Declan, jabbing the point toward him. "You have the flask?"

"Aye." Declan slipped a flask from his pouch, uncapped it, and poured some of its contents onto Alastar's blade. "Brandish your weapons. We should each have a covered blade."

We each tinted our daggers ruby-red with redeemed blood, the lacquer settling in place, but not drying. If I'd ever been one to paint my nails, I'd never want to do it again. Once we were ready, Alastar approached the first throne. The rest of us moved in a collective huddle behind him.

He climbed the steps, his blade readied, as if he expected the carcass to lunge. He brought his blade near the king's arm and swiped. The wound puffed smoke as though it were full of dust, reminding me of stepping on puffball mushrooms as a kid.

The king crumbled into a pile of dust.

"Does that—" My loud voice echoed, and a bat who'd missed his cue earlier took his leave. I lowered my voice. "Does that mean he's not redeemable? Or are they emaciated beyond repair?"

"I've only ever seen fasgadair emaciated to this extent restored by drinking blood." Alastar sidled to the next throne. "We'll have to keep trying."

Alastar cut the next king, and he, too, dissolved into dust.

"Are you sure we shouldn't try something else?" I slid behind Kai, waiting for the fasgadair to realize what was happening and rise to protect themselves.

"Like what, feeding them to plump them up first?" Declan asked. Was he always so sarcastic or was he learning from me?

The next four kings followed the same fate. Only one left.

God, I pray these kings were unredeemable, and we're not killing them.

"Wait." Abracham released his death grip on his beard and approached Alastar. He held a hand out. "Please, allow me."

With his weapon, Alastar motioned toward the final king. "Is this—?"

"My father. I believe so."

He relinquished his blade to Abracham and bowed.

Abracham inched toward the blade, taking extreme care. He held it to his chest, looked to the heavens, and moved his lips in prayer. Then he swiped his blade across the last king's arm. I braced myself for the inevitable collapse, but veins appeared from the spot and fanned out as whatever blood within wound a slow path through his circulatory system. His flesh swelled in a delayed reaction, and the gray skin changed to white, then added a pinkish hue. The slow transformation seemed to stall under his ragged clothing until it crept along his neck, to his face, then to his other arm. Faint crinkling and gushing sounds followed the transfiguration.

Alastar stepped back, joining our cluster. Weapons readied, we barely breathed during the slow change.

Life reached his dead eyes, and the king blinked. With each blink, his dilated, fasgadair pupils shrank to their normal size along with the blue irises, and the whites emerged. He glanced around, moving his neck as if he'd removed a brace and tested it to ensure it had healed. His thin fingers gripping the sides of the throne, he attempted to stand. Cracking bones followed his movement, and he collapsed into his seat. "I–I—"

"You're Kellagh." Abracham's voice broke. "King of Diabalta. Morrigan has returned to Hades, and your kingdom has been restored." Abracham knelt before the throne and bowed his head. "Father."

EPILOGUE

TWO YEARS LATER

I stood with Kai by the cliffs of his paradise overlooking the lake. Peace filled my soul as the lowered sun blanketed the sky in reds, yellows, and every hue in between. Music and merry chatter carried from the celebration elevated me further. Then there was Kai. My heart hammered as he drew me in for another kiss.

"Ehem." Stacy cleared her throat in the most obnoxious way possible.

We peeled ourselves apart and gave Stacy the attention she would receive one way or another.

"There's a party going on." Hands on her hips, she tapped her foot. "You know, to celebrate your marriage? I still cannot believe you're married."

I groaned, then laughed. How I'd missed her. It was beyond my wildest dreams to share this place with her. "We're taking a breather, Stace."

She grabbed my hand then Kai's and pulled us toward the festivities. "You'll hate yourself forever if you miss your party."

"Thanks for thinking of me." I rolled my eyes.

We ducked along the thin path through exotic plants. Floral scents reminding me of jasmine and orange blossoms wafted my way, adding to the intoxicating mood. Flutes, drums, laughter, and chatter grew louder. The foliage cleared, and the place looked more magical as the sky darkened and mason jar lights emitted a fairy-tale aura. People danced on the platform as musicians carried the tune.

Rác bounded toward us, ears flapping, tongue lolling to the side. Kai scratched the dog's side, then petted his head.

"There's the happy couple." King Aleksander raised his goblet. "Where are your drinks?"

Alastar neared with two glasses and thrust them in our hands.

King Aleksander clinked cups and took a swig. Kai and I followed suit, taking baby sips or tonight would end far too soon. "I still can't believe how much the world has changed, Fallon. We owe you a great debt. Not only are our kingdoms and reigns restored, we're united. Something I'd never dreamt possible. But you've done it." He lifted his cup again and took another drink.

I didn't join him in the drink. "It was God, not me. The credit belongs to Him."

"Hear, hear!" Rowan sidled next to her father. "I'm so happy for you two. Congratulations." She smiled as Evan linked arms with hers.

"I'm looking forward to yours." I tilted my head in a slight bow. "I'm sure a royal wedding will be far grander." I'd actually expected them to marry sooner than me and Kai, but it seemed such events involving entire countries took more time.

Rowan waved and scoffed. "I'd much prefer an intimate celebration like this. So enchanting."

"Ours will be too." Evan kissed her cheek.

Rowan blushed. I guess she'd marry for her country *and* for love.

My heart swelled for her. "It's hard to believe I'll be living in a kingdom ruled by such dear friends. I'm glad you'll be close."

"Aye." Rowan wiped a blonde curl from her face. "This worked out perfectly. Bandia is in my father's good hands, and I love this country. It's beautiful."

I couldn't agree more.

Declan and Ji Ah stepped from the dance floor toward us.

"Will you two be next?" I lifted my cup toward them.

"Next to what?" Declan screwed up his eyes at me.

"Marry." Another couple I'd expected to be married already. They'd been inseparable since surviving Ceas Croi.

"If Ji Ah accepts me." He gazed at her as if she held the secret to his happiness.

She smacked his arm and returned his adoring look.

"Speaking of weddings. Where are Maili and Zakur?" Their wedding suspended in Kylemore's trees last year was breathtaking. Nothing could compare to a wedding in a tree village.

Alastar bent around in every direction. "They're around here somewhere."

Colleen ran past waving something in the air. Corwin, Nialla, and Beagan followed, giggling and tripping as they went.

"I love you, Fal." Stacy nudged me as she watched the kids. "But I never, in a million years, imagined you'd get married in another world and have an instant family."

"Me either." I wove my arm through Kai's. "But we both felt called to this next adventure. Those kids need a home, and we can't separate them." I gazed at Kai, my heart swelling with gratitude to have him in this with me.

"Besides, we love them." He patted my hand.

And they loved him, especially Corwin and Nialla. They'd never forget how he rescued them in Bandia. He was their hero as a good dad should be.

"Still, four kids are a lot." Stacy bobbed her head and scrunched up her face into the expression that had oh so many meanings.

I elbowed her.

"But if anyone can do it, you can." Feigning hurt, she rubbed her arm.

"With God, *we* can do it." Kai smiled and planted a kiss on my head. Was it possible to love him more? "And, thanks to our new neighbors' help with the expansion to my house, we have plenty of room."

"Yeah, sorry we invaded." Alastar's smile and swinging arms counteracted his words. "But with all these kids, you'll never know when we'll need the triplet fire. It's best if we're close."

"And I love having my brothers as neighbors." As Wolf and our mother approached, I craned my neck in their direction. "Speaking of neighbors..."

"What are you blathering on about?" Wolf chucked his chin toward me.

"Oh, we're just teasing Fallon about her ready-made family." Alastar winked at me.

"Yes." My mother tugged her sleeves. "You'll need me around to help you care for those kids."

"And Kai needs someone nearby who isn't one of Fallon's blood relatives." Wolf smacked Kai on the back. "I apologize if you enjoyed your solitude, my friend. Those days are over."

"True. Sorry, Kai." I squeezed his arm in mock sympathy, though he'd shared how happy it made him to have his isolation breached. "But Cahal and Pepin will also be around for you."

It saddened part of me that none of those who'd begun this journey with me were planning to return to Notirr. A remnant had returned to begin the rebuilding efforts. But my friends were excited to build a new community with me in Kai's paradise. The first selkie/gachen village ever.

"Maybe I'll be able to visit and have visitors more often with Turas." I raised my voice on the last word to get Pepin's attention.

It worked. His ears perked up. He left his seat with Cahal and sauntered over. "Did you mention Turas?"

"I was telling everyone how great it will be to use Turas to visit and allow them to visit." I folded my arms across my chest.

"Hmph." Pepin grumbled. "You know the rules. An exception

was made for this wedding, but you can't use Turas whenever you please."

I laughed. "I know. I know, O Mighty Keeper of Turas."

"Go ahead and mock me." He waved a pudgy hand that only a fool would underestimate. "We'll see how often I allow you access."

One side of his beard lifted in a crooked smile. Despite his attitude, his new responsibility honored him, and he loved the title I'd given him. He returned to his chair with Cahal, who raised his goblet toward us.

I smiled and took a drink with him across the distance. It's taken me a long time to figure him out. He loves people, but he doesn't need communication, only to be close. I was so glad he decided to take residence in our newly established village.

"We still need to think of a name," Declan said.

"For what?" I asked. "Oh, our village?"

He nodded.

"Yeah." I'd thought and thought and couldn't come up with anything fitting. Perhaps someday. Until then, it was perfect as it was with my loved ones near.

"You know..." Stacy tipped her head and squinted at me. "This place is spectacular. And you've got a great family here and so many friends. I'm beginning to wonder if you made up that stuff about having to save the world."

"Wha—" I slung my mouth open in mock shock. "You never know. The fasgadair might've figured out how to use the megaliths and destroyed our realm too."

"See? There you go being dramatic again." She lolled her head back and forth. "You always were a drama queen."

"Yeah, Stace." I rolled my eyes. "*I'm* the dramatic one."

"Are you suggesting *I'm* more dramatic than you?" Her voice rose in pitch and whininess. She held a hand to her chest as if mortified. "I can't believe you'd say such a thing." Then she smacked my shoulder and laughed.

If only I could keep her here forever. I watched the kids weaving through the dancers, to the royalty in my midst, to a family I'd only recently come to know, to the introverts on the outskirts enjoying the festivities from a distance. Blood or not, they were family now. My heart filled to overflowing. This side of heaven, life would never be perfect, but I had God and His love and His people and their love. I was blessed beyond comprehension.

WANT TO KNOW WHAT HAPPENED BEFORE FALLON'S BIRTH? PICK UP CATALEEN, AODAN, AND FAOLAN'S STORY IN...

FREE SHORT STORY

The story's over? NO!!! Is this you right now? I get it. I hate resurfacing from a story world. But no worries. I've got your back. Here's a short story to ease the withdrawal from Ariboslia.

THE FALL OF DIABALTA

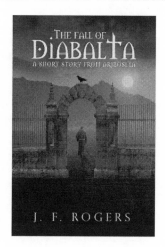

Want to know just how Le'Corenci—eh-hem, sorry—*Ennis* took down Diabalta? Download this free short story to discover the missing piece of the story.

https://jfrogers.com/book/the-fall-of-diabalta/

SHAMELESS REQUEST FOR REVIEWS

Authors need reviews! They help books get noticed, and I love to know what my readers think of my stories. So, if you enjoyed this book, please consider leaving a review where you purchased this book, Goodreads, BookBub...or anywhere you think a review might be helpful. I'm forever grateful!

You are loved,
J. F. Rogers

ABOUT THE AUTHOR

 J.F. Rogers lives in Southern Maine with her husband, daughter, pets, and an imaginary friend or two. She has a degree in Behavioral Science and teaches 5th-6th Grade Sunday School. When she's not entertaining Tuki the Mega Mutt, her constant companion and greatest distraction, she's likely tap tap tapping away at her keyboard, praying the words will miraculously align just so. Above all, she's a believer in the One True God and can say with certainty—you are loved. Connect with her at jfrogers.com.

BB	bookbub.com/authors/jfrogers
f	facebook.com/jfrogerswrites
g	goodreads.com/jfrogers
⃝	instagram.com/jfrogers925
ⓟ	pinterest.com/jfrogers925
⦿	twitter.com/jfrogers5

THE CURSED LANDS SERIES

The King's Curse - Will Colleen turn her back on everyone, including God... or risk her life for strangers.

The Witch's Curse - Coming August 29, 2023!

The Queen's Curse - Coming in fall/winter 2023!

ACKNOWLEDGMENTS

As always, I must thank God first. He is my Creator, my Inspiration, my All.

Next, my husband, Rick, and daughter, Emily. I don't know where I'd be without you. Thank you for your love and patience. I love you both so much.

Special thanks to:

Fantasy for Christ critique group—with a special shout out to Jan Davis Warren.

Deirdre Lockhart with Brilliant Cut Editing.

Mark and Lorna Reid at authorpackages.com.

Beta readers: Jenny Cardinal, William Long, Samantha Sanford, Jen Tate, Lois Wolter.

My ARC team and my clan. I couldn't do this without you.

So many people showed up to encourage me along the way. Your timing was perfect.

God has blessed me and this novel by surrounding me with so many amazing people. *Aloft* wouldn't be the same without you, and I can't thank you enough. I love you all!

STILL HERE?

LOOKING FOR MORE BY J F ROGERS?

Be among the first to know when new books are released.
Join J F Rogers' clan today.

jfrogers.com/join/